Diversion Books
A Division of Diversion Publishing Corp.
443 Park Avenue South, Suite 1008
New York, New York 10016
www.DiversionBooks.com

For more information, email info@diversionbooks.com

First Diversion Books edition June 2014.
Print ISBN: 978-1-62681-355-7
eBook ISBN: 978-1-62681-295-6

Connect with Austin Williams on Twitter **@awilliams_books**

MIS DIREC TION

A
RUSTY DIAMOND
MYSTERY

AUSTIN WILLIAMS

DIVERSIONBOOKS

1.

The bloodstain was shaped like Florida. Rusty didn't know much about geography, probably couldn't point out more than a handful of states on a map. But he knew what Florida looked like, even though he'd never been there. And the mass of drying blood stretching across the hardwood floor, coming to a rounded tip a few inches from his leather boots (this tip just slightly darker than the wide stream comprising most of the stain) was a dead ringer for the Sunshine State.

He knew it was a strange thing to consider, given the circumstances. Hardly an appropriate mental response to such an intensely disturbing situation. He wasn't in shock, exactly, but he had no idea what to do with himself. There was nothing he *could* do until the police arrived. Which should be any minute now. In fact, he was starting to wonder what the hell was taking so long.

Rusty wasn't sure of how much confidence to place in the Ocean City Police Department. When it came to traffic stops and busts for disorderly conduct, open containers, public nudity and the like, the OCPD was surely qualified.

But murder? That had to fall well outside the parameters of what the local law was accustomed to handling on a regular basis. Or so Rusty mused, mainly to occupy his mind and not keep checking his wristwatch every ten seconds.

Rusty stared at the bloodstain's surface congealing in the reflection of an overhead lamp. About two feet in width at the center, it grew wider near its source. That source was the throat of a frail silver-haired woman who lay crumpled on the floor.

The upper half of her body reached into the living room while her legs protruded onto the dull yellow linoleum of the kitchen. One orthopedic shoe lay on its side next to the stove, the other still on her left foot.

Two more minutes and I'm calling 911 again, he told himself.

This house in which he was currently the sole occupant—not counting its recently deceased owner—wasn't technically located in OC proper but in a remote enclave called Ocean Pines, separated from the main town by eight miles of salty bay water. A quiet upscale community, Rusty had a fairly complete knowledge of its character, having spent the first eighteen years of his life here and moving back ten months ago.

Next Thursday would be his thirty-sixth birthday. He had little awareness of that fact, and less interest in it.

For all Rusty knew, this was the first murder to darken the Pines' suburban pastoral facade since the town was incorporated in 1958. And it definitely was murder, of that he had no doubt. No one could conceivably take their own life in such a manner, and certainly not a frail seventy-eight-year-old spinster. The opening in Ms. Garrett's throat was not long, maybe three inches at most. It looked like more of a gouge than a slash. There was no knife or sharp implement anywhere in the room, and Rusty didn't dare step over the body to take a look in the kitchen.

The skin around the gash didn't appear to have been torn with a blade, but hacked away by a cruder implement.

Fingernails? Teeth?

Rusty shuddered as he pondered the options, and forced himself to stop thinking about it.

The hum of a car's engine and pebbles crunching underneath a set of tires claimed his attention. He walked to the front door, pulling aside a sash by the adjacent window to look outside into the hazy afternoon light.

Finally.

An Ocean City Police Department patrol unit sat in the driveway, engine idling. Rusty saw the door swing open, and a powerfully built officer stepped out. He grimaced. The cop didn't appear to be much older than a high schooler. Probably fresh out of the Academy with plenty to prove behind the badge.

Why didn't they send a detective, Rusty wondered, unlatching the door and opening it slowly so as not to make a surprise appearance on the front porch. Well, it was possible the OCPD's homicide unit didn't keep more than one ranking detective on any given shift. They probably didn't need more than that.

The young patrol cop was taking purposeful strides toward the house, fleshy face set tight as he spoke into a shoulder mic, confirming with a dispatcher his arrival at the location. His eyes widened just slightly before narrowing as he made a quick appraisal of Rusty Diamond.

"You're the one who made the call?"

Rusty nodded.

"She's in there," he said, stepping aside to let the patrol officer enter the house.

The cop had not taken two full steps into the living room when he stopped abruptly, one hand falling onto the service revolver holstered on his right hip.

"Jesus Christ."

"Yeah," Rusty said. "That was pretty much my reaction."

For a moment they stood there, two tall male shapes looming over a plump female form in a spattered floral dress.

"Found her just like this?"

"That's right. I didn't touch anything."

"How long?"

"Can't be much more than fifteen minutes. I called right away."

"You know her?"

"Her name's Thelma Garrett. She's my landlord."

The sound of that didn't sit right with Rusty; it was too removed and devoid of any kind of feeling. He almost added something like, *She was kind to me*, but figured that was bound to come out wrong.

The cop finally looked up from the old woman's body, seeming to peel his eyes away by an act of will.

"You live here?"

"No. She owns ... owned a second house not far from

here, on Echo Run. I've been renting it."

Those words brought on a sudden rush of memory. Rusty could see with total clarity in his mind's eye the day he first met Ms. Garrett. Just over ten months ago, on a frigid January morning. The meeting didn't happen here but at the rental house he'd occupied ever since.

At the time Rusty was so disoriented at finding himself back in Ocean Pines after such a prolonged absence that he had some difficulty maintaining a conversation with the chatty spinster. He agreed to her proposed rental fee, which seemed low for a three-bedroom furnished property overlooking Isle of Wight Bay. Location alone must have made the house a highly desirable piece of real estate, and he couldn't figure why she was willing to rent it out for such a reasonable sum.

Speaking in the kindly, crinkly voice he'd come to associate with her in all moods, Ms. Garrett replied she had no use for the property or a large boost in income. Once shared with her husband and the scene of many festive gatherings, it was too big for her current needs. And too lonely. Living as a childless widow in a modest two-bedroom tract house on nearby Heron Lane was much more comfortable.

Thelma (she'd insisted Rusty use her first name) didn't want to go through the hassle of trying to sell the larger house in a lackluster market, and was glad to simply know it would be occupied after many dormant years. It depressed her to think of the house where she and her family had shared so many good occasions sitting dark and forlorn all this time. Rusty signed the lease, feeling halfway guilty for paying so little.

"How'd you happen to find her?" the patrol officer said, yanking Rusty back from his reverie.

A slight whiff of something Rusty didn't like crept into the cop's voice. A taunt, almost, most likely the by-product of youth and rattled nerves. He scanned the badge pinned to the kid's chest.

"Tell you what, Officer Neely. Why don't we go through the whole thing when a detective gets here. Someone's on the way, right?"

"I'm the one you need to talk to now."

"Officer, trust me. I'm going to give my full cooperation. Whoever did this needs to …"

He stopped. The cop was looking at him with a new kind of scrutiny. Now that the initial shock of seeing the dead woman was fading, he seemed to take a full view of Rusty for the first time. The expression on his face didn't make much of an effort to hide a sense of disgust.

Rusty suddenly wished he'd kept his leather jacket on, but the living room had become stifling as he stood here waiting for the cavalry to arrive. The jacket lay draped on a sofa and he was wearing a black tank top, leaving his shoulders and arms open to easy view. *Perusal* would be more accurate, given the snaking tracks of words and symbols tattooed across much of his upper torso, coiling around the back of his neck and splitting into two vines that reached down both arms almost to the wrists.

"Latin, for the most part," he said with a self-deprecating shrug. "Just for looks, really. I don't know what half of it means myself."

Officer Neely's posture tensed visibly. His fingers once again found a place to rest on his gun.

"Turn around slowly, and show me your hands."

Rusty tried to pretend he'd misheard.

"Sorry, what?"

"Come on, do it."

"You're going to cuff me? I'm the one who called this in, remember?"

"Just turn around. We'll keep you nice and snug till backup gets here."

"Look, I'm as freaked out as you are. But I didn't do anything to this poor woman."

"You're resisting? I said let's see those hands."

He unsnapped the button on top of his holster. It seemed like a good moment to do something.

"For the last time, turn around!"

Rusty knew he could disarm this uniformed frat boy in just about 2.7 seconds. The task wouldn't present much of a challenge. He could easily divert Neely's eyeline with a lateral, non-aggressive movement of his left arm.

Momentarily distracted, the cop would never see the fingers of Rusty's right hand extracting a one-inch smoke pellet from a customized hidden pocket in his jeans. Pinched at the proper angle, the pellet would explode in a blinding flash followed by a plume of gray smoke. Utterly harmless but highly effective for misdirection.

The span of time Officer Neely would need to recover from his surprise would offer Rusty ample opportunity to relieve him of the gun. Using his fingertips, he'd grab the wrist and isolate pressure points causing Neely's hand to open involuntarily. From there, Rusty would simply reposition his body at a 45-degree angle and use his left hand to retrieve a sterling set of monogrammed handcuffs tucked in a different hidden pocket. One more second would be sufficient to cuff the young patrolman to a column of the bannister directly behind him.

They were only trick cuffs, but Officer Neely didn't know that. And unless he could perform with great precision, the sequence of twisting wrist movements needed to unlatch them, the knowledge wouldn't do him any good.

So, yes, the maneuver would surely come off. Just as successfully as it had in a thousand performances, even if those all occurred some time ago and Rusty's reflexes were no longer quite what they used to be.

But what would any of that accomplish other than to greatly amplify a sense of suspicion for his role in a brutal murder he had absolutely nothing to do with? Plus bring on a raft of other charges for failing to comply with orders, impeding police business, assault, et cetera. Obviously it was a bad play all around, however tempting.

So Rusty slowly turned 180 degrees and lowered his hands. Audibly relieved, Officer Neely stepped forward and bound them with a pair of un-monogrammed OCPD handcuffs. They closed around his wrists more tightly then necessary, pinching hard on the skin.

Hearing the cuffs snap shut, Rusty glanced up and was

startled by his reflection in a mirror above the sofa. He'd deliberately removed all mirrors from his own residence the day he moved in, and hadn't gotten a good look at his face in many months.

Given his appearance today, he could hardly fault this overeager junior lawman for wanting to lock him in restraints. For a guy who'd once placed such a premium on maintaining a well-cultivated exterior, it was shocking to see just how unkempt he was. Had he really let himself go *that much* in the past year?

Evidently, if the mirror was to be believed.

His long black hair, once treated daily by a personal stylist, was now a ratty mane. The two-pointed devil's goatee, formerly a key visual hallmark of his stagecraft, looked no more than an uneven graying scrub. And all that ink: pentagrams, death's head skulls and weird incantations etched up and down his sinewy arms.

Hell, anyone with a working pair of eyes would find Rusty Diamond a more than credible murder suspect.

2.

Lieutenant Jim Biddison sat at his desk in the sparsely populated squad room of the Ocean City Police Department headquarters, reading through the report for a second time. He'd just clocked in a few minutes ago, and the report practically jumped into his hands the moment he sat down.

There were two reasons for this.

First, the crime itself. Homicide was a blessed rarity in Ocean Pines, which comprised half of his jurisdiction along with the far more densely developed Northern District of Ocean City proper. Violent crime rarely blotted the lives of those with sufficient means to live in the Pines, one of the more exclusive resort communities tucked along Maryland's Atlantic coast. The most recent murder case happened back in 2009, involving an argument between two fishermen on the public jetty. Jim couldn't remember the last time someone was killed in their own home.

The second aspect of the report that grabbed him was the description of an individual who reported the crime and was currently detained on suspicion:

> White male. 5'11" 185 lbs. Hair: black. Eyes: brown.
> DOB: 10/27/78.
> ID: Nevada driver's license.
> Name: Russell Leonard Diamond.

Jesus. Was it possible? Jim hadn't heard or thought about that name in years. Decades, in fact. As far as he knew, Rusty Diamond hadn't shown his face within a hundred miles of this place since they both graduated from Ocean City High in the spring of '96.

The squad room's near silence was putting Biddison on edge. Other than him, there were no more than ten or twelve officers on duty. The room was shared by Patrol and Criminal Investigations. In the peak summer months, up to a hundred bodies might be packed in here on a given night, with phalanxes of seasonal officers filling out the Bike and Patrol Divisions. Now that fall had arrived and swept away the hordes of summer vacation tourists, Ocean City's population shrank to roughly seven thousand year-round residents, and the police force shrank in proportion.

Jim lifted all 216 pounds of himself from the seat behind his desk, stretching out a sore lower back. At thirty-seven, the body that once served him so well as an all-state linebacker was starting to complain about the way he'd treated it during his brief football career. Fifteen years on the OCPD force, rising steadily from patrol all the way to lieutenant, hadn't done his joints a whole lot of favors either.

But Jim wasn't worried about the vagaries of impending middle age right now. All he wanted to do was take a look at the occupant of holding cell 6A to confirm the report's description with his own eyes. He grabbed the 9" x 12" tamper-evident personal property bag that accompanied the crime report and set to find out.

It had to be him. The odds of someone else sharing that name and general description were too long. Yet the alternate conclusion also seemed unlikely. An old friend, long estranged and not seen in this area for almost two decades, was now in a cell two floors below in connection with the first homicide to hit Biddison's desk in five years?

He turned left down the hallway that led to the break room where a pot of rancid coffee awaited, passed by without pouring himself a cup and took two flights of stairs down to lockup.

Stopping outside cell 6A and peering through the small window, any doubts he might have been entertaining were erased. The man sitting on a bench inside, rough and ragged as he looked, was undeniably his old friend. While Rusty could never have been described as having a particularly wholesome appearance, there were no tattoos back in high school. Nor the frazzled goatee. But the long black hair, wiry build, and especially those slightly recessed dark eyes: they were exactly the same as Jim recalled.

It was a jolting sight, even though he half expected it. Taking a deep breath, he pushed the door open.

Rusty's surprise at seeing Jim Biddison was even more pronounced than that of the other man, given that he had no advance warning. But Rusty had once devoted countless hours to the study of controlling his facial muscles so as to never reveal a tell. He hadn't lost the skill; not a ripple of unease troubled his placid expression as Jim stepped into the room and closed the door.

Biddison broke the silence first.

"Even when I saw your name, I couldn't believe it."

"Hello, Jim. Long time."

"That's an understatement."

"You're looking fit."

"I'd like to say the same, but … hell."

Biddison took a seat in a metal chair across from Rusty, a small table separating them. The two men almost shared a trace of a smile. The lack of anything easy to say was palpable. Too much shared history in this small room, and too much time down the drain for any of it to feel relevant.

"Should I address you by rank?"

"It's lieutenant. But give me a minute, I haven't decided yet."

Rusty whistled.

"Lieutenant. Wouldn't expect any less of you. I'm sure captain can't be far off."

"How long have you been back, Rusty?"

The question yielded a short pause.

"Since January."

The corners of Jim's hazel eyes revealed surprise and

irritation in equal measure.

"You've been living in Ocean City for almost a year and haven't bothered to look me up?"

"I don't come into the city all that much. Spend most of my time in the Pines."

"Right, the Pines. All of eight miles away."

"Honestly, I haven't been getting out of the house a whole lot."

That sounded like an incredibly lame excuse, to both of them. But it was true, and Rusty didn't have a better one handy. There really wasn't any particular reason why he hadn't even tried to make contact with the man who was once the closest thing to a best friend he ever had.

"You don't think I did it. Do you, Jim?"

Biddison had been so momentarily taken aback by this surreal reunion that it took a moment for the question's meaning to register.

Instead of a direct answer, he responded with: "What were you doing at the scene?"

"I was worried about her," Rusty said, relieved the conversation had come to the topic of relevance. "Ms. Garrett always stopped by to pick up the rent. Nine o'clock sharp on the fifteenth of the month, like clockwork. It's been the same ever since I signed the lease. She didn't show today, so I thought I'd go to her house and check on her."

"You didn't try calling first?"

"No, I did. Got voice mail. Didn't bother to leave a message. It seemed just as easy to go in person."

"We can verify you made the call, if you did."

"You think I'm lying?"

"Just surprised you felt such concern. If she hadn't shown up after a day or two, I could understand."

"She was an old woman living alone. Could've broken a hip or something. It wasn't exactly an act of heroism to make a three-minute drive and knock on her door."

"The door was unlocked?"

"I let myself in."

"So you had a key."

Rusty exhaled slowly, his patience finally reaching a terminal point.

"Jim, I've answered these questions already. I've been sitting here for over six hours and you've seen the report, so what the hell?"

"Detective Taylor doesn't know you, Rusty. I do, so maybe I can spot something he didn't."

"Am I a suspect?"

"No. Not as of yet, anyway."

Rusty raised an eyebrow, as surprised as he was relieved to hear such a direct reply to the question.

"We lifted an alternate set of prints from the scene. This was most likely a burglary gone bad. We get them once October comes and the summer crowds fade. More than half the single-family residences in Ocean City lie empty for months on end, offering easy targets for thieves. The victim probably surprised an intruder. He freaked and did her in an unplanned moment."

Rusty watched the lieutenant very closely as this theory was laid out.

"I don't think so, Jim."

Now it was Biddison's turn to raise a brow.

"No? Why not?"

"For one thing, the house wasn't robbed. I was in the living room for at least fifteen minutes waiting for one of your people to show. There must've been half a dozen items in plain view any burglar would have grabbed."

"The guy probably panicked and forgot all about tossing the place."

"Have you seen the body? Her throat looked like it was torn open with someone's bare hands. Is that the kind of injury someone inflicts in an 'unplanned moment'?"

He hadn't intended to quote the lieutenant's phrase with such audible disdain. It just came out that way.

"By God, Rusty. You should've told me you'd taken up a career in forensics. Could've saved us all some trouble."

"I'm not a cop, clearly. I just notice things. Even if it was a burglar caught by surprise, something else had to be involved."

The lieutenant just let that suggestion hang in the air for a moment. Then he tore the seal off the tamper-evident property bag.

"Your personal effects. If you want them back."

Rusty held his gaze, noncommittal. Reaching into the bag, Biddison pulled out a pair of sterling silver handcuffs. He examined them, a wry grin stealing across his face.

"Monogrammed, huh? Kinky."

He dropped the cuffs onto the table with a loud clang. Then he pulled three small gray pellets from the bag.

"Took a while to figure out what these are. Why the hell are you carrying them around?"

Rusty almost replied, *Tools of the trade*, but stopped himself because that felt like revealing too much. Besides, it wasn't even accurate anymore. He just shrugged and said, "Old habits die hard."

"You always were into some weird shit. Pranks and magic and whatnot."

"You used to think it was pretty entertaining."

The grin returned to Jim's face, an admission.

"Like when you smoked out the janitor's closet? Still can't believe they didn't suspend you for that. Or the time you rigged that skeleton to pop out of Ms. Hamilton's desk?"

Both men almost let themselves laugh, but it didn't happen.

"I actually feel bad about that one," Rusty said, his amusement fading. "Pretty mean prank to play on the old gal."

"Yeah. As I recall, your favorite targets were always a little more robust."

"I was the target, Jim. For Wagstaff and Holmes and all your other jock buddies. I just found ways to retaliate."

"Sure you did. And I had to stop them from kicking the crap out of you a few times too."

Rusty was feeling uncomfortable with this turn of the conversation. Just seeing Jim Biddison under these circumstances was weird enough. He certainly wasn't in the mood to reminisce about a period of his life he'd made great strides to forget.

So he just pocketed the cuffs and the pellets, hoping Biddison would stand so he could. The lieutenant remained seated.

"Am I free to go?"

"You're free. Plan on staying in Ocean Pines a while?"

Rusty paused, having not considered the matter since making the grim discovery this morning.

"Can't think of anywhere else I need to be right away."

"Good. We might want to talk to you again."

Rusty gave a small nod and made for the door. He laid a hand on the knob, then turned.

"Do me a favor, Jim?"

Biddison didn't answer, waiting to hear what it was.

"Let me know when you catch the son of a bitch."

3.

Five hours later, creeping up on midnight. Rusty still felt unsettled, trying to process the events of the day. Only a few lights were burning in his rented house, a sprawling American Craftsman situated in one of the most secluded corners of Ocean Pines. The address 14 Echo Run seemed somehow apt in describing a hidden place where land gave way to water. His closest neighbor's driveway was half a block up the road, and the whole eastern face of the house looked out directly onto the serene expanse of Isle of Wight Bay.

Tucked behind dense curtains of tall trees for which this community was named, the house had offered him peace of mind for much of the time he'd stayed here.

But no peace was to be found tonight.

Rusty sat in the downstairs den, one of the rooms he used most often. Low ceilings and oak-paneled walls lent a vibe that appealed to him strongly; it was both rustic and gothic in nature. A great place to spend quiet hours, especially in cold-weather months when he could stoke the fireplace and brood in comfort.

For the past twenty minutes he'd been nursing his way through a glass of single-malt scotch and toying with the notion of opening the 15" MacBook Pro on the desk in front of him. When the glass was finally empty except for some melted ice, he gave in.

Flipping open the computer and hitting a bookmark for YouTube, he typed "rusty diamond caesars palace" in the search box. A list of more than two dozen clips scrolled up. Even without looking too closely, he figured they were all unauthorized bits of fan footage shot from somewhere inside the Etruscan Room. Probably the loge section, which offered the best angle for getting the entire stage in frame.

He was just guessing about where the footage came from. In the ten-plus months since last setting foot inside Caesars, he'd never allowed himself to go online and revisit that crazed, triumphantly self-destructive period of his life via the pixilated glory of low-resolution video.

He resisted the impulse now, but couldn't stop his fingers from typing another search query: "rusty diamond chainsaw act." This one yielded fewer results, but each of the videos had at least one hundred thousand views, some close to half a million. No surprise. The chainsaw act had always been his reliable closer, the go-to gag he used to bring down the curtain and leave them gasping before they even had time to applaud— whether performing for hundreds in the Etruscan Room or a scattered dozen on some unlit street corner in downtown Vegas.

What the fuck am I doing searching for this stuff?

With that reproachful thought, Rusty closed the MacBook almost hard enough to crack the screen. Once again he'd managed to avoid the perverse urge to watch any of those videos. Maybe he would tomorrow, or in six months. Right now he could see no point in it whatsoever.

Rusty reached for a half-empty bottle of The Glenlivet 18. A long moment passed as he pondered whether or not to refresh his glass. The option of sitting down to calm himself with twenty minutes of meditative breathing exercises remained viable, but would dissipate with another drink.

Already two down the hatch, an inner voice reminded him like some nagging schoolmarm. The irritation that followed this cautionary impulse made the decision for him.

He poured out a healthy slug, dropped in some ice and swirled, a faint rattle of cubes the only sound audible other than the ticking of an antique grandfather clock by the opposite wall.

Though Rusty had been the sole inhabitant of this house since the start of his lease, tonight it felt lonelier than ever before. Lonely for the first time, really. Ms. Garrett lived about five minutes away and rarely came here other than to collect the rent, yet her sudden absence seemed to permeate not only Rusty's peace of mind but the very walls of this structure that she'd long ago called home. He took his drink across the room to open the sliding glass door and step out onto the wooden planks of the back deck.

The temperature had dropped a good ten degrees since sundown, barely breaking forty, but he didn't mind. His favorite aspect of the house, aside from its seclusion, was this massive deck sitting directly above the western lip of the bay.

Peering due east across the dark rippling water, savoring the sting of night wind on his face, Rusty looked at the broad glowing band that comprised Ocean City's skyline. To the north, a much narrower string of lights indicated the Route 90 bridge, directly linking sleepy Ocean Pines with the bustle of its more traveled sister city.

A lantern moon was pinioned directly above, so bright as to color the night velvety blue against the blackness of the bay. October was always his favorite month when growing up a virtual stone's throw from here. The summers were better across the bridge in the overpopulated madness of OC, at least once he was old enough to go there without parental supervision. But here in the cool wooded embrace of the Pines, October was king.

Finishing his scotch more quickly than wisdom dictated, Rusty decided he wasn't going to sleep tonight. And he knew why.

They're missing something, he thought.

Ms. Garrett's injuries were too savage to suggest a simple break-in gone wrong. He'd been pondering this for most of the day; there was little else to do while warming that bench in the holding cell. Now, emboldened by expensive scotch and a sense of indignation, he knew he was right.

Jim's probably a good cop, but what about the rest of those yahoos on the force? Are they equipped to handle this, to look for any but the most obvious explanation?

Hell, am I?

Maybe not, but either way Rusty had to take some kind of proactive measure to shed himself of the depressive morass he'd been sinking in all day. So he went back inside and grabbed the keys to his Lexus LS 600h.

Exactly four minutes later, he parked half a block away from Ms. Garrett's house on Heron Lane. Sliding on a pair of black silk gloves, he reached under the seat and pulled out a thirty-two-piece stainless steel lock pick set. It occurred to him this would be the second time he'd used this particular set of picks without an audience watching. The second time today, actually.

Closing the driver's door softly, he crept through the moonlight up to the stoop. The house was dark, as expected, but some second-floor lights were on in a duplex across the street.

Rusty watched for a long moment to make sure no one was at the window eyeing his movements. Then he went to work on the lock. It took forty-one seconds, only slightly longer than it had this morning. Pocketing the picks, he stepped inside and pulled the door shut behind him.

4.

He didn't dare turn on any lights, but there was no need. A high-intensity G3 Nitrolon flashlight, no larger than a Magic Marker, created ample illumination. Moving the beam slowly, Rusty made a visual sweep of the living room.

The bloodstain was still there, looking even more surreal and Florida-like now that the body from which it flowed was gone. Rusty couldn't look at it for more than a second, turning the beam away so he could perform a quick inventory.

All the items he'd noticed before, the ones that seemed most likely to entice a burglar, remained in place:

A 22" Samsung TV. An antique gold-leaf clock on the mantle, still ticking. Rows of china lined up neatly across the shelves of an armoire.

Had a thief really broken in here with plans to do no more than loot, and then left without grabbing anything? It didn't seem likely this morning, and it still didn't.

Rusty took a wide step across the stain and placed a hand on the bannister reaching to the second floor. He moved lightly up the stairs, flinching at each creak.

Stepping into the bedroom, he canvassed with the flashlight. Nothing seemed to be missing or disturbed. The queen bed was made up neatly, not a single seam ruffling the smooth blankets. Walking over to a chest of drawers, Rusty honed in on a small jewel box resting on the top at eye level. He pulled off the lid, revealing a tangle of necklaces, bracelets and rings. He couldn't ascertain the worth of these items, but they didn't appear to have noticeable value. A thief might have plucked a few choice baubles and left the rest behind. Or, more likely, never set foot in this room at all.

At the opposite end of the hall was a guest bedroom, sparsely furnished. Rusty didn't bother to look too closely in there.

He was starting back down the steps when he thought to shine his flashlight into the bathroom.

The shower door was pulled partially aside, and Rusty paused the beam on a plastic bath seat Ms. Garrett used when washing herself. Somehow the image struck him as almost unbearably sad.

His buzz from The Glenlivet was all gone. In the clarity that took its place, he could feel a throb of stultifying rage.

Slow down. See what you're doing before you do it.

His breath decelerated, eyes narrowing to a semi-squint even as his legs and torso flexed just slightly. All of the major muscle groups responded in turn, growing perceptively taut but still pliable, like a bow drawn slowly back to let the arrow fly. Rusty knew the sensation—it was the same way his body responded when he stood offstage before a show, feeling the crowd's anticipatory rumblings through the floorboards beneath his feet.

Exhaling, he stepped into the bathroom.

Out of habit from his former life as an avowed drug person, he checked the medicine cabinet first. Ignoring the assortment of expected articles—calamine lotion, aspirin, dental floss, a yellowed box of Band-Aids—he closed the mirrored door. Then he noticed a prescription bottle next to the sink. Made of brown plastic, it was two inches in diameter. He pulled off the cap, revealing a small quantity of white powder inside.

The prescription label had been partially scratched away, but he could read the top line listing the bottle's contents: lidocaine powder. Filled by Trimper's Pharmacy on Wicomico Street with an expiration date that was illegible. The patient's name was almost completely missing, but Rusty could just make out an "ix" in roughly the middle of the space where the last name was printed.

An immediate, if obvious, conundrum presented itself.

There's no "ix" in Garrett, so this wasn't prescribed for Thelma. Living alone as she did, why would someone else's medication be in her cabinet?

His interest now piqued, Rusty ran the flashlight along the floor. He stilled the beam on a small squarish object near the base of the toilet. Translucent and blending in with the off-white linoleum tile beneath, he almost missed seeing it.

Rusty bent down and picked up the item. It was the torn corner of a cellophane gram baggie. Other than a small green stamp on one side, it was colorless and could have easily been missed by a cursory examination, assuming the police even looked up here. Holding the bag close, he saw a thin clump of yellowish crystals inside. Much grainier than the powder in the prescription bottle.

Now his synapses really started firing.

Rusty knew from personal experience that baggies this size had exactly one use: holding drugs, and not the kind found in a spinster's medicine cabinet. Whatever this stuff was, it didn't come with a prescription.

He came up here. Not to steal, but to get high. Maybe he needed to get high to keep his nerve.

Before he killed Thelma, or after?

Securing the baggie in a sleeve of his wallet, Rusty descended the stairs. He really didn't expect to find anything worthwhile on this spontaneous mission, and maybe he hadn't. But the baggie gave him reason to believe his instinct was on target. Its distinctive green stamp was something he could pursue.

Crossing the living room, Rusty laid a hand on the front door. He'd almost started to turn it when the sound of hurried footsteps froze him in place.

Someone was approaching the house.

He turned off the flashlight quickly. But maybe not quickly enough to escape detection from the outside.

Half a second later, a large shadow filled the window adjacent to the front door. The knob rattled once.

Rusty heard a series of erratic ticks and clicks that told him whoever was standing out there was trying to pick the lock.

It seemed to be a rather frantic endeavor performed without much skill.

If the door were still locked, Rusty would have been afforded a few moments to consider his wisest course of action.

But I left it unlocked when I came in.

The intruder seemed to realize that fact at the same moment it leapt into Rusty's head.

The door swung inward with a hard push, a shaft of moonglow lighting up a long section of the floor. The light reached directly to the center of the bloodstain.

Rusty backed across the room with three swift steps. Bumping against a two-seater couch by the fireplace, he pivoted over the back and dropped silently to the floor behind it.

He lay there, forcing himself not to breathe. Waiting to see if he'd avoided being spotted.

The intruder entered the house, pausing to close the door with a bang. An angry, hacking cough consumed the next few seconds.

Then heavy footsteps started moving in Rusty's direction.

5.

He counted the steps as they came closer. Three, then a fourth. Two more and the intruder would be standing directly over the couch. Even in the low light, Rusty would be there in plain view. Lying flat, hardly an ideal posture for defending himself. He pushed up into a crouch, knees bent in preparation to lunge upward at the first sign of physical threat.

After an interminable silence, the steps continued. Moving away from him now. Rusty heard feet clumsily ascending the staircase to the second floor.

He stood quickly and repositioned himself off to the side of the living room, which opened into a snug breakfast nook. From the creaking floorboards above his head, Rusty determined the intruder had gone directly to the bathroom.

No surprise.

He heard the tinkling of glass and a door bang shut—the medicine cabinet. That was followed by an angry curse and more coughing. Then the footsteps resumed, charging down the stairs. Rusty got a quick view of the intruder in silhouette as he crossed the living room: a man of average height, solidly built with a peach-fuzz beard. Then the front door was flung open and the intruder disappeared from sight onto the porch, pulling the door closed.

Rusty counted to five before running to the front door and opening it a crack. Seeing no one on the porch or the walkway below, he stepped outside and bounded down the stoop. Just as he reached the walkway he heard a car door slam. Running onto Heron Lane, he saw a tan Ford pickup turn on its lights a block to the north, just past where his own car was parked.

The pickup lurched forward, cutting a hard right at the end of the block without slowing.

Rusty sprinted to the Lexus and gunned the engine. He wasn't too worried about giving the pickup some lead time. The streets of Ocean Pines, never heavily trafficked no matter the hour, were utterly dead at this time of night. He anticipated little problem in catching up to the Ford. What did concern him was being spotted, so he rolled to the end of the block and turned right with his headlights dark.

Three blocks later he closed in on the pickup. It was heading due north on Cathell Road, as Rusty had expected. This path led directly to Route 90, a state highway dissecting coastal Maryland through the middle. If the Ford turned right on 90, that meant it was heading east across the bay into Ocean City. If it turned left, Rusty had no clue where it might be headed.

The truck was taking these dark residential streets at speeds that made Rusty thank God it was too late for any kids to be out riding bikes. Minimum of fifty-five on the straightaways and barely breaking for turns.

Three miles later, the Route 90 ramp approached. The Ford veered right, heading eastward. Accelerating onto the highway, it easily doubled the 40 mph speed limit and showed no signs of slowing.

Rusty maintained the pursuit, hanging back at a reasonable distance. They weren't the only vehicles on this busy stretch of the 90. He lost sight of the Ford a few times, cursing with frustration, only to bring it back into view. At one point he drew close enough to see there was no rear license plate.

Shit. So much for trying to track it via computer.

By the time they reached the bridge spanning eight miles across Isle of Wight Bay, Rusty wondered if the pickup's driver had a suicidal streak. Most likely he was just high, making unnecessary lane changes and slamming the brakes for no apparent reason before continuing at ever-greater speeds.

Several near-collisions made Rusty wince. His fingers gripped the wheel tightly, sweat beading across his brow. He was starting to ask himself how much damage was worth risking to keep up this hunt when the pickup veered sharply right, cutting off a minivan in the next lane. The minivan swerved left to avoid a wreck, forcing Rusty onto the shoulder.

His foot landed hard on the brake. A barrage of loose gravel sprayed across his windshield, erasing all visibility.

The Lexus skidded, wheels locking. Rusty turned into the skid. He missed the guardrail by a hair, cutting back into traffic at the last moment. A car behind him roared past with an incensed honk.

He swallowed and hit the gas, gradually catching up with the Ford. Soon he could see the lights of Ocean City coming into view across the water. The bridge let them off at Sixty-second Street, and the Ford turned right onto Philadelphia Avenue, heading into downtown.

This came as a welcome relief. Rusty knew he'd have an easier time maintaining the tail with red lights every few blocks. The bars and clubs downtown didn't close for another hour, and even in the off-season there were enough locals about to keep the town humming.

After ten more minutes of stop-and-go pursuit, Rusty saw the Ford turn left at Essex Street and roll into a large public parking lot. Only a block from the beach, with Ocean City's prized boardwalk directly in front.

The surrounding area was almost without light, all the nearby businesses closed. The lot appeared utterly empty now except for the pickup truck. Rusty kept the Lexus back out of sight, idling next to a trash dumpster.

He saw a man emerge from the pickup. The visual impression he'd formed at the house was confirmed: medium build, light beard, flannel shirt and workman's boots. Taking a wild look around as if expecting some kind of attack, the man started walking at an agitated pace toward the boardwalk.

Rusty didn't see much wisdom in parking his car in the lot where it was apt to be so easily identified. But he couldn't leave it here by the dumpster without getting towed. If he didn't continue the pursuit on foot right now, he was going to lose track of his quarry.

So he entered the lot and parked a good ten lanes away from the Ford. Then got out and started hustling toward the boardwalk. He followed the sound of diminishing footsteps in a southern direction along the wide beam of aged wooden planks.

Six blocks to the south stood the entrance to a massive amusement pier closed for the night. Stretching out well past the waterline where the Atlantic lapped against the beach, the pier featured all the usual attractions of its ilk: a creaky Wild Mouse coaster, a Salt & Pepper ride created for the sole purpose of inducing motion sickness in its riders, various fast food kiosks, and arcade booths devoted to Skee-Ball, Whack-A-Mole and similar games of skill and chance.

Rusty couldn't see anyone, but a faint pounding of footsteps told him he was still on the right track. It sounded like the man was heading out straight for the far end of the pier, which stood at least twenty feet above the churning waves and fifty yards from the entrance. At this time of night, suspended over water and far from the nearest source of man-made light, an almost unworldly darkness held sway. All the more so since the moon had ducked behind a towering cloud formation.

Only one attraction occupied the far terminus of the amusement pier. It was one Rusty remembered well from his youth.

The Morbid Manor. A looming two-story spook house the likes of which they stopped building decades ago.

He made his way toward the end of the pier, straining to retain aural contact with receding footsteps drowned out by the crashing surf below. The dark outline of the Morbid Manor rose taller in his vision as he drew closer.

When Rusty got within a few yards of the wrought-iron gate, he stopped. It occurred to him for the first time how hard his heart was hammering in his chest.

Tilting his head, he tried to pick up any sound from the man he'd been pursuing. No more footsteps were audible. There was nowhere else to run at this point other than to proceed inside the Manor.

Rusty deemed that unlikely given the bulky padlock keeping the front gate secure.

He's got to be somewhere close, assuming he didn't vanish into thin air.

The only option was to circle around the back of the hulking structure. Rusty moved at a slower pace now, cautious to keep his tread light.

When he got to the side of the building and turned a corner, he found only a narrow channel down which to proceed. On one side was the large back wall of the Manor, three feet opposite a waist-high metal railing. To go past the railing would be to plunge into the ocean and most likely be dashed against one of many massive wooden pilings.

He paused, sure he'd heard a scuffling footstep.

Whipping his head around, there was only darkness behind him.

Rusty almost looked up in time to see the man crouching in a busted-out windowsill above the Morbid Manor's rear exit. Some intuition, like a sense of being spied upon, guided his eyes upward.

But it came too late, and he lifted his head only in time to see a booted foot swinging at his face.

The blow hit dead center, drilling him between the eyes. Half an inch lower and it would have shattered his nose, but Rusty had no time to be grateful for that. As he staggered back against the railing, the man leapt down from his perch and landed another walloping belt, this time with an elbow to Rusty's right temple.

Then two hands were on his neck, pushing him back against the railing. He could feel the top wrung biting into his back, and his balance started to give.

There was no way to speak, his windpipe completely shut off. Rusty's vision misted and he was unable to make out the face of his assailant. The only aspect he descried was the beard. This had to be the same man he'd followed from Thelma Garrett's house.

For a moment the pressure receded and he thought his attacker had given up, either winded or just deciding to run.

Then a two-handed shove against both shoulders tipped Rusty back over the railing, and the force was too strong to withstand. He felt both ankles lifted from the ground, gripped by strong hands. Then his hips were up over his torso.

I'm going to fall.

That's what he heard his mind say. And he decided to let it happen.

Not resisting against the shove's momentum but moving with it, Rusty let his legs rise up into the air and then over his head. He performed a full backward summersault over the railing, allowing himself to drop, feetfirst, feeling the cold, briny wind rush up to rake his face.

At the last second his arms took over, acting of their own will. Thousands of hours of training and rehearsals paid for themselves in one instant. Both hands shot up to clasp the lowest bar of the railing. Fingers wrapping tight, his descent halted abruptly enough to induce pain in the tendons of his upper arms.

Hanging there in a white-knuckle clench, gusts from below pushed him around like a leaf on a branch. He could hear the footfalls of his attacker retreating.

Rusty didn't know if the guy had seen him cling to the rail, but decided to give him a full minute to get a safe distance away. Assuming his arms could hold out that long.

When the coast seemed clear, he hoisted himself up and over the rail. The creak of uneven wooden boards under his feet never sounded so good. As he tentatively walked back to the front of the Morbid Manor, Rusty was startled to realize he was smiling. It felt like an alien expression shaping his face of its own will.

When he reached the parking lot, the smile faded. The Ford pickup was nowhere in sight, which came as no great surprise but still disappointed him. Tonight's violent chase felt decidedly unfinished, leaving Rusty with a kind of hunger he couldn't quite classify.

Trudging back to his car, the full effect of being kicked in the head started to manifest itself. The pain didn't worry him as much as a weird sense of vertigo, which made the ground slant slightly to the left.

Looking at his Lexus, now the sole vehicle in the entire lot, Rusty really wished he'd had time to park in a less conspicuous spot. It seemed only logical to conclude his attacker knew what kind of car he drove and had possibly even gotten the plate numbers. A Nevada plate was apt to stand out easily enough in coastal Maryland, at least for anyone who had reason to take notice.

Keeping a slower pace, virtually the only car on the road, he drove back westward across the Route 90 bridge. His thoughts meandered, aided by fatigue. Rusty couldn't remember the last time he'd traversed this bridge before tonight. That realization triggered a host of long-buried memories.

Then an unwelcome thought derailed his contemplative reverie. It occurred to him he'd made another mistake.

That prescription bottle. Should've pocketed it along with the gram bag!

Feeling incredibly tired and wanting nothing more than his bed, Rusty knew he had to go back to the house on Heron Lane and confirm his suspicions. So he did just that, remembering only at the last moment to put on his silk gloves before touching the front doorknob.

Back inside, he didn't even notice the bloodstain this time. It had become as much a part of this sad house as the fireplace or the bannister leading to the second floor. He climbed the stairs two at a time, running the flashlight's beam around him to see if anything had been disturbed.

Inside the bathroom, he took a breath before opening the medicine cabinet, allowing himself a moment to hope that perhaps the bottle was still there.

It wasn't.

Right around the time Rusty made that dismaying discovery, a bearded man sat shivering behind the wheel of a tan Ford pickup parked some ten blocks south of the amusement pier. Engine idling, the exhaust pipe belched bluish fumes into the late night air.

The man wore a ratty flannel shirt that did little to keep off the chill. His left hand pressed a cell phone tightly to one ear. The phone performed a miniature jig in his tremulous grip.

"Pick up, goddamnit," he pleaded angrily through frayed vocal chords.

His cheeks quivered with the force of chattering teeth. The night was cold, but that's not why the man shivered. His tremors knew a more malignant source: the inexorable spiral of withdrawal.

The call went to voice mail for the fourth time. Standard factory recording, a robotic female voice saying the person at this number was not available, please leave a message after the tone.

The bearded man ended the call with a harsh curse followed by some prolonged coughing. Composing himself, he started to press redial but paused. A bleak intuition overtook him that a fifth call was not only futile but possibly dangerous.

They'd warned him in the most direct terms never to contact the bungalow again. Only a fool would ignore that kind of admonition.

But he *had* to talk to Fade. Right now.

Earlier today, after his first catastrophic visit to the house on Heron Lane, he never even considered tipping off his former associates in the bungalow about what went down. Why bother? Might as well tie a noose around his own neck and kick over the stool with a move like that.

But after tonight's second visit, and its frantic conclusion at the Morbid Manor, he knew there was no choice.

So he took a deep breath and called again.

Someone picked up on the second ring. It wasn't the person he wanted.

"What the *fuck*?" a guttural voice boomed. "Lost your goddamned mind, Dixon?"

"Got to talk to Fade. Put him on, Nate."

"He ain't talking to you, Kenny. You're what they call persona non gratis."

Jesus Christ, the way Tampa Nate threw out fancy terms to cover up the obvious fact he was a stupid cracker with a third-grade education never failed to irritate. But Kenny Dixon couldn't be bothered with that right now.

"I said I need to talk to him, Nate. It's really fucking important, OK?"

"He's busy. Even if he wasn't, no chance he's wasting any more time on you."

"There's something he needs to know about. Can't wait."

"I really doubt there's anything you could tell him he needs to know."

The bearded man shuddered through the spasms of another coughing fit. By the time it subsided, he was surprised Tampa Nate was still on the phone.

"Fine," Kenny sputtered. "Fade can hear about it on the news tomorrow. I'll be sure to let him know you stopped me from giving him an early heads-up."

Just as he expected Nate to tell him to eat shit or simply hang up without that formality, Kenny heard a new voice come on the fiber-optic line. The one he'd both sought and dreaded, it carried little emotion or hint of any human tendencies beyond a kind of sterile intellect.

"This must be important, Kenny. I thought we'd attained a certain level of clarity on the matter of your obsolescence."

"I'm not looking to get back on the payroll, Fade."

"Well, then?"

Kenny faked one more cough, a long rasping bark with no purpose other than buying him a few seconds to consider his next words with care.

"Some shit went sideways today. It's bad, but I'm clear now. Figured you should hear about it from me first."

A pause elapsed, telling Kenny he hadn't offered enough information to merit a reply.

"Main thing is," he continued unsteadily, "it's got nothing to do with, you know, our association. I don't want you thinking it'll come back to you in any way."

Another pause, more ominous in length. More than long enough to make Kenny Dixon wonder if he'd just made a bad situation a hundred times worse by placing this call.

"Start from the beginning," Fade said.

6.

Rusty sat cross-legged on the floor of his bedroom as an early-morning egg-yolk sun shone in through the east window. Spine straight, chin lifted, eyes shut—every aspect of his posture designed to attain a calm state of detached mindfulness. All was quiet except for some birdsong faintly emanating through the closed windows.

He silently tracked the progress of each extended breath. Seven seconds per inhalation, a three-second hold, then another seven to release the air fully from his lungs.

The well-practiced mechanics of his daybreak meditation ritual were all in place, but their intended effect remained elusive. After a handful of minutes, he felt no more centered than when he'd first lumbered from the bed with an unfamiliar sense of wired anticipation.

His mind simply would not respond to the usual prompts. It was too busy churning with grimly compelling memories and speculations.

They're just thoughts, he counseled himself. *Label them as such, let them go, and return to the moment.*

No dice. Wrinkling his brow in frustration rather than focus, Rusty conceded the process wasn't working today. The dull ache in his forehead provided a constant distraction, each throb bringing him back to that bloodstain and all it signified.

"Try again later," he muttered and rose to his feet.

He'd come to depend on these morning sessions to anchor himself for another day on the straight and narrow, having heard that meditation was a reliable aid for people with tendencies toward heavy chemical consumption. Deeming himself a member of those ranks in the wake of an utterly disastrous series of events in Las Vegas almost a year ago, he'd given it a shot while remaining far from convinced it would work.

Any initial skepticism had quickly faded after his third or fourth honest attempt at meditating, and he now viewed each session as a staple of any healthy day roughly on par with eating.

Despite that, abandoning the effort this morning didn't strike him as a defeat. In truth, he didn't *want* to feel relaxed right now. Not after what he'd been through over the past twenty-four hours. Still amped from the chase, every cell in his body called out for a continuance of that cathartic action. Something entirely opposite to the calming stasis brought on by meditation, and to hell with the risks.

I'm going to find the bastard who jumped me.

That thought brought a smile to his lips, the first of the day. He carried it with him to the bathroom to assess his face in the house's one mirror he hadn't been able to remove; it was bolted into the wall above the sink.

His reflection didn't displease him for a change. A certain light seemed to fire his eyes in a way he hadn't noticed in many months. Flickers of vitality where he never expected to see such animation again.

All because some old woman got her throat torn out?

It made sense even though it didn't. The notion of just forgetting about Thelma Garrett's murder, and his own role in its weird aftermath, repulsed him on a gut level. Rusty knew he faced wildly long odds of uncovering some critical angle to the crime undetected by the police, but maybe he could at least point them in the right direction. Hell, he owed poor Thelma that much.

Yeah, but that's not why, he thought with a humorless grin, staring at the purplish oval bruise covering half his brow.

Last night was good, *no matter what brought it on. A heavy shock to the system, and if I didn't need that no one does.*

He pushed himself away from the mirror. Another thought arose.

Made it too easy for him, stumbling around the Manor in the dark like an idiot. Next time, he won't see me coming.

On impulse, Rusty's hands stretched and balled into fists as he visualized a range of dire payback methods to inflict on his attacker. Whatever means he ultimately chose, that much definitely needed to happen.

Where to start?

First, a closer look at that little green stamp emblazoned on the torn baggie. On a casual glance it appeared to be a simple abstract shape, a kind of rough circle or oval. Only after inspecting it under the glare of a 300-watt bulb did Rusty note the particularities.

It was a snake or serpent of some sort, the design appearing to be of either Chinese or Japanese extraction.

As he examined the stamp, Rusty noticed something familiar. He'd seen variations of this image any number of times. Racking his brain, the name came to him. It was the Ouroboros, the ancient symbol of a snake eating its own tail. Deciding to Google it later, he didn't spend any time trying to decipher some deeper significance. Most likely the snake stamp was a simple branding of the product, no different than the dozens of different Ecstasy tabs in various shapes, sizes and colors with which he was once intimately familiar.

Not much to go on, he thought, setting the baggie aside.

His other possible lead was the Ford pickup, but that struck him as another dead end. Knowing only the make and model, it didn't even seem worth sharing with Lieutenant Biddison. Besides, Rusty wasn't sure how much wisdom there was in telling Jim about last night's activities.

Which left him with the Morbid Manor. He couldn't conjure any clue of how it might fit into Ms. Garrett's death, but for lack of any better options that's where he determined to start looking. As soon as he got himself cleaned up and caffeinated.

For the first time in weeks, Rusty made more than a cursory stab at ablutions, trimming his goatee to a single well-honed edge and combing out the tangles in his hair. As an afterthought, he decided to rub some vanishing cream onto the bruise above his eyebrows. He planned on interacting with a number of people today—a novel concept in its own right—and didn't feel like dealing with a lot of stares or questions.

In the spacious kitchen, he scooped six tablespoons from a ziplock bag of chicory coffee ordered from Cafe du Monde in New Orleans (the only city in the world that produces real chicory coffee, as far as Rusty was concerned). Brewing a pot, he downed two quick cups and poured a third into a travel mug for the car.

Pulling out of the driveway, he decided to make one last trip to the crime scene before driving into Ocean City.

A fresh look at Ms. Garrett's home in the light of day might prove beneficial. In particular, he wanted to canvas the front yard. Given how recklessly the intruder had bolted from the house, it stood to reason he may have dropped something from the stoop to the spot where he'd parked the pickup on Heron Lane. Rusty had no time to inspect the yard when being marched out in cuffs by Officer Neely, and it was too dark to check last night.

He was navigating the quiet wooded streets of Ocean Pines, letting the breeze filter through the open windows, when he first spotted the car behind him. Nothing especially notable about it, just a midsize vehicle painted a dullish silver shade. From the grill he was able to identify the make as a Dodge. Muscle car, probably a Charger.

Turning right onto Heron Lane, Rusty felt a twinge of unease when the Dodge followed him. This was one of the least trafficked streets in all of Ocean Pines, only a block long and containing less than a dozen homes.

Rusty slowed as he approached Ms. Garrett's house, but didn't stop. He pulled over in front of the next mailbox, eyes drilled on the rearview. The Dodge slowed as well, then came to a complete halt two car lengths behind.

He couldn't get a clear read on the driver from this distance, except to determine there appeared to be no one else in the vehicle. A bunched mass of hair behind the wheel could have belonged to either man or woman.

OK, Rusty mused to himself, draining the contents of the travel mug. *What to make of this?*

He was still debating whether to get out and check Ms. Garrett's front yard for any dropped debris when the Dodge revved its engine and pulled an aggressive three-point turn. It roared down Heron in the opposite direction and out of sight. Rusty just had time to see it was a D.C. plate but couldn't make the number.

That was weird, he thought as a wave of tentative relaxation flowed though him. But after the events of the last twenty-four hours, what really classified as weird?

He got out of the car. Took him less than five minutes to scrutinize the rectangular plot of yellowing grass below Thelma Garrett's front porch before satisfying himself there was nothing lying about in the form of a convenient clue. He'd expected as much, but now he could chalk it off his list and hopefully never lay eyes on this house again.

Back inside the Lexus and firing the engine, he turned left onto Harbormist and steered for the Route 90 bridge. Just as the turnoff approached, that same Dodge muscle car materialized behind him.

Son of a bitch.

Rusty accelerated, foot mashing the pedal. If this clown wanted to stay with him, for whatever reason, he was going to make it a little more of a challenge.

He was doing about seventy as he took the ramp to the eastbound highway. The Dodge followed up the ramp, but he lost sight of it as soon as he merged into the middle lane. Traffic was fairly heavy, much more so than last night, and it was impossible to keep track of any vehicle that wasn't directly on his tail.

By the time he'd crossed the bridge and reached the off-ramp for downtown Ocean City, there was no sign of the Dodge. He pushed it from his mind and put all his focus on recreating last night's pursuit with the benefit of daylight.

• • •

The boardwalk wasn't exactly empty this cold morning, with a scattering of joggers and people grabbing breakfast, but it was a virtual ghost town compared to the megalopolis it would be at summer's peak. Rusty had spent a good portion of his youth here. Hours on end he'd stand rooted to these boards, and it was here that inner vistas of a life far richer than anything he'd been given to believe possible first opened in his mind.

The polestar of his adolescent absorption was a motley community of street performers who worked the tourist trade twelve hours a day from May to September. Magicians, jugglers, sword swallowers, contortionists, escape artists, and innumerable variations of all. They were more than just figures of fascination to a withdrawn youth like Rusty Diamond. They appeared almost as living gods, pulling off impossible actions in front of gape-jawed crowds lined up to drop dollars at their feet. The first time he witnessed a well-executed levitating act, it hit him with the force of revelation. He'd found his calling.

But Rusty was of no mind to revisit any long-lost epiphanies right now.

A flurry of activity caught his eye, not far from the amusement pier's entrance. A huge orange banner was in the process of being erected, stretching almost a city block in length. A cluster of men below struggled to secure it in place. Flapping in the breeze, the words stenciled across the banner in bold black letters weren't quite readable, but their message was clear.

Rusty smiled, allowing nostalgia to have its way. The Halloween festival, always an annual highlight, was once again at hand. Or at least in the first stages of preparation.

All around, variations on a familiar seasonal theme were evident. Scarecrows tilted with eyeless heads, lashed to wooden crucifixes planted at odd angles in the ground. Glow-in-the-dark skeletons of outrageous scale were lined up in a grim assembly. A massive inflatable black cat billowed imposingly, just halfway filled with air as a noisy portable generator fueled the pump. Pumpkins abounded.

Turning left onto the pier and away from the festival prep, Rusty walked casually toward the Morbid Manor. Even in the light of an overcast morning, it cut an ominous shape on the horizon.

The Manor was a crumbling dowager of a midway attraction, its tall gables looking ready to heave under a light wind. It had been a boardwalk staple since opening in the late 1970s. Many a parent who took the trembling hand of a reluctant child while forking over admittance could vividly recall their own first foray into its creaking walls.

A throwback to simpler times, the Morbid Manor did not rely on any high-tech special effects. There were no cable-operated cars in which riders could huddle at a safe distance from the scares. You had to walk through the place, both floors, navigating a narrow and sadistically designed labyrinth one step at a time. Much of the trek took place in total darkness, and was populated with real human beings decked out in gruesome garb, waiting to jump from a hidden corner and scare the bejesus out of you.

For more than a generation, a stroll through the Morbid Manor after dark was a bona fide rite of passage. Rusty still recalled his maiden voyage at age seven with crystal clarity, as well as the nightmares that haunted him for weeks afterward. He was hooked by the fright, and never failed to visit the Manor at least once a week during its summer months of operation.

Now, standing just a few yards from the ticket booth, he saw something that escaped his attention last night. Tacked above the wrought-iron gate was a sign reading: *Goodbye and thanks for 38 horrific years! —MM*

He noticed all the windows on both floors were boarded up. Given the intentionally run-down state of the attraction, partly for effect and partly from neglect, the boards could easily have been taken as an exterior design flourish. But it now seemed obvious the Manor had closed for good.

Rusty felt a pang. An icon of his childhood, not thought of for years, had taken the eternal dirt nap. Depressing.

He slowly walked the perimeter of the entire building, stopping to pause near the spot where he'd almost been dumped into the drink last night. There was little to see. The rear double doors used as an exit for patrons were bolted and padlocked similarly to the front entrance. Rusty could spot no way in which someone might enter the building without smashing through the boards on one of the windows, and they all seemed to be intact.

So what was that guy doing last night? he wondered. *Did he have any actual reason for coming back here? Was he trying to get inside the Manor, and if so, why?*

Rusty couldn't conjure a sensible answer. Maybe he'd been spotted at some point during the chase from Ocean Pines—either in the parking lot, or on the road, or even back at the house on Heron Lane. Maybe the guy lured him all the way out here just for the purpose of jumping him and tossing him over the rail.

That theory made sense, sort of. But Rusty knew he was just shooting arrows in the dark.

Ambling back toward the entrance of the amusement pier, he bought a bag of popcorn from a chubby teenage girl in a booth.

"What's happening with the Manor?" he asked.

"Closed," the girl said, barely looking him in the eye.

"For good?"

She nodded curtly.

"Bummer. That was always my favorite thing to do around here."

"Place is gross. And dangerous too. They decided to tear it down before it collapses."

"Maybe they'll build a new version. Make it even scarier than the original."

The girl shrugged like that was the lamest idea anyone had ever presented to her.

"You know when they're tearing it down?" he asked.

"Soon, I heard. After the Halloween festival the whole pier closes for the winter."

"All right, thanks."

Rusty walked away, tossing some popcorn in his mouth. It was unheated and laced with greasy fake butter. He dumped the bag into a trash can. If there was more information to be gained out here about what happened to Ms. Garrett, he was damned if he could think what it might be.

7.

The lobby of the Worcester County Medical Examiner's Office was roughly as cold and sterile as Rusty had envisioned. He really didn't want to be here—wasn't even sure he *should* be here—but it seemed like some kind of obligation. Besides, he still felt demoralized from his unproductive visit to the boardwalk and figured this was probably the best purpose to which he could devote the afternoon.

He'd gone back to Echo Run directly from the boardwalk and spent thirty infuriating minutes trying to calm his mind through meditation. Focusing on the breath, watching his thoughts materialize without getting ensnared in them—normally this required little effort. He'd come to rely on it daily, keeping fiendish memories of Vegas and the self-destructive impulses fueling those memories at bay. The idea of abandoning meditation, losing the ability to reap its protective benefits, truly disturbed him.

But he couldn't muster it today, and was getting too pissed off to keep trying. So he gave up and drove over to this grim building on Ninety-fourth Street.

He had no clue if there were any surviving kin to claim Thelma Garrett's body. She'd been widowed for years and had no children, that much he knew for sure. Surely she had friends, and the staff at a local hospital where she read to sick patients must have known her fairly well. But it seemed eminently possible Rusty was the only one around who could see to it that her remains were dealt with in a respectful manner.

"And what was your relationship to the deceased?" asked

a gaunt silver-haired clerk in medical scrubs seated at the front desk. Rusty couldn't figure out why an administrative type like this was dressed for an operating room. Maybe he was a coroner who double-dutied as a receptionist when the regular was on lunch break.

"She was my landlord."

This response produced a look of surprise bordering on distaste from the man behind the desk. It was the second such facial display in less than two minutes. The first came when he looked up from his monitor and took in the sight of Rusty's long mane and goatee. At least the tattoos were hidden from view under his leather jacket.

"Your landlord," the clerk repeated.

"Yeah. And a friend too, kind of. She lived alone, so I'm not sure if anyone else is going to show up."

"What the hell is it to you?"

This question came not from the man he was speaking to, but from some unseen source behind him. Turning around, he beheld a woman standing less than two feet away across the parquet floor.

She was a stunner. Dressed in a charcoal pinstripe business suit tailored to complement a set of curves, black leather pumps adding an inch to her leggy frame, long amber hair pulled into a tight ponytail tied with a black silk bow. Every inch of her was manicured, primped and painted for some kind of domination, whether in the bedroom or boardroom Rusty couldn't quite say.

"Excuse me?"

"I asked what you're doing here. You had no relationship to this woman. What business is it of yours how she's buried?"

Rusty was a little thrown by the hostility of this inquiry. He tried to keep his irritation in check when answering with a question of his own:

"And you are …?"

"The person responsible for Thelma Garrett."

"OK, fine. I wasn't sure any such person existed. Since I'm not needed I'll be on my way."

"You haven't answered my question."

"I was her tenant. And I'm assuming you're her, what, executor?"

For just a moment the woman's eyes seemed to shimmer, a trace of vulnerability exposed through the cultivated facade.

"Her niece. She was the only family I had."

"Oh, Jesus. I'm sorry."

"Were you the one who found her? I just came from the police station."

"Yeah, that was me. I stayed with her until they showed up at the house."

"I guess I should thank you. Sorry for the third degree. I'm just trying to process all this."

Another wave of emotion passed over her face. Rusty laid a hand on her arm.

"You want to sit down for a minute?"

She gave a partial nod, so he guided her across the gleaming floor to a wooden bench. They sat and he gave her a moment to compose herself, feeling the clerk's curious gaze from across the lobby.

"My name's Rusty. I've been living in the house on Echo Run for some time now."

"Janice Garrett," she said, offering her hand in what seemed like an awkward formality. "Aunt Thelma mentioned she'd taken in a tenant. She used to mention you on the phone from time to time."

"Well, I wouldn't believe half of what she said."

Rusty immediately regretted the flip remark. It yielded a wan half smile.

"She said you looked like a reject from a motorcycle gang, but she liked you anyway."

Now they both smiled just a bit.

"Your aunt was exceedingly nice to me. She gave me a more than reasonable rate on the house."

"I know. When she told me, I said she was crazy. It's an amazing property. You should be paying three times that much."

"Believe it or not, I offered to raise the rent once or twice. She wouldn't hear of it."

Janice gave a skeptical look that quickly faded with a nod.

"Aunt Thelma didn't have much use for money. No husband or kids to leave it to, and she liked to live a simple life."

"She'd sometimes come around with an eggplant casserole she'd whipped up, or a plate of cookies fresh from the oven. She was a damn good cook."

"Yeah, she was. I had that casserole more times than I could count growing up."

"You're from Ocean Pines?"

Janice straightened her posture, her earlier show of emotion tucked back in place.

"I sort of shuttled back and forth between here and Baltimore. My parents lived there, but their marriage was never in very good shape. When things got especially rocky, I'd come stay with Aunt Thelma for a while."

"Do you still live around here?"

She shook her head briskly, as if the idea was unpalatable.

"New York. I caught an early train to Wilmington this morning and drove a rental car straight to the police station."

"Well, if there's any way I can help with the, you know, arrangements. Just say the word. I mean it."

"Thanks. I think I can handle everything."

Rusty felt like he should probably excuse himself now. There seemed little for him to do, which came as a relief. If he'd had to decide how Ms. Garrett's remains were to be disposed of, he'd be left with making a blind guess. It was nice to be free of that burden.

"Do you have any idea what happened?" Janice asked.

"The cops seem to think it was a burglary gone wrong. I guess you've already heard that."

"Is that what you think?"

"I'm not really in a position to question their judgment."

"But you found her. And you probably had contact with her as much as anyone else."

"I was also hauled in on suspicion for doing it."

Janice drew in her breath, a startled look on her face.

"Nobody told me that."

"They let me go after a few hours. I know a guy on the force. He seems convinced it's some local scumbag who probably has a sheet for breaking and entering. Whoever it is, they'll find him."

Rusty wished he sounded a little more convinced in saying that, but Janice didn't seem to hear any hesitation.

"Are you gonna be in town for awhile?" he asked.

She nodded. "At least for a few days, until the funeral. I'd like to be here when they nail the motherfucker."

Rusty couldn't help liking the harsh New York tone accompanying those words. It was kind of a turn-on.

He paused before asking, "Are you staying in her house?"

"God, no. I'm not sure I ever want to set foot in there again."

"Well, it sounds stupid to say since the place I'm living in probably belongs to you now, but you're more then welcome to stay there. Whole lot more room than I need, and three bedrooms as you know."

"Thanks, I hadn't even gotten around to thinking about the inheritance. But I'm staying at the Avalon Inn. It's on Fifth Street."

"I know the place."

"Then you know where to reach me. Let me know if you hear anything from your friend with the police."

"I will. Definitely."

She stood and started walking back to the front desk without another word. Rusty sat watching her for moment, then rose and made for the exit. He could hardly wait to get out of this building.

Savoring a breath of fresh air in the parking lot, he felt a renewed sense of mission bubbling within. This unexpected meeting with Janice Garrett was the trigger, adding a new dimension to the repellent crime of an elderly woman's murder. Rusty tried to convince himself it had nothing to do with the way Janice looked in those pumps and pinstripes, and was marginally successful.

Regardless of motivation, he'd already decided to dig deeper. The Morbid Manor had yielded precisely squat in terms of a lead. Now it was time to focus on that stamped baggie.

MISDIRECTION

Rusty hadn't tried to score any illicit chemicals in quite some time, and never in Ocean City. But he figured a comprehensive survey of every roughhouse boozing establishment in the immediate vicinity wasn't a bad place to start.

8.

Two days passed. Two utterly fruitless, frustrating days and nights.

Since his encounter with Janice at the medical examiner's office, Rusty had worked his way through a substantial amount of shoe leather without unearthing a fragment of new understanding about what may have befallen her aunt. He'd visited every sulfurous gin mill, pockmarked beer hall, back-alley saloon and low dive in all of Ocean City proper. He'd even expanded his search to the adjacent townships of Fenwick Island and Berlin.

He'd been to the Bucket of Blood. Zissimo's. Shenanigan's Irish Pub. The Mug & Mallet. Brass Balls Saloon. Hammerjack's. The Alibi Room. The Purple Moose. The He Ain't Here Bar. The Angler's Rest. The Blue Note Lounge. Ray's Tap Room. Linda's Lair. The Coral Reef.

All these and probably two dozen more swirled in his head. The primary, and depressing, element bonding these diverse establishments was their utter sameness. Same general decor, same classic rock and/or hip hop blaring from the juke either too low or too loud, same mediocre bar service from beefy guys or hot-but-skanky gals, and the same clientele of hard-core regulars: day drinkers, dawn busters, and night owls alike.

Rusty had spoken to maybe fifty people. His first approach was to spark up some chatter with any haggard barfly he could find pouring them down by him- or herself. Attempting to enter a conversation involving two people was trickier, and he didn't even try to insinuate himself with groups of three or more.

After some opening patter in which he ran a quick personality profile (a skill he'd mastered as a street performer recruiting spectators to assist him with various illusions), Rusty would gradually steer the conversation towards drugs. The range of responses he got ran the gamut from walleyed oblivion to plain disinterest to outright hostility. No one came close to offering any insights about where he might procure some of that "sick powder marked with the little green stamp."

When there seemed no likely candidates on the paying side of the bar, Rusty reverted to plan B. He did this with considerable reluctance, knowing how easily it might blow up in his face. Plan B entailed chatting up the barmaid or bartender for as long as it took to break the ice, then shifting to a similar line of inquiry. On two separate occasions he'd been run out of the place with pissed-off oaths to not come back.

It was a clumsy, clunky methodology befitting his status as a rank amateur in the world of private investigation. He was getting nowhere fast, and earning zero friends in the process. But Rusty could think of no more practical way to track down the drugs he was looking for. If they weren't being sold in the kind of shithole bars he'd been canvassing, where the hell *were* they being sold?

That's what he was wondering as he pushed through the smudged glass door of a bar on the 300 block of Dagsworthy Street called The Bearded Clam. Somehow he'd avoided this spot in the early stages of his inquest, which was odd considering it was only four blocks from the boardwalk's amusement pier. So obvious he'd almost overlooked it.

If any narcotic activity took place within these walls, it was more than a fair bet the guy who broke into Thelma Garrett's house was linked to it.

At 3:45 on a Tuesday afternoon, the Clam was basically dead except for a few fossilized specimens holding down stools at the far end of the bar. A dust-covered juke was cranking out some Bob Seger without much conviction. The felt on the pool table looked like it had been worked over with a cheese grater.

Rusty grabbed a stool near the front door and waited for

the mountainous bartender to look up from a copy of the *Ocean Gazette* that was occupying his attention. It took a solid ten-count for this to happen.

Shuffling toward him with elephantine steps, the bartender's eyes glazed over with boredom or something more aggressive.

"Help you," he mumbled.

"Draft beer's good."

The bartender didn't probe for more specifics or offer a list, simply dropped a frosted pint glass under a tap of Yuengling and filled it up.

"Thanks," Rusty said, taking the smallest sip he could manage. There was no one else within earshot, so he opted to get right down to cases:

"Thinking about something strong to chase it with. Can't make up my mind what might scratch that itch."

The bartender raised a fat, hairy forearm to glance down at his Dale Earnhardt wristwatch.

"Happy hour starts in ten minutes. Jägerbombs for three bucks till seven."

Rusty smiled and took another nip. The beer was cold but skunky beyond redemption. They probably cleaned out the tap lines once every other presidential election cycle.

"Tell you what," he said, leaning forward just slightly and dropping his voice, "I was thinking about maybe something a little stronger. Maybe something I'm willing to pay extra for."

The look of disdain on the bartender's face grew another layer.

"You a fucking cop or what?"

Rusty didn't respond but almost had to laugh at the ungainliness of his approach. He probably wasn't cut out for this kind of assignment after all.

"Do I look like a cop?" he said, locking eyes with the bartender.

"Look like a fucking loser. Finish your beer and walk. There's no kind of action you're looking for in here."

As Rusty was pondering a prudent response or whether to even bother with one, the front door opened and a young man of skeletal build hurried in, a ratty scarf trailing in his wake and almost getting caught in the door as it swung shut.

"What the hell, Ronnie!"

"Not my fault, Big Bill," the emaciated kid said, a trace of weak defiance in his voice. "Goddamn bitch Rhonda took the car again. I had to use the bike."

"Unload that shit in the back. There's at least ten cases to be inventoried."

"Just let me get a Coke first."

Ronnie circled around the bar to pour himself a glass of soda from the dispenser. Big Bill the bartender's eyes never left him, practically glowing with anger.

Rusty thought the distraction might pose an opening.

"One more question," he said quietly.

The bartender planted both hands on the bar and leaned forward in a posture that announced an imminent explosion.

"Suppose someone *was* looking for the kind of action that can't be found here. What's his best bet?"

This question seemed to amuse Big Bill, like an unknowingly naive query from a precocious youth. He pointed to the beer.

"You gonna drink that?"

Rusty shook his head, pushing his stool away from the bar. He knew walking out without touching the beer only made him that much more glaringly suspicious, but he didn't care. Big Bill had pegged him for a narc or a drugged-out loser already, and he didn't plan to darken this door again.

"Dump it with the rest of the dishwater."

With that, he turned and made for the exit. Heard the bartender mutter "asshole" under his breath as he reached the door.

Outside, a cool sea breeze came in strong off the beach. Clouds overhead threatened rain. Rusty was just glad to be released from the clammy interior of the bar.

Probably how they came up with the name, he thought.

He was half a block down Dagsworthy, making for his car with a sense of gnawing frustration, when he heard someone whistle behind him.

Turning, Rusty saw the skinny kid who'd walked into the bar. He was standing near the far corner of The Bearded Clam, most likely having emerged through a back exit.

The kid gave one furtive yank of the head in signal for Rusty to approach. He did, and didn't have time to speak first.

"You gotta tell me if you're a cop, right?"

"That's right," Rusty replied evenly, figuring he wasn't speaking to a future Mensa candidate. "I'm no cop. It's Ronnie, right?"

The kid nodded, lighting a cigarette. "What're you looking for?"

Rusty dug the torn baggie from his pocket. He held it up, displaying the green stamp.

"Seen these around?"

A squint and another nod.

"Anything you can tell me?"

"That sounds like something a cop would ask."

"I'm just trying to score. Don't know much about this shit."

"Looking to re-up?"

"Hell, yes. I'd like to know what it is first."

This stuck Ronnie as improbably amusing.

"You don't know?"

Rusty laughed. "Buddy of mine came by the other night. He cut me a few bumps and left the bindle. Whatever the hell it was, I dug it."

Ronnie grinned, dragging deeply.

"Intense, huh?"

"No shit. I didn't know what fucking planet I was on."

"Guess you never done bath salts before."

Rusty kept his poker face, glad to have finally gleaned at least one small nugget of intel.

"Tried it once. Didn't do dick for me so I must've got burned." He waved the baggie. "Nothing like this, tell you that much."

"That's next-level shit right there. It's all I'm doing now."

"Been around long?"

"Since last month. Hadn't seen it before then, and I'm

pretty connected."

"No doubt. Always the same bag when it comes with the stamp?"

"Always so far."

"Glad to hear that."

"I can get you some. Forty a gram. Cash now, come back tonight."

Rusty pretended to think it over.

"Probably better if you could hook me up direct," he said. "That way I don't have to hassle you every time. I'd make it worth your while."

Ronnie's brow furrowed, clearly not liking this suggestion.

He was about to answer when a jarring slam made him jump. They both turned in time to see Big Bill emerge out of The Bearded Clam's back door.

"Goddamnit, Ronnie! Get the fuck in here!"

"I'm just having a smoke," Ronnie protested, trying to sound tough with a quiver in his voice.

He cast a quick look at Rusty and started walking back.

"We're having words," Bill snarled. "Inside, now."

He cuffed Ronnie on the side of the head as he passed, hard enough to induce a yelp.

The kid spun around in a brief surge of defiance that didn't die fast enough to escape Bill's notice. A hard slap to the face rewarded him for the aborted effort.

Disgusted, Rusty watched as Ronnie disappeared inside the bar. Then Bill turned his way with a look of cold fury.

That familiar coiling of Rusty's major muscle groups kicked in as the big man stomped across the gravel toward him. Breath growing a bit shallower, feet spreading, eyes focused on the coming confrontation, he assessed the options.

Try to take him out straightaway?

Bad choice. One solid punch wouldn't fell this man. Rusty doubted he could hit him hard enough, and he wouldn't have time to follow up with another.

Misdirection was the proper tool. Use body language to divert Bill's gaze leftward for a fraction of a second, then land an openhanded blow to his Adam's apple. Three to five seconds of painful but far from lethal incapacitation, guaranteed. From there, plenty of time to heel it to the Lexus or strike again at leisure.

No.

His breathing slowed further, rationality taking over.

Stay loose and let him figure how this plays.

Squaring up, Bill jammed a hard palm into his chest. A warning shot, not an outright assault. Rusty absorbed it vertically, releasing the energy into the ground by bending his knees almost imperceptibly to avoid retreating a half step.

"Stay the fuck away from here, asshole. That kid's got enough problems."

"My guess is I'm looking at one of them."

"Just mind your goddamned business. Next time I see you, you're done."

A minute repositioning of Rusty's right shoulder attracted Bill's gaze for a blink. Time enough, but Rusty didn't strike.

Touch me again, fatass. I want you to.

The threat unspoken, Bill read it clearly enough in his eyes. Or maybe he just wasn't in the mood to tangle this early in the day. He spat at the ground and turned and stalked away, not feeling Rusty's left hand slip a two-inch circular mesh screen into his hip pocket.

Big Bill reentered the bar, slamming the door with enough force to loosen the hinges. Rusty stood there for a minute, processing it. Allowing his posture to resume a nondefensive stance and wondering why he'd even bothered planting the screen.

It was a rudimentary street magician's gag. One he'd used to hilarious if ethically dubious effect on unusually obnoxious hecklers back in the early Vegas days.

In roughly an hour, aided by the bovine bartender's body heat, the screen would dissolve into a scorching, gooey mass of black tar-like Polyethylene. Mildly toxic, it would leave a stain about two feet in diameter, ruining his filthy dungarees and raising an inflamed prickly rash on the skin underneath not likely to fade for days. Harmless, but more than a little bit uncomfortable.

Bold move, Rusty thought with a wince of self-derision. *Really big-league stuff.*

What the hell, he should've either fought the man outright or just walked away. Almost embarrassing to resort to such a juvenile ploy, but his fingers had placed the screen before he'd thought better of it.

Well, it was done now. With a little luck, Big Bill's misfortune would unfold with the maximum number of spectators on hand to witness it. Especially that young wastrel Ronnie, who looked like he could use a good laugh almost as much as a good meal.

As the first scattered raindrops dampened his brow, Rusty turned and walked back to his car. Perversely disappointed the encounter with Bill hadn't escalated to a more violent plane. But also relieved to feel for the first time in days like he might not be expending utterly useless effort with all this.

9.

Back in the downstairs den of 14 Echo Run, Rusty spent a solid hour doing some online research on bath salts. Having steadfastly removed himself from the drug life since leaving Las Vegas over a year before, he had no firsthand experience with this relatively recent addition to that culture. Other than seeing the occasional news item or tabloid horror story heralding the extreme danger of ingesting such substances, he was as clueless as the average straight citizen.

It wasn't hard to dig up information on the subject. He learned the innocuous term "bath salts" was slang for an entire platform of designer drugs. Intensely psychoactive compounds that penetrated the blood-brain barrier with pernicious speed and efficacy, they were known to trigger intense hallucinations, rapid heartbeat, feelings of dissociation from reality, and violent outbursts among those under the influence. Whether snorted, smoked, or injected, bath salts were all too easily devoured by anyone with a mind to do so, and equally potent regardless of the method of consumption.

Sometime not too long ago, someone in desperate need of getting high discovered that a couple of chemicals developed in the 1960s but never green-lit by the FDA for any approved medical use (specifically mephedrone and methylenedioxy pyrovalerone) can get a person good and ripped.

This revelation spread like a rash, and soon drug cookers great and small were working to manufacture derivative compounds containing these two core ingredients. Thus the term "bath salts" entered the lexicon of drug use for all time.

Some dealers even labeled their product with familiar names like Vanilla Sky and Ivory Snow and sold them in gas stations and convenience stores to reinforce the wildly false perception that these narcotics had to be harmless since they were identical to a staple product found in your own home.

The craze grew quickly. The DEA classified bath salts as a controlled substance. And the nightmare stories started hitting news desks coast to coast.

Rusty read with grim fascination an AP report of a veteran user of psychedelics in Seattle who, on his first experience with bath salts, stabbed himself in the face and stomach with near-fatal results. Another report from Reuters told of a Memphis teen shooting himself in the head after doing the same to both his sleeping parents, this eruption being the final stage of thirty-six hours of nonstop raving delirium.

These sounded like the old government-issue scare stories from the *Reefer Madness* era warning America's youth of what they faced should they commit the grave error of smoking marijuana. Except these were all true, and they only indicated the tip of a massive, growing iceberg.

A possible chain of connection formed in Rusty's mind: the brutality of Ms. Garrett's murder could be linked with utter plausibility to the powder in the torn baggie, if in fact it turned out to contain some variation of bath salts. That remained a big if. Rusty hardly considered young Ronnie a reliable source of information.

But if the baggie did contain salts, that offered a direct link to the brown prescription bottle. Lidocaine powder was often used as a cutting agent for illicit drugs, particularly those of unusual potency. It had a range of other legitimate uses as well, which made it something easily obtained with a prescription.

Suppose the killer had brought the bottle of lidocaine powder with him, intending to dilute and consume a portion of the salts at some point during the break-in. Out of an excess of caution or paranoia, he had scratched away his name from the prescription label. Which actually turned out to be a good idea, since he ended up leaving the bottle at the crime scene and had to risk coming back that same night to retrieve it.

Someone with an "ix" in the middle of his surname.

Who are you, fucker?

That was a question Rusty couldn't begin to answer. Not yet.

But finding out who sold him the baggie might be a hell of a good step in the right direction.

Getting up from his desk, Rusty felt a keen urge to move past this pointless zone of pure speculation. Without knowing exactly what was inside that gram bag, he really couldn't establish a direct link to the murder.

There's one sure way of finding out what's in there.

This thought had been circling the back of his mind for a while now. Despite a protective sense of better judgment, he was finding it harder to ignore. Studying the yellowish grains with an expert's eye, he weighed risks versus benefits.

On the one hand, sampling this substance would be an utterly reckless and stupid thing to do. Quite possibly catastrophic.

On the other hand, judging the psychoactive effects of drugs was a pursuit with which Rusty had a wealth of firsthand knowledge. If academic institutions offered degrees in this field, he'd have a Ph.D.

The prospect of reverting back to his former epoch of heavy usage didn't cause him too much concern. That had been a very specific time in his life, loaded with specific pressures. He was much better now, more in control.

Going with that rationalization without committing to any irreversible decision, Rusty carried the baggie down to the basement.

He rarely came down here. An open, cavernous space, he'd turned it into something of a dusty showroom from the past. The basement was filled with artifacts from his days as a performing illusionist. Detritus of a life abandoned.

A framed poster leaned against one wall, showing Rusty in dark-lit close-up, his eyes burning with a red tint. Beneath, in a wild looping font: *The Strip's Most Dangerous Magician—Rusty "The*

Raven" Diamond, Live at Caesars Palace.

A collection of throwing knives gleamed with polished perfection against red velvet in a glass cabinet. He placed both palms against the glass, feeling the weight of each knife in his hands like an amputee feels a phantom limb. He turned away, resisting an impulse to test his aim after many months of neglect.

Rusty ran his eyes across an adjacent worktable, its unfinished surface holding various small props—everything from smoke pellets to invisible string to loaded dice. A bronze plaque read: *Las Vegas Entertainer of the Year, Runner-Up 2012.*

A porcelain raven, thirteen inches in height and handcrafted by an artisan at the Gallerie Versailles, kept silent watch from the top of a massive bookcase across the room. The shelves beneath its black talons contained a range of well-thumbed volumes, including some rare first editions: *The Expert at the Card Table*, written in 1902 by S. W. Erdnase, 1911's *Our Magic* by Nevil Maskelyne and David Devant and a much later book, *The Thirteen Steps To Mentalism* by Tony Corinda.

The top shelf of the bookcase held one item, a blue velvet case the size of two shoe boxes. Written across its face in skeletal white letters: "Property of St. Louis Cemetery No. 3, New Orleans."

Rusty reached for the case and opened it, yielding to an unexpected impulse. This wasn't what he'd come down here to do, but once the action had been initiated he couldn't seem to stop.

The silk-lined interior was divided into two equal halves, each indented with the same tapered hexagonal shape nine inches in length and three inches deep. The left indentation lay empty, while the right contained a miniature coffin carved with handcrafted precision from dark amber teak.

Rusty almost opened the coffin, pinching two fingertips together to lift the lid by its curved brass handle. He halted, shuddering as if a chill wind had materialized in the musty basement.

He couldn't bring himself to look at the tiny body within. Not now, nor at any time during the many months leading up to this moment. The thought of seeing that piece of mummified handiwork, which always appeared somehow more than lifelike despite being obviously artificial, soured his stomach.

Maybe if its companion was still here, he could steel himself for a quick glance. The two bodies, and everything signified by their exquisite decay, belonged together. To see them separated felt indecent, like a lapse of conscience he'd never find a way to redress.

Sentimental bullshit, he scolded himself in a weak stab at dispelling his unease.

The illusion for which this velvet case had been created was ancient. In one form or another it had existed since the days of the pharaohs, or so an impressionable young Rusty Diamond was once told. It had proven the most difficult trick for him to master during his long apprenticeship in the Crescent City, which began a few days prior to his eighteenth birthday.

What made the trick so challenging was that it required a partner—not a simple spectator from the crowd duped into a fraudulent sense of collaboration, but a genuine co-creator without whom "The Dance of the Deathless Lovers" could never be performed.

Rusty had found such a partner. Actually, she'd been there since the first day of his tutelage; it just took him some time to fully trust her with sharing the tasks of preparation, misdirection and execution.

He could not have asked for a better partner, onstage or off.

"Yeah, and she's long gone now," he murmured to himself, wondering where the urge to vocalize that obvious fact came from.

Hell, she'd been gone for well over two years. And their shared illusion was permanently ruined the moment she'd taken that matching coffin. Stolen it, in the middle of some hazy day or blackout night while Rusty slept off some long-forgotten debauch. All the velvet case could offer him today were recriminations silently screaming from the vacant hole on its left side.

She didn't steal it. It was hers to take.

He shut the lid and returned the case back to the top shelf where it could fade into obscurity once more. Then he knelt down in front of the bookcase.

Cut into its bottom, beneath the lowest shelf, was a cabinet covered by an ornate brass lock in the shape of a spade. Twisting the lock left ten degrees, right fifteen, and another forty to the left, he yanked the cabinet open with a loud click.

Rusty thrust his hands into the cabinet and pulled out the sole item stored within its sealed darkness: a portable leather kit bag. Ten inches long and almost deep enough to hold a football. Crafted from the finest artesian leather and black as night.

He lifted the bag slowly, as if it possessed a slippery life and might squirm free of his grasp. Carrying it to the worktable, he set it down and ran his fingers over the grooved leather.

"Miss me?" he said, the words coming out in a rough half whisper.

This bag, nondescript except for the quality of its manufacture, was once his daily companion. A portable pharmacopeia, it carried whatever was required to operate at full capacity under the glare of an increasingly bright spotlight, when twelve shows a week both energized and enervated him.

The bag always held coke for energy and focus, Vicodin for relaxation and pain relief, and a range of barbiturates to help bring him down when he'd been going for more than three nights straight and simply had to sleep. Plus a host of more benign curatives ranging from ibuprofen to Imodium for any minor issues that might crop up and threaten his ability to keep the show going.

In all the time he'd been living in this house, Rusty had never felt remotely tempted to come down here and dip into the kit bag for old times' sake. Nowadays he could enjoy a nice stiff drink and not even toy with the idea of upshifting to something heavier than scotch. That alone gave him confidence his days of flirting with outright addiction were relegated to the past.

This would be a controlled exercise. It required a good mixing agent to ensure he didn't consume anything close to a full-strength dose.

He grabbed a vial of harmless baking soda from the leather kit bag. From the stamped baggie he extracted a tiny amount on the tip of a knife, smaller than a #2 pencil's eraser. Mixing this into a larger quantity of baking soda at a ratio of roughly 3:1, he applied the knife in cutting a three-inch line.

Simply performing this action for the first time since swearing off drugs produced a palpable rush that both excited and nauseated him. He'd almost forgotten what it felt like to look down at a well-cut line of ingestible powder, the anticipatory rush that started in his brain and produced an involuntary tightening of the bowels.

He extracted a small tube, gold plated and monogrammed with his initials, from a side pocket in the kit bag. It felt heavy in his fingers.

You're sure you want to do this, right? Not too late to back out.

Whenever that kind of prudent inner voice would whisper in his mind's ear just as he was getting ready to perform some wildly dangerous stunt onstage at Caesars, Rusty always politely told it to fuck off.

He did the same thing now.

Without allowing time to weigh the matter further, he leaned down and inhaled the line in one long snort.

10.

He started to come back to his senses about two hours later. Lying half naked on the cold cement floor of the basement, the glare of an overhead lamp gradually wavered into focus. He'd been staring up at it for the last twenty minutes, forcing the glowing orb to reshape itself into something he could recognize.

It was finally starting to do that, and Rusty was able to remember where he was and why he was in this condition.

That's pretty much where the memory stopped. He retained few coherent impressions of what happened after knocking down that line. Or rather, the memories he had were disjointed and separated from time. Individual moments could have been an hour long, or seconds.

The one thing he recalled with a jolt of clarity was how *fast* it kicked in. Almost immediately, he'd barely had time to return the gold tube to its pocket in the kit bag before he felt it. The first wave was overwhelming, both physically and psychologically. A blistering sensation of pure white energy coursing through every pathway in his body, lighting him up like a pinball machine.

Goddamnit, he'd thought, the word echoing loudly through his ballooning head. *This shit's* good.

And indeed it was, for a while. Surges of humming pulsations, from the surface of his skin to deep within his innards, felt weirdly satisfying. The high was downright playful; it took turns messing with his head and his body, then both together. Like a mix of improbably pure speed and something from the hallucinogenic category rendering effects that overlapped one another like a line of dominoes falling with ever-increasing velocity.

Now, as he tried to rise from the floor and clear away the cobwebs, Rusty couldn't tell exactly when the ride shifted from pleasurable to terrifying. There was no sudden plunge but a gradual morphing of those two contradictory sensations into something he'd never experienced before.

His limbs had started vibrating as if hooked up to electric cables. He tried to still them and couldn't. They were alien entities, alive of their own malevolent will. Pupils widening to blot out his corneas, a sense of panic rippled across his fuzzed-out consciousness. He remembered hearing a guttural scream only marginally recognizable as his own, then falling to a crouch as everything in his vision separated into a starburst.

And then, total darkness. A black pit of incomprehension, which didn't start to abate until Rusty's focus locked onto the overhead lamp, seen directly above from his prone position on the floor.

He slowly sat up, taking a cautious assessment of himself. It seemed he'd been quite active while touring the abyss.

Both hands were badly bruised, skin hanging from the knuckles. Scrapes and gashes covered his naked torso, deep fingernail imprints here and there as if he'd tried to rip away his own skin. The Magicopolis T-shirt shirt he'd been wearing lay in shreds (which pained him, as it was a personal favorite picked up on his first visit to the West Coast in 2003).

Looking around, Rusty saw the basement itself was in shambles. Almost everything breakable smashed to pieces—one whole end of the wooden worktable, the glass covering his cherished framed poster, several of the less sturdy props. Thank God the display cabinet holding his knives was made of three-inch glass. Rusty shuddered to think of what might have happened if he'd been able to reach those blades. From the smudged fingerprints on the cabinet's face, it looked like he'd made a go of it.

All of this irreplaceable stuff—smashed, shattered, and wrecked. It was a fairly impressive display of destruction for a single person. With a great sigh of relief, he saw the porcelain raven had somehow survived intact.

Rising to his feet and gingerly stepping to the staircase, Rusty felt his head clearing by minute but noticeable degrees. Balance and motor function seemed more or less normal, if a bit stiff and slow. He allowed a stab of hope that whatever damage he'd just inflicted upon his cerebral cortex would not prove permanent.

Climbing the stairs to the first floor, he considered himself very fortunate, if not exactly smart.

Well, what did we learn from this little experiment?

There were only three conclusions he could draw at the moment.

One. Whatever was in that baggie—whether technically classifiable as bath salts or not—was incredibly dangerous stuff. The pleasurable fuzziness of the initial rush was probably enough to entice repeat customers among OC's hardiest or most desperate users, though the hellish crash seemed likely to dissuade more cautious types from braving a second taste.

Two. Anyone under the influence of a dose equal to or greater than what he'd just consumed could easily rip away a woman's throat without having any conscious desire to do so. Especially during the period of yawning blackness that kicked in once the drug shifted gears in the bloodstream.

Three. It was time to call Jim Biddison. Rusty's fantasy about personally dishing out payback to Thelma's killer now struck him as not just immaterial but to some degree ludicrous.

After cleaning himself up, which required some patience and much rubbing alcohol, he picked up the phone and dialed the central station. Biddison sounded dubious when Rusty said he had something urgent to discuss, but agreed to meet for a late lunch.

11.

An hour later they occupied a corner booth at the Wilhelm Diner on Fifty-eighth and Baltimore Street. A round-the-clock greasy spoon on a block dominated by two liquor stores and a laser tag arena, the Wilhelm never seemed to attract more than a few patrons at a time but somehow managed to stay in business year after year.

After a few minutes of strained small talk, Rusty got to the point, describing his actions on the night of the murder: entering Ms. Garrett's house, the discoveries made in the bathroom, the intruder, the Ford pickup, the crazed pursuit into OC and the Morbid Manor. He didn't mention getting kicked in the head or the little guinea pig routine he'd just endured in the basement. The lieutenant didn't need to know everything.

The whole narrative took less than ten minutes, and Biddison clearly didn't like what he was hearing. He raised a large callused hand for silence.

"Hold it, hold it. Start over, and tell me up front this is all a joke. I want to believe I missed that part."

Rusty looked wearily across the table. The hangover from his experiment had mercifully faded but was far from totally gone. He wasn't too interested in the hoagie on his plate, and the coffee, while passable, was a long way from Cafe du Monde's chicory blend.

"I went back to the scene, Jim. I let myself in and ..."

"No, you broke in. If I'm hearing you, you just confessed to breaking and entering. Not to mention tampering with an active crime scene."

"It didn't look all that active."

Biddison picked up half a sandwich, then put it back down.

"Rusty, choose your next words very carefully. If you say something that forces me to act as a cop, not as an old buddy from OC High, then I'm going to act that way."

"Jim, listen to me. I found something that ties in."

He pulled the stamped baggie from a pocket and laid it on the table between their two plates. Biddison returned his attention to the sandwich and shot barely a glance at the baggie.

"In the upstairs bathroom," Rusty said, "almost hidden behind the toilet. And there was something else, a prescription bottle of lidocaine powder."

The look on Biddison's face didn't give Rusty much encouragement his spiel was making any impact, but he kept on.

"The label was scratched away. I couldn't read the name but it had an "ix" in it. The prescription wasn't for her, Jim. It was for the same tweaker who dropped that gram bag in haste, either before or after killing Thelma."

"His name's Kenny Dixon. Or had you figured that out too, Sherlock?"

That stopped Rusty cold for half a beat. Of all the responses he'd anticipated from Biddison, angry skepticism seeming the most likely, he really wasn't prepared for this one.

"You heard correctly," Jim said with a sardonic grin. "We're probably not quite as incompetent as you'd like to think."

Rusty let that pass, taking a sip of coffee and finding it lukewarm.

"So what do you know about this guy Dixon?"

"That he's a piece of shit from way back. Took us less than a day to match his prints to the ones lifted from the scene. He's got a jacket that fits this charge almost too well. Two B & E's, an aggravated assault that somehow got dropped last year, and half a dozen drug busts."

"Think you've got a good handle on finding him?"

"There's a manhunt covering the entire Delmarva Peninsula underway as we speak. He's done, just a matter of time. And I'm expecting hours, not days. But that's not your biggest concern right now. What you should be worried about is whether I'm willing to forget this conversation ever happened."

Rusty used the end of his fork to push the baggie closer to Biddison.

"You're welcome for the evidence. If you can pull a clean print, I imagine the DA will find some use for it."

"I can't include that in the case file. It wasn't obtained as part of a formal investigation."

"Hold on to it anyway. That would be my advice."

Biddison picked irritably at the fries on his plate.

"What about the prescription bottle?" he asked at length, sounding reluctant but unable to resist. "Lidocaine powder, you said?"

"I fucked up there," Rusty said with a grimace, still bothered by the mistake. "When I went back to check, it was too late. That's what Dixon came to get, maybe the baggie too if he knew he'd dropped it."

Jim looked ready to unleash some harsh words, almost recoiling in the leather booth for a strike. He then seemed to stop and calibrate his response.

"Rusty, I know you're trying to do the right thing here. In a way, I respect the effort. But it's not for you to handle."

"Maybe not, but I'm worried about more than just Thelma at this point. These drugs have to be some real nasty shit. If I were you ..."

"We've got a very effective narcotics unit. I promise you they're aware of whatever's being sold on the street, which probably isn't a whole lot this time of year."

"That's the wrong attitude, Jim."

"Just stay out of it, OK? You've already crossed the line and put both of us in a bad spot."

Rusty was too wiped to keep arguing, and he wasn't even sure what there was to argue about anymore. They'd identified the suspect, and with any luck he'd be locked up soon.

"Fine. I'm sure we should all feel safe with cops like Officer Neely walking that thin blue line."

Jim had to smile. He knew full well of the incompetence

Brad Neely had shown on duty thus far, but he wasn't going to give Rusty the satisfaction of mentioning it now.

"I'll let you know when we bring in Dixon. Meantime, just go back to whatever the hell it is you do with yourself and leave the police work to us."

Rusty pulled out his wallet to pick up the check.

"That sounds like a warning."

"You wouldn't be wrong to interpret it that way."

12.

The electric sign above The Bearded Clam buzzed against the darkness of the night. A gust of cold ocean breeze made Rusty shiver and check his watch. 12:57 a.m.

Almost time. Bars had to close by law at one o'clock in Maryland, which seemed like a bizarrely truncated schedule for nightlife compared to what he'd become accustomed to in Vegas. Good thing he didn't frequent bars these days anyway.

Jim Biddison had been pretty clear this afternoon about not digging further into Thelma Garrett's murder, but that didn't mean Rusty had to sit around the house waiting to hear something had happened. There was no law against walking the boards and perhaps picking up a nugget or two of information about the black market trade in this town.

Besides, he'd spent the whole afternoon feeling unsatisfied and vaguely pissed off about the meeting with Jim. The walls at Echo Run kept closing in tighter with the passing hours, promising nothing but a night of purposeless frustration.

On top of which, some lingering aftereffects from the salts still had him jittery. Not entirely unpleasant, but disconcerting. An hour ago he'd been halfway tempted to revisit the basement for another bump—maybe play it safe with some garden-variety coke instead of the salts—and that scared him.

So this was not a night for inactivity. Meditation was out of the question; he hadn't even attempted a session this afternoon. In fact, his daily practice was starting to feel like something he could no longer rely on for a stabilizing influence. Not right now, anyway. He needed to channel his amped nerves into some kind of action, fruitful or otherwise.

Which explained, at least partially, his current chilly monitoring of The Bearded Clam. He figured it was a coin toss whether to scope the front or back door for Ronnie. When he sat at the bar earlier today, the kid had come in through the front, so that's what he put his money on tonight.

The sign flickered off, and fourteen seconds later Rusty saw that he'd bet right. Ronnie stepped out the front door, turning around to lock it. Hands in pockets, he started walking briskly east on Dagsworthy toward the boardwalk. Rusty hung back a moment, making sure there was no sign of Big Bill or anyone else. Then he followed.

Ronnie turned left on the boardwalk, keeping his pace. The amusement pier reached out over the ocean four blocks to the north, its hundreds of multicolored popcorn lights extinguished hours ago. Rusty could just barely discern the dark, looming bulk of the Morbid Manor stationed at the far end of the pier.

The boardwalk was virtually deserted, all the shops, restaurants and arcades closed. The only light other than that shining from streetlamps came from some of the hotel rooms where people were continuing the party in private after being ejected from public venues.

Rusty's plan was to trace Ronnie as far as he walked, whether to his home or, preferably, to the place where he scored. He followed him up to the amusement pier and well past it. Luckily, there were still enough stragglers on the boards for him to maintain the tail without drawing attention to himself. Not that Ronnie would be apt to notice. The kid was moving with a very telling kind of forward-leaning pace. He was on his way to see the man.

Six blocks north of the pier, Ronnie took a sharp left at Ninth Street. He hustled down this narrow residential lane, lined on both sides by time-share condos and apartment buildings. Two blocks farther away from the boardwalk, the apartments gave way to a short stretch of modest single-family homes, many of them rentals empty until next summer.

Rusty watched as Ronnie unlatched a gate in front of a

slant-roofed bungalow on the right. It was a simple one-story box of a building, no frills but with a certain dilapidated charm. The front walkway was empty of any items that might hint at a family in residence: bikes, a basketball hoop or the like. Two windows faced the street, both shuttered. Taking up the driveway was a black Chevy van built for cargo, not passengers.

Ronnie walked up to the front door and gave a series of four quick knocks, glancing nervously over his shoulder as he waited for someone to answer. He looked ready to bolt at the first unexpected sound.

Rusty hung back by a telephone pole across the street, shaded from the nearest streetlamp by two poplar trees. It was about as close as he could go without drawing attention. He noted the mailbox in front of the bungalow had been stenciled with a street number that was no longer visible. Either faded with time or scratched away on purpose.

Ronnie knocked again, four rapid taps. The door swung open with a jerk, and he retreated half a pace like he expected to receive a blow. Rusty made out the shape of a man filling the doorframe, outlined by some dim reddish glow from inside. He stood well over six feet, with wide shoulders and big, muscled arms underneath a T-shirt that looked at least two sizes too small.

The guy was white; there was no question about that even in the low light. Incongruously, a long spray of dreadlocks fell in unruly tangles from his head. It wasn't a look you were apt to come across every day, Rusty mused, then decided the same could be said of his own look.

A terse conversation unfolded on the doorstep, peppered by some heated words. The big guy with the dreads leaned forward in a vaguely menacing pose. He flicked a cigarette butt into the front lawn, missing Ronnie's head by an inch.

Rusty couldn't make out any specific words, but he gathered this wasn't an anticipated visit, or one that was welcomed. A plaintive note in Ronnie's voice was counterbalanced by gruff interruptions from the guy in the doorway. Rusty thought he made out the word "rule" being uttered once or twice, but it was impossible to be certain. He stood there in the shadows waiting to see the door slam in Ronnie's face, or something more hostile.

Instead, the dreadlocked dude looked over his shoulder into the bungalow, then gestured for Ronnie to come inside. They both disappeared into the dim red light and the door closed soundlessly.

Rusty leaned against the phone pole and waited.

He didn't have to wait long. Six minutes later Ronnie reemerged from the house, walking as fast as before and with a noticeable buoyancy Rusty recognized immediately. It was the happy tread of someone who just scored and now had nothing to worry about but getting high at the soonest possible moment. The kid was so amped he forgot to swing the gate closed when he barged through, and doubled back after a few paces to tend to it.

Rusty tailed him in the direction from which they'd come, up to the boards. Ronnie turned south and headed back, following the same route. Now that it seemed likely the score had been made, Rusty saw no point in concealing himself any longer. He'd already pinned down a physical location where he felt confident drugs were being sold.

And he really wanted to talk to the kid, not just to pry loose information but maybe impart some good advice. Rusty wasn't enough of a hypocrite to launch into some rant about the evils of narcotics, despite feeling certain these salts were unusually dangerous. It just seemed clear Ronnie was a woefully misguided youngster who might benefit from some straight talk that wasn't accompanied by a slap in the face.

He waited until they'd gone two more blocks, passing the Mug & Mallet, which appeared to still be open in defiance of the alcohol ordinance. When they reached a section of boardwalk on which no other person could be seen within a hundred feet, he silently crept up behind Ronnie and whispered his name.

Ronnie flinched like someone had ignited a firecracker. He wheeled around, eyes wide with alarm, letting out a long exhalation of relief when he saw who it was.

"Jesus! What're you sneaking up like that for?"

"Sorry. I just came out of the Mug & Mallet and saw you passing by. Thought I'd make sure you were alone. Didn't want to get you in more trouble with your friend the bartender."

Ronnie snorted with disgust. "Bill's an asshole. Thinks he can treat me like that just 'cause he's with my ma."

An insight dawned in the kid's uncombed head, short-term memory coming to his aid.

"You pulled that shit today."

"Come again?"

"Had to be you," Ronnie nodded, smiling at the memory. "Fucking hilarious. Like Bill sprung a damn oil leak, nasty black shit all over the place. Strips off his pants right there at the bar, screaming like a little girl. Whole place in stitches. 'Cept for Ma, of course."

"Not really sure what you're talking about," Rusty said, a casual grin belying the denial.

"Yeah, right. Scorched him pretty good, whatever it was."

"Call it a character builder. Maybe he'll dial down the macho crap a notch or two."

Shaking his head doubtfully, Ronnie uttered, "He knows it was you. Wouldn't recommend drinking at the Clam anytime soon. Like, ever."

They walked in silence for a few more paces.

"You on your way to score?" Rusty asked.

Ronnie halted abruptly.

"Ask a lot of nosey questions, dude."

"Just curious. And, you know, always on the lookout."

Another moment passed, the wheels in Ronnie's noggin turning at their own sluggish pace. Rusty could see he was calculating the benefits of telling the truth. Apparently he couldn't conceive of a worthwhile lie because he finally nodded.

"Just did now, as a matter of fact. Still looking, huh?"

"Damn straight. Lucky timing for me."

"Let's sit," Ronnie said, jerking his head toward a nearby bench. "I need a smoke."

They occupied the bench underneath the sickly glow of a streetlight. Gentle ocean sounds carried clear across the empty beach.

"Only got a gram. I can sell you half. That's twenty."

"Think we could run back to your connection? I've got enough scratch for two grams at least."

"Nah, fuck that. I hate dealing with those guys. Not even supposed to go there, but it's too late to score on the boardwalk. Everyone's in for the night."

"Well, shit. You were just there …"

"I said I'm not going back," Ronnie rasped, voice spiking a bit. "And I'm sure as hell not bringing some dude they don't know. Probably kill my ass."

"OK, I get it."

"Fuckin' Fade's so paranoid, practically shit a brick just now."

Ronnie flicked his smoke away angrily before deciding he'd let it go too soon. He almost retrieved the butt. Stopping to consider how that would look, he dug out a fresh one instead.

Rusty could tell he'd almost pushed too hard. The kid was on the verge of bolting, and he wanted to at least get a look at what just got procured from the bungalow.

At any rate, he'd picked up a name.

Fade. Won't have trouble remembering that one.

"Forget I mentioned it," he said to Ronnie. "I appreciate you splitting your bag, if you're still up for that."

Ronnie dragged deeply on his cigarette. He kept one knee bouncing madly, like a hyperactive third grader. Rusty couldn't tell if he was high already but doubted it. There was a cogency to him that seemed to rule it out.

"Tell ya the truth, I'm not sure I even *want* this shit anymore. Last couple times haven't been so good. Shit's making me really aggro, know what I mean?"

He raised his left hand. Rusty saw for the first time it was wrapped in a bandage, dried blood soaked deep.

"Put my fucking fist through a car window last night." Ronnie laughed without mirth. "Don't even know whose car it was. Poor bastard must've been pissed when he found it."

"Have you been cutting the bag with anything?"

"Hell, yes. Think I want to go out of my mind? One part

salts to four parts baking soda, that's the rule."

"What about lidocaine?"

"What about it?"

"It's all I have to cut with. That'll work, won't it?"

Ronnie shrugged. "Dunno, never tried it." He scratched the bloody wrap around his hand. "Gotta change this, itching like crazy."

An aura of abject misery wafted off him. Rusty could practically smell it.

"I'll take the whole bag, if you want to get rid of it."

This proved to be the wrong tactic. Ronnie shook his head vehemently, all traces of ambivalence gone.

"Fuck that. I need a taste. Been taking shit from Big Bill all goddamn night, then I gotta deal with those assholes at the house." He turned to face Rusty, expression cold. "Half, take it or leave it."

"I'll take it, man."

"Gotta eyeball it. I don't have a fuckin' scale with me. Keep lookout."

Rusty watched for any approaching bypassers as Ronnie dug a gram baggie from his pocket. Under the street lamp's glow, he caught a clear glimpse of the familiar green stamp on the baggie's bottom left corner.

Ronny pulled a piece of paper from his pocket—part of a pizza menu—ripped off a four-inch square, and folded it into a bindle. Then he opened the baggie and tapped out roughly half of the yellowish grains inside. Sealing the baggie and returning it to his pocket, he folded the bindle three more times so it was tight.

"Let's see the twenty."

"Sure. Now you see it …"

Ronnie actually laughed when Rusty produced a twenty-dollar bill from thin air and palmed it to him.

"That was cool. You a magician or some shit?"

"Just a hobby."

"Nice hobby. I don't know how the hell you pulled that stunt with Bill, but I dug it."

A small smile of unguarded delight held on Ronnie's face. Seeing it, Rusty felt something that caught him completely off guard. It was a feeling he once got on a daily basis, was actually the main thing that used to propel him out of bed each morning.

A good magic trick, no matter how simple, does something very specific to the brain. When a person confident in their grasp of reality witnesses something their intellect can't explain, a tiny moment opens up when the impossible seems possible. This moment reveals itself on the spectator's visage in a way Rusty recognized instantly.

He hadn't produced that look on anyone's face in a long time. It called him back not just to his days as a professional illusionist but much further into the past—when he was a kid himself standing out on this very same boardwalk and going pie-eyed at the feats performed by the street magicians.

Ronnie was still grinning in the same way.

"Want to learn the bill trick?" Rusty asked.

Quickly returning to a state of cool, Ronnie shrugged like he didn't care one way or the other.

Rusty held his hand out.

"Give me back the twenty."

Now the look on Ronnie's face turned to icy suspicion. He retracted a little on the bench.

"I'm not gonna burn you, man. It's just easier to show how it's done by doing it."

Ronnie gave back the bill with visible hesitance.

"It's one simple move. The key is to prep beforehand."

Rusty held up his hand to show how the bill, folded down the middle, was tucked between his ring and middle finger, laying flat against the back of his hand.

"A little misdirection is needed, but not much. Something simple, like repositioning your other arm by a few inches while you set the bill. Then just do this." He illustrated a twist of his right hand at a deliberately slow pace, about five times slower than he'd done it before. The bill slowly crawled between his two fingers to lie flat in his palm.

He gave it back to Ronnie.

"You try."

Ronnie fumbled with folding the bill behind his knuckles, tossing away his cigarette in frustration as he failed to secure a tight fit.

"That's right. Now curl the knuckles and open them just enough for the bill to slip through as you turn your hand so the palm's facing me."

They sat there for the next ten minutes as Ronnie attempted the maneuver with varying degrees of success.

"Shit's hard."

"You're getting the hang of it. Keep practicing, and do it slow. Once you get the mechanics down, you can start speeding up. Chicks will dig it, trust me."

Ronnie tucked the bill in his pocket.

"Thanks."

"The salts?" Rusty asked.

"Right. Here ya go."

He handed over the bindle.

"I'm out," he said, standing up. "See you around."

Rusty stood as well. "Go easy, brother."

Ronnie started walking away at the same accelerated pace, pausing to turn when the sound of Rusty's receding footsteps stopped. He was nowhere in sight.

Thirty-one minutes later Rusty was back at the house on Echo Run typing with focused intent on the MacBook. Earlier today, in hopes of getting his hands on exactly the kind of sample he'd just scored on the boardwalk, Rusty had started a thread on the online message board for the toxicology department at the University of Maryland's Eastern Shore campus, located an hour away in the town of Prince Anne.

The title of the thread was simple:

Cash assignment for qualified student, chemical analysis.

In the body of his message he wrote the following:

Seeking toxicology major in graduate department to perform private analysis of a small amount of granular material (less *than 1 g). $500 cash paid for expedited assessment of chemical properties. Material will be delivered to campus, preferably for same day analysis. In exchange for cash payment, student will provide a complete printout of findings and agree to ask no questions.*

Checking back as soon as he got home tonight, Rusty saw a total of thirty-seven replies, all expressing interest. Must be a lot of hungry students out there.

Scrolling through the first half dozen, many of which oozed a certain academic disdain he loathed on instinct, he settled on one from a user named *sxylabchik.*

The message was direct: *I'm in. Will be in lab all day Friday if that's not too soon.*

Rusty's fingers froze over the keys. An inner caution stopped him from typing a reply.

Rereading his original message, he wished he'd been more artful with its phrasing. Some shading of the language might have gone a long way to conceal, or at least divert attention from the fairly naked fact that the material he wanted analyzed had to be illegal.

Agree to ask no questions? Yeah, that's subtle as hell.

As part of the university's IT system, this message board undoubtedly had moderators keeping an eye on all postings. They were apt to take a dim view of anyone contacting students for such shady purposes.

For all he knew, *sxylabchik* was a member of the campus security department posing as a student. The same unknown person who might well be waiting, accompanied by a few Maryland State Troopers, to pump some pointed questions at Rusty the moment he set foot on campus.

Maybe. But how else to get a handle on what's in this shit?

Racking his brain, he could find no reasonable answer to that query. Nor any indication of just how obvious his message's tacit intent might read in the eyes of another person.

Taking a moment to weigh his paranoia against the urge to continue pushing forward in defiance of all risk, he let his fingers hover over the keyboard.

Why bother maintaining this half-assed investigation? The question nagged. In plain truth, he needed to keep going because the only other outlets for release close at hand either bored or scared him.

Take the knives out of that glass case and try a little target practice? Rusty had considered doing that countless times since relocating to Ocean Pines, but the idea of hurling a blade with no one to applaud his aim struck him as hopelessly depressing, like an over-the-hill bodybuilder flexing in the mirror.

Revisit the kit bag downstairs? Christ, no. Over the past several hours he had come to feel incredibly, stupidly lucky to have not only survived his experiment with the salts, but to have resisted the "chaser" effect so familiar to anyone ever who tried shaking off chemical dependence. One little taste, just for old times' sake, invariably leads to a major bender, and from there a full-blown relapse can't be far off.

What about Janice Garrett? She hadn't strayed too far from his thoughts since their awkward meeting at the medical examiner's office. A memory of the way she'd filled out that tailored suit, and the gradual easing of their conversation, almost prompted Rusty to grab his keys and make for the Avalon Inn right away.

But what did he have to say to her? Not much, yet. She'd opened the door for him to reach her with any information about Thelma's death. The cops were hunting some faceless scumbag named Kenny Dixon; that part was well out of his hands. But with some specialized intel about the drugs he found at her aunt's house, Rusty would have a legitimate reason to make contact.

Still wrestling with this limited series of options and finding none of them satisfactory, Rusty's fingers tired of waiting for him to decide. Almost without realizing what he was doing, he typed out a quick reply to *sxylabchik* and hit Send.

13.

The illuminated blue spires of the Indian River Inlet Bridge, recently rebuilt in a $150 million contract with Swedish construction behemoth Skanska, rose into a brilliantly clear night sky about twenty-five miles north of Ocean City, just across the border into Delaware. At its foot, on the western side of Route 1, sprawled the Indian River trailer park.

Roughly a hundred travel trailers, mobile homes and RVs formed a pattern of uneven lanes across a large swath of dusty ground. The trailer park, which thrived as a year-round destination for those who by necessity or preference made their home on wheels, was something of an eyesore as it sat directly in the shadow of the magnificent new span. But there was little talk of relocating to a less conspicuous area, except among the wealthier owners of some bayside mini-mansions who felt the park diminished their sunset views as well as their property values.

Fuck those assholes, thought Kenny Dixon as he stood at the western edge of the trailer park, looking across the bay at the opulent homes stationed along the far shore, their lights faintly reflected on the calm waters.

Kenny wasn't happy to be here, though he could think of several alternatives that sounded a lot less desirable. Indian River wasn't nearly far enough from Ocean City to allow him any peace of mind, nor half as far as he planned to go once he had a chance to get his shit together.

Just a few minutes before ten, the trailer park stood virtually empty of any people milling around outside. Everyone was huddled up inside their units. On a summer evening the place resembled an arena parking lot before a rock concert, with smoke rising from the barbecue pits, keg beer flowing, and Frisbees arcing through the air. But it was too cold for any activity tonight, and would remain so for another five months at least.

Kenny had stepped out of the mobile home parked in spot 29-C a few moments earlier to take a piss and have a smoke. His bitch sister Laurene and her douche husband Dwight didn't allow smoking inside their double-wide. Typical tight-assed move on their part, which was one of numerous reasons Kenny hadn't bothered to come visit them in months despite living a short drive away.

Technically speaking, he wasn't visiting them at the moment. He was hiding out from a tri-state manhunt sweeping the entire Delmarva Peninsula. The cops had certainly raided his home by now.

There was also the possibility Fade and Tampa Nate had come calling, which rattled Kenny even more. He'd made a bad mistake in telling Fade about that nasty business in the old woman's house on Heron Lane. The news was not well received, to put it mildly. Not that Fade or Nate threatened Kenny outright, but he wouldn't put anything past those fuckers if they felt he'd jeopardized their operation.

So Kenny was keeping his head down nice and low here at the trailer park. Not for long, just until he could arrange for some travel money to get him out west. He knew some rough dudes, former associates in petty crime, living in Flagstaff.

The leader of the pack, a 'roided-out gym rat named Rife who used to bounce at Seacrets in OC when he wasn't jacking cars, told Kenny he could crash anytime he felt an inclination to see the far side of the Rockies. No need to phone ahead before arrival.

It was only right, considering all the solids Kenny had done Rife over the years—mostly in the form of forged prescriptions for brand-name human growth hormones including Nutropin, Humatrope and Genotropin.

That was Kenny's bread-and-butter for a while, selling

'scripts of all kinds. He sorely missed those days. Didn't take much work or entail any real risk, thanks to three fat prescription pads he'd lifted from a psychiatrist's office in the nearby township of Berlin.

In a weak moment last spring, Laurene made the error of confiding that Dwight was seeing a shrink to combat some severe anxiety brought on by their failure to conceive after more than three years of increasingly frantic effort. This revolted Kenny, who did his best to limit any exposure to family crises.

But it turned out to be one hell of a good stroke.

Playing the dutiful brother-in-law, he grudgingly drove Dwight to a session one afternoon when Laurene was busy at a friend's baby shower. While he waited for the session to end, Kenny chain-smoked and casually cased the office building.

Finding the place almost insultingly easy to break into, he drove back to Berlin that very night for that very purpose. Simplest heist he ever pulled, just a damn shame the quack only had three 'script pads in his desk.

The bulk of Kenny's customers predictably wanted Vicodin and Oxy, but Rife and his crew of muscle-bound dimwits just couldn't get enough of that brand-name HGH. "Massive gains, bro!" they'd bellow every time he tore them off a fresh sheet. No charge, since Rife was a dude you could count on in a tight spot.

Feeling he owed Kenny, Rife extended his kind offer six months ago before striking out to 'Zona for bigger and better things. Since then, Kenny had received about four emails a month with photo attachments showing Rife and his posse surrounded by an ever-growing roster of babes. Rife had found a new career cranking out a boatload of low-budget porn he shot and cut and uploaded to considerable profit entirely on his iPhone.

Each email contained a reminder that he could always use a hand in recruiting new girls, as the dual jobs of producing and starring in his z-grade videos taxed most of his time.

An enticing proposal, but Kenny wondered what the rest of those gym rats would think of him arriving at their doorstep unannounced. He wasn't too tight with any of the crew but Rife, and if the shoe was on the other foot he sure as hell wouldn't welcome another swinging dick to what sounded like a pretty good party.

It didn't matter. Any port in a storm would do. Who knows, he might discover a real aptitude for wrangling talent. Homemade porn sounded like the ultimate growth industry the way Rife described it, even more than narcotics. Kenny was looking forward to his westward relocation.

Laurene and Dwight had no idea he was wanted by the law. They'd have ejected him from their pathetic mobile domicile if they had any inkling what he was wanted for. That's why it was so important to scrounge up some money soon, preferably within the next day or so. If his sister learned what was going on, she'd kick him out in a heartbeat. As for Dwight, that asshole would probably call the cops looking for a reward.

Lighting a fresh Doral on the burning tip of one he'd already smoked down to the filter, Kenny cursed his lousy luck. Why'd that old bitch have to confront him? Hell, why did she even have to *be* there in the first place?

Fucking Fade. It was all his fault, really. He had no right to cut Kenny loose, even if Kenny had dipped into the stash once or twice. Hell, for a cooker like Fade that was part of the cost of doing business. He could afford a little skim from the top and still haul in maximum profit.

But no. Fade went apeshit when he caught Kenny in the act of liberating a few measly grams for personal use. Fired him flat, leaving him no means of income with which to feed his perfectly moderate and well-controlled habit. So Kenny broke into a house he thought was empty with the intent of pulling a nonviolent burglary and ended up taking a life, so stoned at the time he still couldn't remember the deed.

Unbelievable. How bad could a guy's luck get?

Standing now at the lip of the trailer park, Kenny was musing bitterly on the unfairness of life when he heard the sirens. Just a faint hint at first, quickly drowned out by a gust of cool wind off the bay.

He went rigid for a moment, then scolded himself for being

paranoid. It was probably just a seagull.

Then he heard it again. Undoubtedly sirens, as in plural. They were coming from the south, a realization that made Kenny's stomach catch in his throat like he'd been pushed off a ledge.

Fuck. There was no way. The trailer park was a perfect place to hide, and he'd only been here since this morning. They couldn't possibly have traced him so quickly.

As the sirens grew louder and Kenny saw the first flashes of red light rise above tall marsh grasses in the distance, it came to him.

Fucking Dwight. He must have heard something on the radio and tipped off the cops. No other explanation made sense.

Flinging his cigarette to the ground with an angry curse, Kenny started running toward their trailer. He wasn't going to be taken in, no way. There was still time to run and plenty of dark marshland nearby in which to escape. But he needed a few things from the trailer—his gun and the paltry roll of bills stashed in his clothes.

And maybe he'd have time to split Dwight's fat head open while he was at it.

Some of the park's inhabitants were stepping out of their trailers dressed in robes and sweaters to see what the commotion was all about. A young couple clinging naked underneath a thick down comforter saw Kenny racing past their unit and nodded to each other; that scruffy dude was in some serious trouble, and there might just be some entertainment around here tonight.

Kenny didn't notice them or any other onlookers as he stumbled madly toward Laurene's double-wide. Thirty more staggered paces got him there. He threw his body against the front door, knocking it off the hinges.

The first thing he saw was Dwight, standing in the kitchen nook with an aluminum baseball bat clutched in his hands.

"You motherfucker!" Kenny shrieked.

"Get out of here, Kenny. Run if you can, just go."

"Where's my cunt sister?"

"Safe in the bedroom. She didn't want to do it. It was

my idea."

Scrambling through a pile of clothes he'd stashed next to the rollaway sofa, Kenny found the cash and stuffed it in his jeans. He tucked the gun, a compact 9mm that wasn't even loaded, into the back of his belt.

"I'm gonna kill you for this, Dwight. Know that."

Without another word he barged out of the trailer and started retracing his path back to the park's western side.

That was his sole hope for escape. The park had only one entrance, directly underneath the bridge to the east. The cops would have no choice but to come in that way. From the roar of their sirens they'd be here in seconds.

The blue spires of the bridge were bathed in flashes of crimson from the approaching cherry tops. There wasn't a single person inside their mobile home at this point. Everyone was stationed outside to see the show.

Kenny ran like hell, knowing if he could get to the western perimeter there was a chance of diving into the deep marsh grass and working his way up along the edge of the bay. He might be able to elude capture long enough to emerge onto the highway a mile or so upstream. At that point, he'd flag down a motorist by standing right in the goddamn middle of Route 1, pull the stupid fuck from his vehicle and start driving northward at a reasonable speed. If he could make it as far as Rehoboth Beach, about ten miles away, he could ditch the car and find a cheap place to hole up for the night.

It was a long shot, but it was all he had.

Kenny charged across the muddy ground, his body deprived of drugs for days but moving with the manic speed of someone who'd just taken down an entire gram in one bolt. He could see the tall grass through his blurred vision, maybe twenty yards directly ahead.

Some bright, irrational hope filled his chest. He was going to make it.

He halved the distance with a dozen more strides and could almost smell the briny tang of bay water. It smelled like freedom, wildly improbable freedom.

Then the whole area lit up in the glare of a spotlight. No choppers circling above, so the light must be coming from a patrol car. Not daring to glance back, Kenny knew his pursuers had to be close enough to see him as easily as in a midday sun.

He kept running. A garbled voice boomed through a megaphone, commanding him to drop on the ground. Warning him if he didn't drop they'd fire.

No fucking way. He was so close.

The light grew brighter, falling across the curtain of tall grass he'd imagined as a route to escape. Exposed in the high-wattage glow, Kenny saw with dismay what flimsy cover it would offer him. Probably not enough to delay capture by more than a few minutes.

In a single ragged exhalation, all the fight fled from him. From euphoria to exhaustion in the space of one breath.

His pursuers were so close he could hear their leather shoes pounding the muddy ground. The sirens were like a sonic wall of defeat. It was over.

Even with the marsh grass now less than ten paces away, he couldn't possibly escape by diving into that wet thicket. All he'd do was soak himself and have to endure his ride to the police station in muddy, wet clothes.

Suddenly feeling as tired as he'd ever been in his thirty-four-year life span, Kenny Dixon let his legs go limp mid-stride. He fell flat on his face in the damp grass, enjoying one final unmolested moment.

Then the kneecaps of a patrol officer landed on his shoulder blades like lead weights, knocking the wind out of him, and Kenny gladly entered oblivion.

14.

Jim Biddison pulled an unmarked Pontiac service unit into the driveway of 14 Echo Run. He stepped out and took an admiring view of the property, a fine two-story wood frame in the Craftsman style he liked but couldn't quite afford on his cop salary. Surrounding him were stately pines, their lush fragrance almost intoxicating in the crisp afternoon breeze.

Rusty was clearly doing all right for himself if he could afford this place. The rental had to be near ten grand a month, probably spiking from May to September.

Ruth and Edgar Diamond were both dead as far as Jim knew, and they didn't have much to pass on to their only adopted child. Rusty's biological parents had been killed in an eighteen-car pileup on the Baltimore-Washington Parkway when he was four years old. Miraculously, young Rusty had been pulled from the wreckage alive. He'd spent the next few years shuffling between foster homes until the Diamonds adopted him at age seven. They brought him to their modest home in Ocean Pines and enrolled him in first grade at Tidal Elementary.

Jim still remembered Rusty's first day of class. The way he separated himself from the rest of the students, withdrawn without seeming shy, just detached. It wasn't long before they'd struck up a friendship, though that required Jim making an effort at pulling the new kid from his shell. It was clear Rusty was kind of weird, but he was also smart. And funny in an offbeat way, sort of like he'd walked out of a Charles Addams cartoon.

Struck by memories long forgotten, Biddison closed the Pontiac's door and walked up to the house. A black Lexus was parked in the drive.

He didn't know exactly why he'd driven out here. The ostensible reason was to share the news of Kenny Dixon's arrest. That was perfectly legitimate, given what seemed to be earnest interest on Rusty's part to see his elderly landlord's killer brought to justice.

But Jim could have just as easily shared that information on the phone. So why had he chosen to come in person? As he marched up the steps to the porch, two ulterior motivations occurred to him. First, he wanted to assert the skill of the Ocean City police force about whose competency his old friend seemed to harbor some doubt. Maybe rub it in just a little, without making too big a deal of it.

The second reason embarrassed Jim slightly to consider. Seeing Rusty these past few days, bizarre as the circumstances had been, reminded him of old times. If Rusty was going to be living in the area at least for the foreseeable future, Jim thought it was worthwhile to see if they could get on good terms again. They might not be going out for beers or driving into Baltimore to catch a Ravens game, but at least they could feel no bad blood existed.

A knock on the front door yielded no response. Jim thought about dialing from his cell until a noise caught his ear. Faint and muted, it sounded like some kind of engine being revved in the near distance. Could be a motorboat in the shallows that lapped just on the other side of the house, but Jim knew crafts of that type were prohibited in this section of the bay.

It sounded like a chainsaw. Actually, it sounded like *multiple* chainsaws, all going at the same time and overtaking one another in a wavelike pattern of sounds.

A mildly unnerving cacophony, no question. But he wouldn't necessarily call it ominous.

Casually taking the flagstone pathway around the house's long southern side, the noise grew louder in his ears. Ten more steps brought Jim around the rear corner of the house and confirmed his suspicion.

Rusty was indeed operating multiple chainsaws. Three of

them, to be precise. At the same time. Big mean ones, with frenzied sixteen-inch bars capable of God knows what kinds of damage.

He was juggling them. Standing on a narrow stool about four feet in height and with a base at the top maybe ten inches in diameter. He stood on one foot, the other tucked behind his knee.

And he was blindfolded.

Jim Biddison hadn't been left dumbstruck too many times in his adult life, and he'd seen plenty on duty with the OCPD that would make the average person blanch. Dead bodies, car wreck casualties, juvenile victims of domestic abuse, and any manner of nasty sights had greeted his eyes. He'd always been able to filter it through his professional veneer as a peace officer.

But right now, watching someone engaging in an activity as stupefyingly dangerous as it was pointless, Jim just froze for a moment. He was scared to keep looking, and scared to look away.

After what seemed like a very long time, Rusty let each of the saws fall to the ground in an orchestrated sequence, throwing up clumps of grass and dirt where they landed. Then he removed himself from the stool by way of a perfectly executed backflip, his feet landing inches away from where one of the chainsaws continued to angrily tear up the lawn.

Pulling off the blindfold, his eyes immediately went to the spot where Biddison was standing, not twenty feet away. As with their first meeting in the holding cell, if Rusty experienced any sensation of surprise at seeing Jim here, none was revealed on his face. He simply went from one saw to the next, killing their motors and placing them on a wooden picnic table. Then grabbed a towel to wrap around his sweat-soaked shoulders and walked over. He was smiling.

Jim spoke first, with the only words that came to mind:

"Got a beer?"

• • •

Rusty didn't have any beer, in fact. His daily alcohol consumption was a regimented affair, limited to two strong glasses of single-malt scotch on the rocks, maybe a third on certain days that demanded it. But never before five. That was his rule, and though he knew how arbitrary it was, he adhered to it with the fidelity of a religious zealot. Such measures are necessary for people who recognize a potential for serious addiction but don't want to abandon the pleasures of chemical mood enhancement altogether.

So he and Biddison drank iced tea instead, standing somewhat awkwardly in the kitchen. Jim refrained from commenting on the weird spectacle he'd witnessed in the backyard. Instead he got right to the point by laying out the details of Kenny Dixon's apprehension.

"Did he confess?" Rusty asked, pulling a pitcher from the fridge to refresh their glasses.

"Not yet, but he'll crack. There's a mountain of physical evidence against him, from prints at the house to blood in his pickup truck. We're confident it'll match Ms. Garrett's."

"What about the baggie?"

"I told you I can't use that, Rusty. And I don't think we'll need to. Whether Dixon confesses or not, the county prosecutor has a strong hand. Especially with his career rap sheet to buttress the case."

Rusty raised his glass in a toast.

"Congratulations, Jim. I'm glad you caught the fucker." After a beat he added, "And I appreciate you coming over to let me know."

A long silence passed. Finally Jim said it:

"What the hell were you doing out there?"

Rusty smiled, abashed.

"I know, weird. It's how I blow off steam sometimes. Good cardio, too."

"Try jogging."

"There's a little more to it than exercise. I …" He paused, not sure what he wanted to say. "I guess I just want to see if I still can."

"One of these days I might ask you just how you spent the last twenty years. Something tells me it would make a good story."

Rusty didn't respond. A sense of conflicted sentiments overtook him. On the one hand, he'd love to tell Jim—to tell anyone—about all the things that occurred in the years since leaving Ocean Pines. On the other hand, that notion repelled him.

"You know," Jim said, "I was pretty pissed when you took off. It's like we're friends and then, bam. Right after graduation, you vanish."

"I figured you'd do all right without me."

"That's not the point, asshole."

"I know."

"Your folks were pretty torn up about it too."

"I left them a note," Rusty said, feeling a familiar sting of shame. "When I started making money in New Orleans, I'd send some back every few weeks. By the time I was really pulling it in, out in Vegas, they were both gone. They died within three months of each other. I guess that happens a lot to couples who've been together a long time."

"Did you come back for their funerals at least?" A pause. "Hell, it's none of my business."

"Yes, I came for both of them. Didn't spend the night either time, just paid my respects and got the hell out."

"If you can't stand this place so much, why'd you move back?"

Rusty drained his glass, a contemplative look on his face.

"That's a pretty good question."

He left it there. Jim picked up on his unease and changed the subject.

"You don't seem particularly relieved about Dixon."

"No, I am. It's reassuring to know Thelma's killer will stand trial. But there's a bigger problem out there. Not for me personally so much, but for you and the Department."

"What's that? These hyper-drugs you've been looking into? You really missed your calling, Rusty. I swear you've got the nose of a bloodhound."

"It's no joke, Jim. These drugs are bad, tainted. The threat they pose isn't limited to whoever takes them but anyone who might cross their path. Just look at Thelma."

"That was an isolated incident. It was terrible, but isolated. Dixon's a fucking piece of shit, and he'll probably get life."

Rusty looked across the kitchen with those dark eyes Biddison sometimes found slightly unsettling, especially when they assumed a kind of weird intensity they had now.

"Take my word, Jim. This isn't over yet. As long as those salts are on the streets, you're going to have more problems."

15.

Navigating some moderately heavy traffic in downtown Ocean City shortly after Lieutenant Biddison left the house, Rusty decided he was being followed. This time he was damn near certain about it, and he didn't reach that conclusion on a whim. Only after keeping one eye welded to the rearview mirror for ten city blocks did he make the decision.

There was no doubt. The same Dodge he'd caught a glimpse of several days ago was once again on his tail.

He wasn't sure how long it had been there. For most of the drive since leaving Echo Run, he'd been distracted by troublesome thoughts of what Jim had told him about Kenny Dixon. They overlapped with other thoughts about the best way to share the news with Janice Garrett, who he was on his way to see now.

Before leaving the house he picked up the phone and started to call the Avalon Inn. She'd asked him to let her know of any developments in the case, and news of Dixon's arrest seemed to qualify. He hung up before the front desk answered, figuring this was a conversation best had in person. And if she felt like maybe grabbing a bite or taking a stroll on the boardwalk, all the better.

He spotted the Dodge behind him just after entering downtown. Still couldn't identify the model, but the color was definitely that same dullish silver.

Rusty kept driving another six blocks down Baltimore Street toward the Avalon. The muscle car stayed with him all the way, maintaining a steady distance.

He didn't consider himself a person given to irrational

fancies, but he was starting to feel pretty unnerved. And angry. Accepting the premise that he was being tailed raised two obvious questions: why and by whom?

He thought back to the other night when he'd left his car in such a conspicuous spot after following the pickup from Thelma's house to the boardwalk.

His worry at the time, that someone might spot the Lexus and possibly track down its owner, now seemed justified. Anyone with access to DMV records could run his Nevada plates in the national database. Which would make finding and following him a feasible task. Not an easy one, but doable by someone with sufficient motive.

Just for the hell of it, still not willing to fully believe the premise, he made a rapid series of turns. Four hard rights in a row: at Twenty-second, again at Philadelphia, one more on Twenty-fourth, and then back south onto Baltimore. In less than three minutes he'd executed a precise and pointless square pattern comprising about eight blocks.

The Dodge stuck with him all the way.

OK. I think I can get pissed now.

The sun was just falling over the high-rises to the west, streetlights coming on in unison. Pulling up to a red light at Baltimore and Eighteenth, Rusty decided to test the intensity of this pursuit. The Dodge was directly behind him now. As when he'd spotted it the first time, there appeared to be only one person inside, but it was too dark to get a decent read on the driver.

The light turned green. Rusty didn't advance an inch.

Angry honks started to rise from the cars behind. He stayed put, watching the rearview mirror for a reaction. His pursuer in the Dodge was animatedly gesturing for him to go.

Fuck you. Go around me so I can get a look at you.

The light turned yellow.

The honks continued, then doubled. Someone yelled an obscenity to the effect that Rusty should learn how to drive or get off the road.

His eyes flicked upward briefly to check the light. Returning his gaze to the mirror, he flinched as if given an electric shock.

No.

The Dodge had crept much closer, almost nudging the rear bumper of the Lexus. Bathed in his taillight's red glare, he got his first good view of the driver.

I'm not seeing this.

A woman clutched the steering wheel behind him, dark hair pulled back to reveal her entire face. And it was an unforgettable face. Wide almond-shaped eyes. Smooth mocha skin set tight with anxiety or a more extreme emotion, over features so delicate they might have belonged to a porcelain doll.

It's not her!

Rusty jerked his head around to see more clearly. To prove he was wrong.

No time. The Dodge suddenly swerved into the next lane and plowed ahead just as the light turned red.

"Marceline!" Rusty yelled at the top of his lungs.

The Dodge missed a head-on collision with an approaching vehicle turning left by mere inches, then disappeared from view.

Blocked by the cross traffic, Rusty couldn't advance through the intersection. He pounded the steering wheel, pulse racing even as he kept telling himself he was wrong.

Think it through, idiot! How could it be her?

Counting the seconds with mounting frustration, he slammed the gas the moment an opening appeared.

All thoughts of dropping by the Avalon Inn fled from his mind. The only thing that mattered was catching up with that Dodge. He still didn't believe he'd seen Marceline Lavalle behind the wheel. It was impossible, a self-imposed illusion. Stupid trick of the mind rendered by poor visibility and his overamped nerves.

But he had to know for sure.

Transformed in one confused eyeblink from quarry to hunter, Rusty drove as fast as any modicum of safety allowed. Aggressively changing lanes, he wove between cars with a sinking feeling in the pit of his stomach.

After a dozen blocks, he knew it was futile. Spooked by

his stall tactic at the intersection, the Dodge's driver had almost certainly pulled off onto one of countless side streets.

Give it up, he told himself. *It wasn't her.*

Gradually calming down, Rusty's mind returned to tonight's original purpose. He slowed the car to a more reasonable pace and continued on toward his destination.

By the time he turned right on Fifth and parked in a gravel lot behind the Avalon, he'd convinced himself of being mistaken in identifying the driver. It was just too ludicrous to take seriously, and he bristled at his own gullibility.

All of which still left him with the same question: why was he being followed, and by whom?

A certain sequential logic arose in his mind.

Someone spotted my car when I parked it at the boardwalk and got the license number. Either Kenny Dixon or a confederate of his. Now Dixon's locked up and I'm being tailed. That could have been his girlfriend, or some random drug skank, or God knows.

As a theory regarding the who, that seemed reasonable enough. But the why remained unanswered. Was this tail put on him just to return the favor, or with more malicious intent?

Rusty knew he wasn't going to figure it out by guesswork. Only if and when that Dodge reappeared on his back bumper would the truth present itself. Because at that point, he would be taking far more hostile countermeasures.

16.

Rusty was up the stairs leading to the Avalon's spacious porch and halfway through the front door when he stopped and turned. Janice occupied a rocking chair at the far end of the porch. She was looking at him with a faint, unreadable smile, waiting to see if he'd notice her before going inside.

Letting the door swing closed, he walked over to her.

"I was about to ring your room from the desk, see if you had a minute to talk."

"I guess it's pretty urgent, the way you charged up those steps."

"Well, I'd say so." A pause. "Am I intruding?"

"Have a seat," she said, nodding to the empty rocker nearest hers. "You look a little wrung out."

"Thanks. The drive over was kind of stressful."

She didn't probe for more details as Rusty seated himself. For a brief interval they just rocked in silence. The corner of Fifth and Baltimore constituted a prime location in downtown OC, but on this chill October evening most nearby establishments were closed, adding a melancholy overtone to what was often a lively scene.

Despite the temperature, Janice wore only a light summer dress and sandals. Her figure made a powerful impression on Rusty at the medical examiner's office, but that day's designer business suit didn't reveal nearly as much as tonight's cotton dress. The asymmetrical hemline favored his vantage point, dancing a bit in the offshore breeze to reveal a pair of tanned, toned legs.

"I've got a crazy intuition," she said, turning to look at him.

"You've come to tell me about the man they arrested last night."

"You heard already."

"Detective Taylor called me a little while ago. I thought that was considerate."

"I'm sure he was glad to share the news."

"Is he the friend you mentioned?"

"No, but I know the guy you mean. He interviewed me when I was brought in."

"I guess this means you're officially off the hook."

Rusty allowed a moment to let that comment pass like a disagreeable odor.

"It's good to know this asshole Dixon is behind bars," he eventually said.

"Assuming he stays there. Maryland's judicial system is pretty lenient from what I understand. Almost as bad as New York's. It's always the criminal whose civil rights need to be protected."

Rusty didn't have any particularly intelligent comment to offer on that subject, so he switched gears by asking, "Do you feel any better at all?"

"I don't know that I'd say better. Obviously it's a relief to know they caught him, if he's the one who did it."

"Seems like a pretty clear-cut case. They've got his prints all over the house and a bunch of other evidence."

"No weapon, though. That's what Detective Taylor said."

Rusty almost mentioned that Thelma's wounds appeared to have been made with someone's bare hands, but thought better of it. Instead he replied, "I don't know that they'll need one to get a conviction."

"He also told me this is the first murder to hit Ocean Pines in over five years." She paused. "Can you believe that? Of all people to break that streak, why her?"

"I don't know. I'm not sure there's any good answer to that question."

Another interval of silence. Rusty really wished he could offer some words of comfort or reassurance, but he was way out of practice when it came to such matters. Not that it was ever his forte to begin with.

"When's the funeral?"

"Tomorrow. I've already had her cremated. It's going to be a small service. Don't feel you need to come."

"I'd like to," he said, though in fact he didn't want to at all. Funerals were one of numerous socially dictated events he had a hard time attending. It wasn't a callous lack of empathy, just a sense of having no idea how to behave on such formally ordained occasions that caused him unease.

"No, really," Janice said. "It's just going to be me and a few people from the hospital where she volunteered."

There was a tone of finality to that, and Rusty decided with some relief not to pursue the issue further.

He was starting to get the feeling his presence, if not unwanted, was something of a distraction. Any nascent ideas about seduction were miles from his head. If they'd met under different circumstances, he would undoubtedly give it his best shot. But the timing seemed hopelessly off, and he didn't have the stomach to field even a mild gesture at flirtation.

"Well," he said, rising, "I'll be on my way. I'm glad we had a chance to meet, Janice. Hope you're able to put this behind you soon."

At first he wasn't sure if she'd heard him, still gazing into the night. Just as he was turning away, she spoke.

"I think you should stay in the house, for as long as you want to. I'm not going to raise the rent."

"That's good of you. I'm happy to pay whatever you think is right. It's a comfortable place to live, and I don't have any interest in moving at the moment."

"Good," she said, turning to drill him with her deep blue eyes. "That means I know where to find you."

He couldn't quite read the intent of those words, delivered in such a flat tone as to be rendered fairly cryptic. Was it a come-on? A joke? Or even, improbably, a veiled threat of some kind?

He just nodded and stepped off the porch.

Reaching the parking lot, Rusty suddenly remembered tonight's unnerving encounter with the Dodge. He'd completely erased it from his mind while on the porch, but now he couldn't resist doing a 360-degree visual pan of the area to determine if his supposed stalker was anywhere in sight.

He didn't see any sign of the pursuing car. It almost came as a disappointment. With his night wide open since leaving Janice behind, the idea of getting into some kind of confrontation at this moment was strangely appealing.

And he really needed to find out who'd taken such a dogged interest in tracking his movements.

17.

Ronnie crouched on the floor in the back storeroom of The Bearded Clam staring at the dripping object in his hand. He wasn't sure what it was, how it had gotten there, or whose blood was dotted across not only the object but much of the trembling fist that clenched it.

The object was a box cutter. The blood came from Big Bill. Deep down, on some core plane of awareness untouched by the drugs in his system, Ronnie knew that. But it was all so unclear, and that nightmarish pounding on the door made it impossible to think.

His whole 132-lb body was shaking so hard he struggled to keep his balance even in a low crouch. Fluorescent lights overhead flared in his vision, creating a strobe effect. The storeroom's air was fetid, clinging to him like a slimy second skin the rivulets of sweat pouring from his brow could not wash away.

He wanted to reach in his jacket pocket and see how much he had left. Even just a little taste to rub on his gums would help right now. Or maybe it would make things worse. Ronnie wasn't sure what he needed more—to gain a sense of clarity about what was happening or to blast himself into utter oblivion.

In order to maintain some measure of control, he was staring at a spot on the floor between his feet. It was clean, or at least cleaner than any other part of the storeroom. Ronnie should know, he was the one who pushed the broom around here. And that spot on the floor was spic and span. Not a trace of blood on it anywhere.

He kept his eyes welded to that one area by a major force of will. He didn't dare look left or right even a few inches for fear of what he might find. As long as he focused on the clean spot, he didn't have to think about the box cutter.

Suddenly his will broke, and his eyes darted to the left. All he saw at first was a pair of size sixteen Timberland boots. They belonged to Big Bill. Inching his eyes further leftward, Ronnie beheld the rest of the bartender.

Bill was lying facedown on the floor, head jerked to one side. The back of his stained wifebeater was covered with dark red splotches.

Ronnie knew he'd killed him. He retained trace memories of repetitive motions made with his right arm, plunging down to cut deep and then rising again with renewed force. He didn't know the exact number of times he'd struck, nor the corresponding quantity of wounds opened on Big Bill's well-fed body. It didn't seem to matter now, anyway.

Today had started normally enough. He remembered coming to the Clam at three o'clock sharp, making a point of leaving home early so he'd get here on time and not give Bill an easy excuse to chew him out.

All for naught. A chew-out is exactly what happened the minute he set foot in the door. Ronnie wasn't pleased to see his ma sitting at the bar making small talk with the man he despised more than any other on earth. Why'd she have to fall for an a-hole like Bill? Ronnie didn't know if they'd consummated the friendship (the very thought made him want to vomit) but it hardly made a difference. Given how much time they spent together, Big Bill and his ma might as well be married. Granted, he wouldn't have this job if that weren't the case. But Bill wouldn't feel free to yell at him all the time either, or cuff him about the ears whenever the mood stuck.

For the past two days Ronnie had managed to abstain from touching the salts. He'd gone cold turkey, and it wasn't even hard. After he sold that half gram to the weird dude with the goatee on the boardwalk the other night, Ronnie went home to bed and didn't take so much as a little gummer. Waking the next morning and not feeling like shit for a change, he decided to see what a day on the straight side felt like.

It felt pretty good. And so did the next day. The best part was knowing he had that half gram sitting right there in his wallet, and not touching it. Just letting it ride, being in control of it and not vice versa. Ronnie started to entertain thoughts of never touching the stuff again. He didn't really believe that, but it was a pleasing notion.

His optimistic mood crashed today when he walked into The Bearded Clam. Just seeing Big Bill and his ma holding hands all lovey-dovey, and both of them tossing him acid looks before he was even inside the damn bar, he knew it was going to be a tough day. A day that demanded he get high in order to function.

Then Bill started bitching about how dirty the back room was. Top of his lungs, too. Couldn't express enough frustration at how it hadn't been swept in over a week and there were cobwebs in every corner.

That was true enough, but there was no reason to be a dick about it. And Ma just sat there and didn't say a thing, not even in defense of her own son. It was sickening.

Ronnie didn't utter so much as a word to express his contempt. He just poured himself a Coke from behind the bar and said he'd get right to it. And then he'd walked back to the storeroom with the intention of doing just that.

But he needed a taste first. No question about it. There was no way he could put up with Bill's shit for the next nine hours without some chemical help.

It wasn't easy cutting up the lines with his left hand still wrapped in gauze. Ronnie was starting to wonder if he should've gotten stitches for the cut he'd earned smashing that car window. He still felt guilty about that, another negative emotional current waiting to drag him down.

He finished cutting the lines. Two big fatties, one for each side of his face. Didn't bother with any mixing agent; there was no time and he'd left it at home anyway. He was going to clean the almighty shit of this room, and Bill wouldn't have a choice but to commend him on a job well done.

The rush hit him full bore, and in an instant those last few days of sobriety seemed like utter folly. Why on earth would he give up *this*? This lurid uncovering of shimmery clarity, this galvanizing rush of fearless focus? He could literally hear the blood coursing through his veins, pumping him into something much larger and stronger than he ever was when sober.

Ronnie spent the next fourteen minutes riding a blissful haze, all thoughts of Bill and Ma and sweeping up this shitty storeroom wiped from his mind. Hell, the room already looked clean to a degree of excellence beyond his ability to describe. Each slow inhalation made him taste the very motes in the air, and they were as perfect as he was.

Twitching happily, Ronnie enjoyed near-total ignorance of the crash that was already on the way. It arrived soon enough and with disorienting power, a widening blackness that reminded him where he was and what he'd come here to do.

No way in hell he could be even marginally productive without forestalling that crash for at least a while longer. Fortunately, his pocket held the means of achieving such a delay.

Ronnie had just snorted the second of two more bumps when a large shadow fell over him. What happened next was hard to sort out, even now that it was all over.

Bill's reaction to seeing the drugs was volcanic. He stormed across the cement floor, knocking the straw from Ronnie's hand with an open slap. Another one struck Ronnie in the face with enough force to disrupt his balance. He fell to one knee, crying for Big Bill to chill out. His protestations were cut short by a kick to the stomach that completely stole his breath.

He rolled over onto his back, gasping, vision rupturing into a million pixilated fragments as the second round of salts kicked in hard.

Big Bill loomed over him like a mountain, showering down heated words and spittle. As Ronnie's pupils dilated further, Bill took on the aspect of a grizzly bear, huge paws swinging in the air, killer fangs bared.

A sense of utter panic coursed through Ronnie's body. This beast was going to kill him, he had no doubt. Hand reaching wildly, his fingers found the plastic grip of a box cutter.

The first slash went across Big Bill's right shin, the blade cutting almost to the bone.

The Bill/Beast roared and doubled over in pain. Ronnie knew he'd only angered it with a glancing blow. He had to finish the job or be torn limb from limb. As Bill clutched his shin and screamed blue murder, Ronnie rose to his full height and brought the box cutter down in a plunging motion to the base of Bill's neck. Droplets of blood sprayed into his vision like a flower blooming at time-lapse speed. He couldn't even hear the screams anymore; his head filled with a dull roar like two conch shells had been fused to his ears.

He kept at it with the box cutter, swinging and slashing many, many times. He vaguely recalled turning to see his ma standing in the doorway, her face an ivory mask of shock. Then she disappeared as quickly as she materialized, and Ronnie returned to the task of slaying the beast.

At some point he stopped and walked over to bolt the back door of the storeroom, and then did the same to the front door where his ma had been standing. When was that—an hour ago? A year?

Ronnie had no clue and he was too tired to even think. So he retreated to a far corner to sit down on the cement and just be still. That's where he was right now, straining to hold his gaze on that one clean spot on the floor.

The pounding kept getting louder. Ronnie wished it would stop. His heart was thumping in his chest at a hundred beats per minute, and he really needed to clear his head.

He finally realized the pounding was not coming from inside him, but from an external source. The front door of the storeroom. There seemed to be voices accompanying each thump, but the words were too muffled to hear or understand. All that came through was a sense of urgency.

Then Ronnie picked up one word that froze him clean through.

Police.

In a sudden merciless unveiling, everything became clear.

He knew where he was. He knew what he'd done, even without looking across the room at Bill's legs.

And now the police were here. Called by his ma, undoubtedly.

A much greater pounding shook the door, ending with one huge bash that rattled the frame. Ronnie figured the cops had given up on their fists and resorted to a battering ram.

Another massive slam twisted the steel lock a few degrees. It would only take one more, maybe two. The door would give way, removing any cloak of protection from the consequences of what went down here today. The police would be inside, descending upon him like a crazed herd, and Ronnie would have to fully accept what he'd done. Not just today, but for as much of his sorry life as he could recount.

No. That was too much. Ronnie felt a brief flash of something like lucidity, a sense of cold purpose. No matter what happened next, he was not going to be hauled in by any cop. He'd take another way out.

Fingers closing around the box cutter's handle, he knew what to do. And just as the door finally gave way with a splintering groan, he did it.

18.

Rusty stood outside Room 345 on the third floor of the chemistry building at UM's Eastern Shore campus in Prince Anne, his hand frozen on the knob. A thin vertical window ran down the door's right half, two inches in width. It offered a sliver of a view into the lab on the other side, but the view didn't tell him much. All he could see was an empty chair on rollers next to a white tabletop and some cabinets built into the wall behind.

Rusty had no way of knowing who might be occupying that room right now. He'd gotten a brief glimpse of someone in blue clinician's scrubs walking past a minute ago, but couldn't make out any specific features or tell if anyone else was in there.

Campus security officers? State Troopers? His paranoia hovered vexingly in the silent hallway, but Rusty wasn't biting. He hadn't driven all the way out here on a drizzly morning just to turn back. The bindle of salts felt like it was about to burn through his pocket, begging to be analyzed.

Rusty glanced at his watch. Eleven on the dot, exactly the time scheduled for this meeting.

Exhaling, he opened the door.

Four hours later, he entered Room 345 again with significantly less trepidation. To his great relief, the online username chosen by *sxylabchik* turned out to be highly apt. She was, in fact, a sexy lab chick. Long, dark hair matching soft brown eyes and tawny skin, she could have been of Latin, Asian or Mediterranean heritage, or an almost unimaginably ideal blending of all. Her name was Carmen. A third-year grad student in inorganic chemistry, she filled out her scrubs in ways that surely were not conducive to maintaining focus on toxicological studies, at least not for any of her male classmates.

Carmen had the lab to herself all day, one of the reasons she'd responded with interest to his post on the message board. Clinical and sparse, everything in the room was eggshell white with a half-dozen workstations spread around a hexagonal table in the center.

Rusty found Carmen only too eager to let him know she was recently single, having dumped a self-absorbed poli-sci major who was more interested in heading meetings of the Young Democrats Club than spending time with a highly intelligent and willing girlfriend. He'd deflected these pleasant overtures by pulling out the drug sample sold to him by Ronnie.

Before she could ask the questions he saw forming on her full lips, Rusty politely inquired how long her analysis would take. She offered a brief outline of how to study granular material on a molecular level through gas chromatography-mass spectrometry, then told him to come back around three.

Now he was here again, after killing the time with a meandering drive through Queen Anne and a long lunch at Doc's Riverside Grille.

"I know I agreed to no questions," Carmen said. "But I'm really curious where you got this stuff."

"It's been making the rounds. What can you tell me about it?"

Carmen flipped open a manila folder containing the six-page report she'd recently completed.

"Well, on the one hand this is a pretty standard mixture of synthetic cathinones commonly referred to as bath salts. Cathinones are a natural beta-ketone amphetamine analogue found in the leaves of the Catha edulis plant. Synthetic cathinones are derivatives of this compound. There's nothing illegal about eighty percent of the properties in here."

"What about the other twenty percent?"

"The chemicals most commonly used in street bath salts

are MDPV, and a newer kind called alpha-PVP. This sample has a healthy dose of the latter."

"Which people use to get high."

"Correct."

"So is there anything notable about this particular … *strain* of salts?"

Carmen's face lit up like a star pupil ready to show off.

"In fact, there is!"

She flipped forward a few pages in the report and directed Rusty's eyes to the top paragraph with a polished fingernail. The jumble of chemical text formulations meant nothing to him.

"What's interesting are these two isolated components."

"You mean stuff you wouldn't expect to find in standard-issue product?" he asked.

"Correct again. This right here indicates the presence of pure methamphetamine."

"Crystal meth?"

"Yup, and a massive dose of it. A typical dose of street meth might contain 50 mg, depending on the purity. This sample contains about four times that much. Making it potentially lethal for anyone dumb enough to ingest it."

"But not necessarily lethal."

"It would depend on a number of variables. The amount consumed, a person's body weight, any tolerance they might have developed to the drug, et cetera. Assuming it didn't kill you, it would induce a vastly intensified high. Probably followed by a hellish crash."

"Makes sense," Rusty said. "I know meth can cause all kinds of aberrant behavior in users. Violence, a lot of the time."

"You bet."

"So would this stuff be likely to bring on even *more* violent episodes?"

"Again, it would vary from person to person. But that seems like an outcome that would fall within predictable boundaries."

"I think that was a yes."

"Let's put it this way," Carmen said, pointing to the pile of powder. "This stuff is to regular bath salts what a double espresso is to decaf. Whatever bad reactions a person is apt to experience would be exponentially more powerful."

"Got it. What about the second component?"

Carmen let out a sigh, seeming a bit perplexed. She flipped to another page of her report.

"This one's harder to explain. I couldn't identify it as belonging to any known narcotic category. But there's something strange about it."

She pointed out a line of text marked with a yellow highlighter.

"See this? It's a generation code that's embedded in the molecular structure of certain synthetic compounds. Like a stamp, a way of identifying the manufacturer. I haven't had time to dig into it fully, but this code's six-character prefix makes me think whoever this stuff came from is somewhere close."

"How come?"

"Because I recognize the prefix. Or at least I think I do. All these formulations start to blur together after a while."

"I can imagine," Rusty said. "Tell you what, it'd be a big help if you could prove this was produced locally."

She looked at him, brows lifting with unhidden curiosity.

"Why are you messing around with this stuff, Rusty? It's seriously bad news."

"That sounded like a question. Don't tell me you're reneging on our deal."

"I'd just like to know if you're paying me with drug money."

"Don't worry. I've got nothing to do with the sale or manufacture of this shit. That's a promise."

"Well, I can try to track down a matching code," she said, "if you'll let me hold on to a sample for a while longer."

"Sure. Just get rid of it when you're done."

"Don't have to tell me that twice."

She used a polypropylene spatula to separate a small portion of the salts for her use, then folded up the bulk of it in the paper bindle. Rusty pocketed the bindle.

"I'll call you if I come up with anything interesting."

"Awesome. You're an amazing resource, Carmen."

"Oh," she said, revolving just far enough to grace him with some fairly brazen elbow tit. "I'm much more than that, Rusty."

He was very close to taking the bait. Hell, why not? This amateur gumshoe business was wearing him down, and a lazy afternoon with the sexy lab chick sounded like a superb way to put some spring back in his step.

Maybe later, he admonished himself. *Got a few more pressing items on the agenda right now.*

Carmen took his nonresponse to her advance agreeably enough. She heaved a mock-heavy sigh of disappointment, rotating her guns away from him.

Definitely later.

"That's pretty much all I got for ya," she said, closing the manila folder and sliding it across the table. "Is it worth your five Benjamins?"

"Absolutely. I really appreciate you handling this so fast."

"No sweat. It was a nice change from my usual lab work."

Rusty picked up the folder and gave her a friendly nod.

"I swear," she said, "you look really familiar. Are you in a band or something?"

"No, but I get that from time to time. Some people think I look like Rob Zombie."

She wrinkled her nose, mulling the comparison.

"His younger brother, maybe."

"Thanks again, Carmen. You've been a big help."

"You know where to find me," she said with a wink as he turned for a final wave at the door.

"That I do."

19.

Walking from the chemistry building to the lot where he'd parked, Rusty found the campus quad humming with midday activity and at the same time quite peaceful. Rays of warming sunshine broke through the patchy clouds. He gave into the temptation to recline on the grass and relax for a short while, watching the carefree flow of youthful bodies zigzagging across the quad by means of foot, bike and skateboard. Having never experienced college life himself, he felt a certain envy for these fresh faces, seemingly empty of angst or regret.

Where was I at that age? he mused. *Still working the streets of the Quarter, or had I already lit out for LV at that point?*

Reflecting further, he decided he must have been in New Orleans at the age of a typical undergrad, not venturing to the Nevada desert until shortly before his twenty-second birthday.

That first week in Las Vegas was a brutal eye-opener. Arriving in the spring of 2000 as a fledgling illusionist, his naive hopes of working in a major casino or nightclub crashed into the reality of what it took to reach that plane.

He shared a stifling apartment in a seedy off-Strip part of town with two people—his mentor, a stately Bourbon Street magician named Prosper Lavalle, and Prosper's daughter Marceline, Rusty's first love, with whom he shared a febrile romance almost as important to him as magic. Both Lavalles had accompanied him westward despite serious misgivings about the relocation. Buttressed by their support, he went from one failed audition to the next until he finally got the message.

As far as the Vegas decision makers were concerned, he

115

was persona non grata. Whatever notice young Rusty Diamond may have garnered as a street performer in New Orleans didn't hold the slightest value in the big leagues. His odds of getting booked in any but the smallest and sleaziest of venues were nil. No references, no agent, no chance. Forget the newer palaces on the Strip. Rusty couldn't even land a graveyard gig in one of the dilapidated casinos in old downtown.

So he took his act to the only place it could find an audience: the street corner. To ensure notice, he specialized in wildly dangerous stunts. At Fremont and First, he'd startle bypassers by hurtling himself through the lid of a glass casket bottomed with six-inch nails. Or summersaulting off the roof of a two-story garage, disappearing in a cloud of gray smoke the moment his feet made impact with the asphalt below.

He found an audience. Not rapidly, but growing by steady increments. Street performers were nothing new on Fremont, but few ever attempted the kind of stunts and illusions Rusty seemed to knock out on a whim. Bug-eyed spectators couldn't believe the risks he took. Who was this maniac, they asked, and was his act even legal? Prosper didn't approve of the needless danger Rusty seemed to thrive on, but could already see his protégé was pulling beyond the reach of his influence.

Over time a grapevine effect kicked in: *you gotta see Rusty Diamond before he kills himself.* A persona emerged. Dark, gothic, stylistically closer to Ozzy Osbourne at his bat-biting decadent peak than the cheesy velvet-cloaked suavity of David Copperfield. The location of his impromptu performances, whether an unlit parking lot or the back room of a machine shop off Paradise Road, was rarely known more than twenty-four hours beforehand. You had to be one of the initiated to see it, and then spread the word.

He finally got busted in the summer of 2008 for driving a motorcycle through a plate glass window at a defunct shopping center due for demolition. It did wonders for his reputation. Membership to Rusty's website, featuring videos of stunts too flagrantly illegal for him to perform in public (such as ingesting a near-lethal quantity of barbiturates and then traversing a narrow wooden beam from the roof of one high-rise to another), made a six-digit jump following the arrest.

He was eventually found guilty of creating a disturbance and wanton destruction of property, with massive fees accompanying each count. He never paid them, because by that point he'd signed an eighteen-month exclusive contract with Caesars covering such troublesome work-related expenses. Tossed in as a sweetener, a two-bedroom suite on the seventeenth floor of the west tower, rent-free.

It wasn't an easy call for the honchos at Caesars to bring such a loose cannon onto the payroll. Eight pages of meticulous terms regarding what he *could* and could *not* do on their stage were central to the agreement. They knew Rusty represented a potential bonanza in ticket sales, but only if he was insurable and stayed alive long enough to repay their investment. So they took the risk, offering him a deal for twelve shows a week in the Etruscan Room. He signed without bothering to read the fine print.

It was in the run-up to his debut at Caesars that he acquired his stage name. Just a gimmick to match the carefully cultivated goth/metal persona suggested by a talent manager briefly hired and discarded. He had to admit it was catchy: Rusty "The Raven" Diamond. An alliterative adornment that fit the tattoos, black leather wardrobe and two-pointed devil's goatee. He embraced it whole hog.

By that time, both Prosper and Marceline had been gone for months. Alienated by some unsavory character changes impending fame spurred within him, they'd returned to Louisiana early one morning while Rusty was out carousing in a North Vegas bordello. Neither father nor daughter saw the need to leave a note explaining their departure—and Rusty didn't allow the sting of their abandonment to derail his breakneck momentum.

For about sixteen months, it was a pretty sweet run. He was a dark star rising in the Vegas firmament. A magnet for rabid, youth-driven crowds spellbound by his notoriously unhinged performances where magic and masochism collided in an array of profoundly unnerving stunts.

Knives, guns, explosives, high speed collisions, dangerous drugs, hairbreadth escapes, fiendishly inexplicable acts of slight of hand and mentalism … after almost two decades of constant study, these had become Rusty's stock in trade.

It was his penchant for dodging a grisly demise at the last possible moment that made him something not seen before in the world of professional conjurers: Houdini with a death wish, orchestrating imminent doom with a deafening heavy metal soundtrack. Selling out the house every night and almost burning it down half as often. Never taking his eyes off the prize long enough to worry about anyone who might get singed by the flames.

Only after the lines separating his performing life from his private life started to blur did Rusty feel some tremors of unease about his alter ego. The Raven seemed to grow ever larger, stretching its mordant wings across his entire landscape. He'd sometimes wake in the blazing sunlight of midday Nevada to find himself decked out in full stage regalia even when he had no show to perform.

These episodes should have been troubling, along with the abrupt departures of his mentor and lover months before. But he took no notice. There were way too many showgirls, contracts, champagne rooms and bumps of cocaine clouding his immediate vision.

With the benefit of hindsight, Rusty realized what should have been his breakthrough was the beginning of the end for him as a performer. He couldn't have imagined at the time just how bad it would become, but now it was obvious that signing his contract at Caesars signaled a precipitous downward spiral that only started to abate more than a year later when he scrawled another signature—this one on the lease for his house in Ocean Pines.

Yes, very heroic. Crawling back to the place I once swore I'd never call home again.

With a jolt of self-reproach, Rusty snapped back to the present. He'd been lying on the grassy quad replaying old mental tapes for almost half an hour.

All of a sudden he'd had enough of the UM campus.

He was halfway to the parking lot when his cell phone started vibrating. Not an incoming call but a message from his web browser. Last night he'd set a notification preference so he'd know whenever there was a Google News alert for any items containing the words: "ocean city maryland drugs violent crime."

He opened the browser and saw an article from the AP. Rusty's shoulders sagged when he read the headline:

GRISLY MURDER/SUICIDE ON OCEAN CITY BOARDWALK; YOUTH KILLS EMPLOYER, SELF AT LOCAL BAR.

OCEAN CITY, Md. — A young man apparently murdered his employer and then took his own life at The Bearded Clam Saloon located adjacent to the popular boardwalk where families flock by the tens of thousands each summer. Nineteen-year-old Ronnie Wilson is believed to have used a box cutter to kill William Langston in the storeroom of the bar owned by Langston where Wilson was employed as a barback.

Ocean City Police arrived on the scene after receiving a 911 call from Wilson's mother. She'd overheard the two men getting into a violent argument, and walked into the back storeroom to see her son stabbing Langston.

When police arrived on scene, they found Wilson had barricaded himself into the room. Using a battering ram, officers broke through the door. As they were attempting to subdue Wilson, the young man took a sharp blade to his own throat, fatally injuring himself. It is believed to be the same box cutter used to slay Langston.

No motive is known at this time. Wilson's mother, a friend of Langston, says the two had a contentious relationship. She indicated her son had struggled with narcotics for some time, but he had never shown any violent tendencies. Wilson had never been arrested before.

Turning off the phone, Rusty just stood there in the parking lot for a long moment, oblivious to everything around him. The news stung in ways he could not have predicted.

Slowly resuming his walk to the car, he hit upon what it was that so disturbed him. He'd been thinking about Ronnie quite a bit the past day or so, in the back of his mind. Rusty felt like he'd established some kind of rapport, however fleeting, with the troubled kid.

Ronnie, without knowing or intending to, had given him a gift. That look of uncool enjoyment lighting up his face after seeing the bill trick had sparked something precious. A reminder of what once fueled Rusty with purpose, when he'd had the power to move large crowds to similar states of wonder. It had been a long time since he let himself indulge a forgotten sense of pride that used to come from performing.

Thelma Garrett was a victim, plain and simple.

Her killer, Kenny Dixon, was a villain.

Ronnie Wilson was both victim *and* villain.

The common denominator connecting these three unfortunate souls was the drugs. The same strain of ultra-toxic poison that someone by the handle Fade was cooking up and peddling for profit.

Rusty's fingers closed around the bindle. Feeling the crystallized bumps of powder contained within its folds.

He could still hear Carmen's words:

Whoever this came from is somewhere close.

20.

Jim Biddison spent the afternoon plowing through a stack of paperwork and struggling to stay awake. There was nothing remotely interesting in the collection of arrest reports and case files he was looking at, which covered the most common complaints to come across his desk in an off-season shift: DUI, petty theft, the odd domestic abuse incident. Given the boredom this pile of crap induced, Jim wasn't sure if he should feel lucky or cheated not to be dealing with another homicide.

He had no direct oversight of the gruesome double death from two nights ago that still had many of the officers in the squad room buzzing with lurid interest. The Bearded Clam was located in the Southern District and thus the concern of his colleague Lieutenant Lineweaver. Captain Briggs was putting her hands on this one as well, with arguably more urgency than had accompanied the Garrett case.

Three civilians dead of extraordinarily violent means in one week was more than an anomaly for Ocean City and its environs. It was the center of a full-blown media shitstorm. Mayor Boyle's office felt a mounting avalanche of pressure to find some effective means of calming a rattled base of taxpaying voters.

None of that was Jim's headache, for which he had to feel grateful. And with the suspect in the Garrett killing safely incarcerated, that case was in the county prosecutor's court now. Leaving Jim with the pleasingly unstressful but dull task of sorting through this morass of mundane casework.

He shared a cramped office with two other ranking officers, sergeants both. Jones was off today and Burnett was out in the field, leaving no one to talk to and help Jim fight the urge to lay down his head and grab some shut-eye. He'd made the mistake of eating a huge lunch at Fager's Island, accompanied by two beers. Jim never drank alcohol on duty (well, almost never) but it seemed downright criminal to feast on Fager's signature crab cakes without a few cold ones to wash them down.

Now he was paying for it. Of all the items on his desk, the only one that held any interest was the 8 x 10 photo of his wife Kim holding their ten-month-old daughter Danielle. He'd taken the photo a few weeks ago and just got around to having it framed. It brought a much-needed dose of life to this charmless space. Looking at their smiling faces made Jim want to nod off in happy slumber.

Just as his eyelids started performing a flutter than might actually lead to a loss of consciousness, Rusty Diamond barged into the office.

Jim snapped to with a start, chin jutting up from where it had briefly settled on his chest.

"OK, listen," Rusty said, not bothering with any kind of greeting. "I know you told me to keep away from this, but I found something you really need to look at."

At first Jim thought it had to be a gag; Rusty was trying to get a rise out of him.

"I'm telling you, it's pure poison," Rusty was saying, shaking a manila folder like Exhibit A. "Forget the damage it does to users. They should know what they're getting into. The real concern is what happens to anyone unlucky enough to cross the path of some tweaker out of his mind on this shit."

Rusty stopped talking, looking faintly out of breath. Apparently he'd said his piece, or at least what he felt was sufficient to get a response from the lieutenant.

Biddison rose from his chair, wincing at the familiar complaint of his lower back, and walked around the desk.

"Didn't I warn you about staying clear of police business?"

"Fuck that, Jim. I'm trying to help you out."

"There's nothing I can say that will sink in, is there? Do I really have to charge you to get my message across?"

Rusty ignored that, reaching into his pocket.

"Still got that baggie I gave you? Here's more of the same."

He dropped the bindle onto Biddison's desk. Jim looked at it for a moment, head shaking in wonderment.

"You're really out of your fucking mind, aren't you?"

"Know who sold me that? Ronnie Wilson. Name ring a bell?"

Biddison paused just half a beat.

"The kid who snuffed that guy at the Clam."

Rusty nodded. "And then himself. How about you draw some blood from the body? We can lay friendly odds on how much of this garbage is in his system."

"Rusty," Biddison said, "when this was about your landlady, I could almost understand. Now you're messing around with this Wilson kid? Buying drugs off him, for Christ's sake?!"

"I bought it so I could have it analyzed." Again he held up Carmen's report. "This info is verified from the toxicology department at UM. You're not gonna believe what's in here."

"I don't believe any of this. What the fuck are you doing? You really want to get booked, don't you?"

"What I'm trying to do is draw your attention to a commonality that links two crimes together. I told you the other day, as long as these toxic salts are being sold more people are going to die. Now we've got two more corpses."

"*We* don't have anything!"

"Just tell your lab guys to take a look. There's a good chance this stuff is being produced locally."

"I wouldn't doubt it. Coastal Maryland has its share of homegrown narcotics like anywhere else."

"So find out who the damn cooker is. I got a name for you to start with, or a nickname. Fade. Mean anything to you?"

Jim just shook his head. He didn't recall anyone brought in using that handle.

"Do a little digging," Rusty said, sounding irritated and almost derisive. "Shake down every known drug cooker in your files. Raid their shit, run some analyses and compare them with this sample. Whoever's making it is ultimately responsible for Thelma, Ronnie Wilson and the other guy."

"And God knows how many future victims, right?"

"That's right," Rusty said, not sure if Biddison was humoring him or not.

"Anything else we should do, in your professional judgment?"

"Sure. Release a public statement. Warn people an unusually lethal strain of bath salts is being sold on the boardwalk. It's a serious public safety threat."

Jim decided he'd heard enough. This had been something of a shit day to begin with. He'd woken in a foul mood momentarily leavened by his lunch at Fager's Island, which had only yielded regret once it was over. The last thing he felt like dealing with right now was this off-the-wall visit from Rusty Fucking Diamond.

He laid a heavy hand on the back of Rusty's neck and turned him roughly toward the door. Rusty flung the folder; it sailed through the air and landed on top of Jim's desk next to the bindle.

A few cops looked up from their desks at the sight of Jim Biddison physically hustling some weird cat across the squad room.

"I'm warning you for the last time. Stay out of this. You just burned your last pass with me, Rusty. Next time you stick your nose in, I'm booking you for tampering with a police investigation, and fuck old times' sake."

They approached the double doors leading from the squad room to a hallway outside.

"OK, fine. I got the message."

"Better hope you do."

With a firm push on the shoulder, Biddison propelled him toward the exit.

Walking back to his desk, all traces of his earlier fatigue had vaporized in response to Rusty's uninvited appearance. What the hell was with this guy? He'd always been weird, but was he actually touched in the head? That seemed more and more likely. Biddison thought maybe on some level Rusty really did want to get locked up, but didn't have the gumption to commit an outright act of criminality.

Jim sat there for a moment, letting himself calm down and staring at the two items Rusty had deposited on his desk. He reached out for the manila folder and flipped it open. The six-page report appeared credible enough to his eye upon a brief glance. Maybe sending it down to chemical forensics to see what they made of it wasn't the worst idea in the world.

The name Rusty had mentioned returned to his mind. Fade. Musing further, Jim was certain he'd never heard it before. But a simple database search couldn't hurt, and would only take a few minutes.

Detective Theo Taylor poked his head in the office.

"You look like you're enjoying the hell out of yourself," he said, leaning against the doorframe. "Ready for some good news to cheer you up even more?"

Jim wasn't in the mood for Taylor's wiseass sense of humor right now.

"What is it, Theo?"

"Kenny Dixon just made bail."

"What?" Biddison said, almost lurching forward in his chair. "How the hell …"

He didn't finish the question. The answer had already come to him, and the look on Taylor's face seemed to confirm it.

"Andrews."

"That's right," Taylor said. "Judge Compassion himself."

"What was the bond?"

"$400K."

"Shit," Jim muttered. "Hard to believe Dixon has enough collateral to cover that."

"Wonders never cease."

Dark clouds formed over the lieutenant's brow. He was known around the squad room to have a short fuse, once shoving a bike patrol officer up against the break room's wall hard enough to crack the plaster.

Detective Taylor could see the news he'd come to share was being received by Biddison even more poorly than he'd expected. He saw no sense in poking an angry beast in its cage, so he just backed away from the desk.

Jim barely seemed to notice.

21.

Rusty swerved a hard right onto Echo Run, just a few blocks away from his house. Gripping the wheel tightly, he still felt agitated by his encounter at the police station, having only started to calm down once he'd reentered Ocean Pines.

Most of his anger was self-directed. He'd approached it all wrong with Jim, stupidly. Thinking back through a host of memories, Rusty could clearly picture how much Biddison despised feeling like he was being taunted, or played for a fool. All throughout grade school and into their years at Ocean High, Jim responded with the same sore temper against anyone dumb enough to try to get his goat. Not once did he just laugh it off and let it go, as far as Rusty could recall.

That's what he thinks I'm doing with all this. Taunting him for my own entertainment.

Rusty drove on, wondering how he might be able to reset his contentious relationship with the lieutenant.

He forgot all about that as soon as he pulled up to the house.

A car was parked in the driveway. A car he didn't recognize. In all the months since moving here, he'd never had an unannounced visitor. Never had *any* visitors except for Ms. Garrett and an exterminator who came by last spring to handle a fledgling termite problem. And then there was Jim's surprise drop-by two days ago.

But this wasn't the unmarked unit Jim had driven then. And it wasn't the silver Dodge.

It was a white Buick sedan with Maryland plates.

Feeling his pulse quicken, he willed it back to normal

through a controlled breathing exercise.

Rusty knew, rationally, he shouldn't have any cause for alarm. Nobody knew he lived here. Maintaining privacy and seclusion had been one of his top priorities for the past year, and he'd put into practice any number of routines to maintain anonymity since moving in.

So maybe the car didn't belong to someone who'd come looking for him.

Then who the hell does it belong to?

Deciding an excess of caution might not be such a bad thing right now, he shifted into reverse. Backing up, he parked about fifty yards away on Echo Run, where his Lexus would be blocked from view from the house by a bushy wall of pines.

Walking back to the driveway, he made a quick examination of the sedan. Nothing of any interest inside. No possessions at all, or a scrap of debris on the floorboards. A tag in the windshield identified it as a rental car from Avis.

Once again Rusty couldn't help but think of how he'd left the Lexus in the parking lot when pursuing Kenny Dixon to the boardwalk. Had someone taken note of the plate number and tracked him to this house? It wouldn't be easy, but not impossible either. He'd switched the utility bills to his name last year, figuring he'd be around for a while and there was no need for Ms. Garrett to be bothered with forwarding the bills to him. Someone with access to billing files from the DWP or the gas company could find him here. Assuming they'd been able to get his name from the license plate, which would involve some kind of access to police or DMV records.

To hell with this uncertainty, he thought, stepping away from the sedan.

Still feeling mildly spooked but ignoring it, Rusty approached the front door and found it unlocked. His sense of alarm shot up a few degrees. He definitely didn't leave it that way when heading out for the campus this morning.

Entering through the front door didn't seem wise, so he loped around the eastern side of the house, which fronted the bay. There was a bathroom halfway from the front door to the back deck, the window of which he thought was probably unlatched. He was right, and with a quick two-handed vault he pulled himself up and through.

Stepping into the bathroom, he removed his boots and set them quietly on the floor. He opened the door slowly, revealing a narrow hallway that led to the living room on the left and kitchen on the right.

Before walking through the house, Rusty figured it wouldn't hurt to have something blunt in hand. So he gingerly opened the hallway closet and pulled out a croquet mallet. Part of a vintage set that came with the property, it was a relic of Garrett family gatherings from happier days. Thelma told him when he signed the lease she hoped he'd set up the wickets in the backyard, for sentiment's sake.

He never bothered to do that. But now, hoisting the sturdy mallet over a shoulder, he was grateful not to have relegated the whole set to the dumpster.

The wooden handle felt good in his grip, like a surprise meeting with an old friend. It carried similar heft to a huge customized hammer he used nightly in his showstopping "Smashed Mirrors Escape" routine at Caesars.

Rusty's eyes narrowed as he shut the closet door. A flash flood of adrenaline washed any nascent fear out of his bloodstream.

OK, pal. Let's see who you are.

Moving with utter silence, he stepped into the front foyer and saw nothing out of order. Ditto the living room off to the immediate left; it was probably the one room he frequented least often in the entire house and appeared utterly undisturbed.

A metallic sound caught his ear. Short and sharp, like two pots knocking together.

The kitchen.

He'd just started to turn the corner where the hallway's hardwood floor gave way to the kitchen's checkerboard tile when a flurry of movement in his peripheral vision stopped him.

"Who the hell's there?" he said loudly, raising the mallet. He stood flat against the wall, out of view from anyone in the kitchen.

For a moment there was no reply. Then Rusty saw a long and elegant female leg step into view, quickly followed by the rest of Janice Garrett's elegant frame.

"Is that your standard greeting?" she asked, eyes flicking upward to the mallet then back to lock on his.

"Jesus," he said, lowering his arm as a palpable wave of relief rolled over him.

"Sorry, did I surprise you?"

"What gave you that idea?"

"I figured you'd see my car and know it was me. Left the door open too."

"Good thinking," he said, wondering how quickly he could make a move for the bar. It wasn't quite five yet, but he was willing to make a small concession. It had been an unusually weird few days.

"I just thought I'd take a look at the house. Make sure you haven't done too much damage."

Rusty appreciated the smile; otherwise, he'd have no way to read the intent of her remark.

"Fix you a drink?" he asked.

"I was just boiling some water for tea. That loose leaf sencha in the mason jar looks pretty high quality."

"Best money can buy. I order it online from the Kagoshima Province in Japan."

"Impressive."

"I might go for something a little stronger."

She seemed to think about it, glancing at her Rolex.

"Fine, twist my arm."

"Bar's sort of limited, I'm afraid. I don't do a lot of entertaining."

"Then I'll have what you're having," she said, following him out of the kitchen, down a half set of stairs into the den.

"God, this place is just as I remembered it. You haven't done much in the way of redecorating."

"Didn't see any reason," Rusty said, pulling down two glasses. "I dug the decor the first time your aunt showed me the place. She had good taste."

"A little stuffy for me," Janice said, looking up at a large oil painting over the fireplace depicting a rustic fox hunt: red-jacketed riders whipping their steeds over a darkening countryside with a pack of baying hounds at the lead.

"Water? Soda?" Rusty asked, holding up a fresh bottle of The Glenlivet's 18-Year single malt.

"Not with top-shelf scotch. I see you prefer the finer things."

"Sometimes."

"Rocks will do."

He handed Janice a glass with two ounces and three ice cubes.

"Seems weird to raise a toast, but I'm glad you stopped by. It's a nice surprise."

"A surprise, anyway. Glad you didn't club me with that mallet."

"That makes two of us. I'm just not that used to having other people in the house."

"I'm starting to pick up on that. Have you always been such a loner?"

Rusty didn't say anything to that. They touched glasses lightly in a toast, barely making contact.

"On days like today I usually catch the sunset out on the deck. Is it too cold for you?"

She shook her head, silently appraising him, or maybe just the offer. The look in her eyes was, as ever, unreadable. Rusty wasn't sure he liked that as much as he thought he did at first.

"Well then," he said. "Shall we?"

She nodded, smiling. He opened the sliding glass door and they stepped out onto the deck.

22.

Three hours later, they were still sitting out there in a pair of wooden Bermuda chairs. The Glenlivet bottle stood somewhat drained on a circular glass table between then. Sunlight was a memory but the sky was crystal clear, a ripple of moonlight dancing across Isle of Wight Bay. The temperature couldn't have reached much over forty, and Rusty was starting to feel a bit chilled himself. He'd asked Janice twice if she would prefer to go inside and toss some logs in the hearth. She declined, saying the cool air was invigorating.

They'd worked their way through several glasses of scotch apiece, and were feeling no worse for it. The conversation flowed easily, much more so than their last encounter at the Avalon Inn. They made each other laugh with some shared stories of growing up in the area. Enough common points of reference existed, especially regarding summer activities in Ocean City, for a sense of connection to arise.

Untying the bow behind her head to let her amber locks dangle freely, Janice inquired about what he did for a living.

"I almost want to guess writer," she said. "Crime novelist or something. Not that you really fit the image, but it seems like this would be a good place to do that."

"It probably would. I'm not currently employed."

"Then you either made a bundle in your former job or inherited it. Even at the criminally low rent you're paying, this place isn't exactly cheap."

"I did well in my last gig, and I was smart when it came to saving. One of the few areas where I practiced some discipline."

"Any more specifics you'd like to share? I can't pretend not to be intrigued."

"Do you often find yourself intrigued?"

"Depends on the situation, and nice dodge. If you don't want to tell me, that's fine."

Rusty swirled some scotch around his mouth, loving the burn as always.

"I was in the entertainment racket for a while. It was great, and then it wasn't. Things got away from me in a hurry in ways I still don't fully understand. It's not really my favorite story."

"Fair enough, but you haven't done much to dampen my curiosity. I can be pretty tenacious when there's something I want."

"That must serve you well in New York," Rusty said. "What do you do to pay the rent up there?"

Smiling at his absence of tact in changing the subject, Janice described her job as a senior account rep at Rawling + White. Rusty knew the name in a general sense. He was at least sufficiently aware to recognize it as one of the more high-profile advertising agencies in Manhattan, which meant in the nation at large.

She didn't seem interested in discussing her work at length, mentioning only that her top clients were in the pharmaceutical and medical services industries. This piqued something in Rusty's mind, but before he got a chance to follow up on it Janice raised a dismissive hand.

"Trust me, my job's not all that exciting. And I don't think you're really interested in hearing about it."

"Got a business card handy?"

"Why? You think I made it all up because I'm ashamed of my real job selling pens in Times Square?"

"Maybe," Rusty said, deadpan. "Or maybe I'd just like to stay in touch after you leave town."

Amusement lighting her eyes, she laid a monogrammed silver card case on the table. Rusty reached over to refill her glass and handed it to her as she extracted a business card printed on thick, glossy stock. She slid it across the table toward him, taking a small sip of her drink.

Rusty picked up her card. Without even a cursory glance at the text, he ripped it in half. Then halved it two more times, dropping the eight torn pieces onto the table.

"Very mature," Janice muttered, shaking her head.

"Sorry. Sometimes I do stupid shit, can't seem to stop myself."

After an awkward silence passed, just long enough to milk the moment, Rusty reached across the table and very delicately took hold of her left hand. She wrinkled her brow but gave no indication of wanting to free herself.

He picked up the torn card fragments, placed them in her upturned palm and pressed her fingers closed. Then he sat back in the chair.

Janice opened her palm. The business card was back in one piece.

"I bet that impresses at least some of the girls," she said, making a marginal effort to hide her enjoyment.

Rusty just shrugged and raised his glass.

"I should have guessed magician. How else to explain the, um, *theatrical* appearance."

"I'm retired, like I said. But sometimes it's fun to dip a toe back in."

"Pretty good trick," Janice nodded, turning the card over in her fingers. "How'd you do it?"

"I'd love to tell you, if you were an inducted member of the international illusionist's society. But then you wouldn't have to ask."

"Hmm. The BS is piling up pretty quick around here."

When he made no reply, she continued, "I want to know how you did it, Rusty."

"We all want something, Janice."

"I'm more than willing to make a fair trade."

"That's nice, but I'm not sure you have anything to offer that's of equal value."

"Bastard," she said with a laugh. "I'll get the information out of you. One way or another."

"Yeah. You just might at that."

She proffered the card between two polished fingertips, smiling in a different way now.

"So do you really want my card, or was it just an easy prop?"

"I want it."

"Prove it, magician."

He reached out and she pulled away slightly, like teasing a cat with a ball of string. Rusty advanced more slowly, plucking the card from her grip just as she leaned in to meet him with a kiss. It lasted longer than either of them anticipated, pointing toward a decided change in the evening.

Rusty's cell phone started vibrating. He grumbled but made no move to answer it.

"Perfect timing," Janice grinned, breaking the lip-lock.

Rusty glanced at his phone. The area code and prefix told him it had to be Carmen calling from Prince Anne.

"I should take this."

Janice nodded, taking the opportunity to check her own phone.

"Hey, Carmen," Rusty said. "Didn't expect to hear from you so soon."

"I've been working on your sample all day. If I fall behind on midterms I'm holding you personally responsible."

"Fair enough. Did you find anything noteworthy?"

"Big time. I was able to identify that second element. It kinda caught me off guard, but I knew my hunch was right."

"I'm all ears," Rusty said, glancing at Janice. She'd set down her phone, and he had a sense she was keeping tabs on his conversation.

"So this element, it's a chemical bonding agent with a funny name. Sephinordome-H."

"Is it dangerous?"

"It's definitely not intended for human consumption. In large enough amounts it would be toxic."

"Why would someone bother to use it in the sample we're talking about?"

"Like I just told you," Carmen said with mock impatience,

"it's a bonding agent. You need those in this kind of mix; otherwise, there's no way to stabilize the end product."

Rusty waited for her to continue.

"Here's what's so weird. This stuff is not generic, or easy to come by. It's a proprietary solvent made exclusively by Tilly Pharmaceuticals. You're familiar with them?"

"No. Should I be?"

"They're the biggest employer in the region, hands down. The plant's just a few miles from here in Salisbury. The patent for this agent belongs to Tilly, and it's hard to imagine how it could end up in some street drug."

"Does that tell you anything about the sample?"

Janice was now looking at him openly, not disguising her interest.

"Just that it had to have been produced locally," Carmen said. "There's no other way Sephinordome-H could have gotten into the mix."

"How sure are you about that?"

"Positive," she answered firmly. "I'd bet on it, but gambling isn't one of my vices."

Rusty stood and tossed the melting cubes from his glass into the bay. He leaned against the deck's rail, continuing in a slightly lowered voice.

"OK, I'm convinced. But how'd you figure out where this, whatever, *solvent* was made? Seems like a pretty rarified bit of information. Trade protected, I'd imagine."

"No mystery," Carmen said casually. "If you're a toxicology major at UM and you want to stay in Salisbury after school, there's one option. I plan on working in Tilly's R and D unit as soon as I get my degree."

"That's sensible enough."

"Damn straight. Starting salary in the high five figures and three weeks' paid vacation. I've made a point of studying Tilly's product line in preparation for the gig."

"Smart girl."

"And then some." There was a pause before Carmen continued in a warmer tone. "So, I'm just kicking it at my place now. Bored. What are you up t …"

"Actually, I've got to run," he said, cutting her off. "Got some company I've been neglecting."

"Oh," Carmen said, her disappointment clear as a bell. "Well, whatever."

He thanked her again for putting in the effort and ended the call rather abruptly. Felt like a dick for being so rude, but the timing was less than ideal.

Rusty idly reached for the bottle with no intention of pouring another. He could feel Janice's gaze on him. Grateful as he was that Carmen tracked down the information so quickly, he really wished she'd waited till tomorrow to share it.

"That sounded like an interesting call," Janice finally said.

"Yeah, I'd say it was."

"None of my business, but when I hear words like sample and evidence it makes me a little curious. Is that out of line?"

"No," Rusty sighed. "You're entitled to hear this."

Taking it one step at a time, Rusty told her about the baggie he'd lifted from Thelma's bathroom. He described having its contents analyzed at the UM campus and what he'd learned there. Then he summarized what Carmen just told him over the phone.

Janice listened with quiet focus, not interrupting. The last bit really grabbed her attention. She set aside her unfinished glass of scotch and shot out some very precise questions about the toxicological analysis.

"So this student …"

"Carmen."

"She was sure the drugs are being made locally?"

"Seemed pretty sure," Rusty said, leaving it at that and wishing there was some way to unring this bell.

"*How*, Rusty?"

"Well, this bonding agent had to come from someone working at Tilly Pharmaceuticals. It's a proprietary compound, not something a run-of-the-mill drug cooker would be likely to use. I guess it's possible someone working there is making salts on the side for some extra income."

"Someone working at Tilly?"

"Whoever it is, they got their hands on the chemical somehow."

A long silence passed, Janice staring off at the lights across the bay. She'd assumed an oddly rigid posture, almost clenching the arms of her deck chair.

"Something bothering you?" he finally asked. "Aside from this whole sad situation?"

"I'm just tired of thinking about it all."

"Can't blame you there. Let's talk about something else."

"No," Janice said, her voice soft but firm. "Let's not talk at all."

He let her lead the way into the house and up the stairs. There were three bedrooms on the second floor, and any one of them would have suited him just fine, but Rusty wanted her to choose. Having spent a good amount of youthful nights in this house, Janice might feel a specific resonance for any or all of the rooms. The king-sized bed in the master room he occupied was damn comfortable and more than big enough to suit their needs, but the idea of Janice selecting one of the smaller rooms where she'd once slept as her younger self was vaguely arousing.

She chose the master, its huge bay window letting in ample moonlight for Rusty to see her remove her top in a single fluid motion. Less than a minute later they were both naked, feeling the 1200-count Egyptian cotton sheets envelope their bodies.

Reaching a wordless agreement to take it slow and grind out every last ounce of pleasure, they let the night fade into morning with no awareness of time's passage. Only when the first hints of eastern light touched the tops of the pines outside did they slip into a conjoined sleep.

23.

He awoke to the sound of the shower running. The bedside clock read a little before nine. Rusty thought about crawling out of bed and joining Janice in the hot water, but something was bothering him. Something small at the back of his mind, he'd been vaguely aware of it last night but was distracted by better things.

Rusty rolled over and reached down to the floor where their clothes lay in a heap. From a pocket of his jeans he extracted her business card, the one he'd used for the trick last night.

Janice Garrett, Senior Account Representative, Rawling + White, New York. A Madison Avenue address in the Fifties, and contact information.

He heard the water shut off and returned the card to his jeans. Then just lay there a few minutes, staring at the ceiling while Janice dried her hair. His attention was split between a stubborn hard-on and the unnamable intuition that had been bothering him.

Janice walked into the room, leaning against the doorframe with a grin on her face and a towel around her waist. She dropped the towel, still wet underneath, and Rusty's attention was quickly undivided. He pulled the sheet aside to show her his motives, but she shook her head coquettishly.

"Sorry, gotta run."

"What could possibly be so important for you to do right now in Ocean City?"

"I've been neglecting work for the past three days. About a dozen phone calls I need to return and God knows how many emails. Radio silence tends to make my clients nervous."

"They can wait another hour, can't they?"

"I just got cleaned up, mister."

"All right, be like that," Rusty said, rising from the bed and pulling on some clothes. "You at least got time for some java? If you've never had Cafe du Monde's chicory coffee, you really don't know what you're missing."

"Sweet offer," she said, leaning in for a quick kiss. "How about a rain check?"

"Sure. You gonna be around awhile longer?"

"I have to be back in New York by Monday. Should really go back today, but since the weekend's almost here I might just stick around."

"Solid plan. Give me a call later."

He walked her downstairs. At the front door she surprised him by wrapping her arms around his neck. She pulled him in tight and whispered in his ear.

"Is it too early to ask for a promise?"

"Guess that kind of depends on what it is."

She didn't respond for a moment. He could feel her heart beating fast beneath the sheer dress shirt she wore.

"This is serious."

He pulled back to look her in the eyes. They focused on his with unblinking intensity.

"Name it."

"Find out who's making these drugs. It's got to be someone in the area. That's what the toxicologist said, right?"

"Well, yeah. I'm not really sure how I'd go about that. Already handed over her report to the police."

"Are they going to do anything about it?"

Rusty shrugged.

"I don't know. It didn't make quite the impression I'd hoped for." He paused. "I can keep bugging this lieutenant I know, but only so much. He's just about had enough of me."

"Then keep digging on your own. You've learned more than the police have so far."

"I've also been warned in no uncertain terms to stay out of

it. Gotta admit that sounds like pretty good advice."

Janice broke contact with him, a flinty detachment stealing across her face. He hadn't seen that look since she'd first accosted him at the medical examiner's office.

"If you're not interested in helping, I can't make you. I thought maybe you'd want to, but if not ..."

"Hey, hey. Calm down."

Her eyes softened a bit, but the intensity was still there.

"I won't be able to let this go, Rusty. You don't know me. I'm like that. This is going to eat away at me like cancer."

"The man who killed your aunt's sitting in a cell right now."

"Obviously I'm glad they arrested Dixon. But he was just the weapon, the knife in a killer's hand. Whoever's putting this stuff out on the street is ultimately responsible."

Rusty sighed, wishing he could mount some argument that carried any conviction.

"I tend to see it that way myself."

"So you'll keep digging?" she asked, arms encircling his neck.

"Yeah," he said.

"Promise."

The way she said it sounded like a command, not a request. He nodded. "It's a promise."

She pulled him in for a last kiss. It was as moist and heated as anything they'd done in bed last night, and Rusty started to think maybe she wouldn't be leaving so soon after all.

But then she broke the kiss quickly and stepped outside.

Rusty watched her get into the Buick, and they traded a wave before she pulled out of the driveway.

Taking his first mug of coffee into the den, he tried to feel a greater sense of contentment. Last night was good. It had been so long since he'd been with a woman, longer than he wanted to calculate. Janice was the first woman he'd taken to bed since relocating to Ocean Pines at the start of the year.

Back in Vegas, during those final months when he was selling out twelve shows a week, never more than two nights passed consecutively without him burning the sheets with someone or someone else. He didn't keep a close tally on names or faces, nor did he distinguish showgirls from starstruck fans who'd line up outside his dressing room hoping for an autograph on their whatever. Granted, showgirls were his favorites, as they tended to keep the same weird performing hours. And their costumes, along with his own wildly varied wardrobe both on and offstage, made for some pretty zesty role-play in the sack.

Those days were long gone. It's hard to meet prospective bedmates when you spend weeks on end sitting in a big empty house, doing your best not to think about all the wrong turns and bad decisions littering the past.

Well, Janice might signal the beginning of a new chapter. New York was an easy commute, either by car or train. Maybe they'd get a semi-regular thing going. If she was too busy to come down this way, the idea of spending weekends in the big city had a lot of appeal for Rusty. This monastic routine had definitely grown old, and he was starting to do the same.

New York.

The idea itself stirred a sense of excitement, of possibility. Shit, maybe he'd even start performing again. Nothing major, just some small clubs downtown. Using a different name, of course. He wasn't prepared to fully reemerge into the public spotlight. Not now, probably not ever.

Thinking of New York troubled Rusty as much as it excited him. The same niggling suspicion that had been eating at the back of his mind resumed with thoughts of the Empire City.

Something wasn't sitting right. Something he'd seen or heard over the course of the past day, it kept butting up against the back of his mind like a needy child that won't be ignored.

Rusty thought he knew what it was, but he hoped his intuition was misplaced.

Flipping open the MacBook, he Googled the name of Janice's company. Rawling + White. The corporate website was as slick and comprehensive as he would have expected from a high-powered ad firm. He skipped past the opening flash animation and got to the home page. The menu directed him to separate pages devoted to expected items like mission statement, executive profiles, sample clients & campaigns, and a raft of media reports. Rusty spent a good half hour clicking through the R + W site until he figured there was no more to be learned from it.

Returning from the kitchen with his third mug of coffee, Rusty started a fresh Google search for the most recent web pages related to Janice's firm. Something he'd seen on the corporate site—minor, but hard to dismiss—triggered a connection in his mind, and he was hoping there would be no more timely information to verify it.

I could be reading this all wrong, he thought in a bid at consoling himself. *Wouldn't be the first time, God knows.*

He brooded for a few minutes. Then a pop-up window announced a news item hot off the wires. The story matched the same Google search terms he'd entered earlier. It was a breaking story from the online version of the *Ocean Gazette*.

Rusty only had to scan the headline to see all he wanted to see:

ACCUSED KILLER GRANTED BAIL; DIXON OUT ON $400K BOND, PROSECUTOR EXPRESSES OUTRAGE AT RELEASE.

He closed the MacBook softly. Somehow this development didn't even surprise him. It seemed to be a logical extension of everything that had happened so far.

The system, such as it existed in Ocean City, wasn't going to address the problem it faced. The cops and the courts, no matter how well staffed and intentioned, seemed unable to act in a proactive manner. Capturing Kenny Dixon in the first place had been a matter of luck more than competent investigative work. How often could you count on getting a tip-off from the suspect's brother-in-law?

Even with that boon, the system had failed to keep Kenny Dixon behind bars. Rusty almost took it for granted that he would run again, and maybe the cops wouldn't be so lucky next time.

He's just the weapon in the hand of a killer.

Janice was right about that. The real villain, the one who needed punishing, was the one manufacturing the tainted drugs.

Jim Biddison clearly wasn't making the pursuit of this dealer a sufficiently high priority. If something was going to be done, Rusty felt a kind of gravitational pull to do it himself.

But why?

Absently plucking an apple from a wicker basket on the kitchen table, he interrogated himself with that question. Why not just let it all go? Was it really because he mourned Thelma Garrett so much, or because of some ill-considered promise to her niece that justice would be done in the dead woman's name?

Bullshit. If I do anything at all, it's because I haven't felt this alive in too fucking long.

This inner admission yielded an involuntary nod. It was liberating, in a way. Why con himself, here in this empty house? He had no audience to persuade or manipulate. No one waiting to applaud his feats of miraculous deception. Even after being off the stage all this time, Rusty sometimes had trouble remembering that.

He almost took a bite of the apple in his hand, then set it down on the table's edge and reached into a coat pocket. He'd unconsciously stuffed a fresh deck of playing cards there yesterday afternoon and just remembered it now.

This was becoming something of a habit: grabbing various artifacts of his former craft and keeping them on his person without being aware of it. A sign of early-onset senility, perhaps? Rusty still recalled the look on Biddison's face when he pulled those cuffs and pellets out of the evidence bag at the station. He couldn't help feeling a little embarrassed.

Peeling the cellophane wrapper off the deck, Rusty extracted a card at random. The nine of diamonds. His favorite suit, for obvious reasons, but the card in particular had no special meaning for him.

Slipping the card between the index and middle finger of his right hand, he stepped out of the kitchen into the breakfast nook. The apple sat on the table about fifteen feet away.

Haven't tried this one in a while. Should I, or will it piss me off too much if I can't do it?

That was the same inner nag he'd made such a point of ignoring over the years. Doing the same now, he raised his hand, holding it perpendicular to the ground, then flicked his wrist with jackrabbit speed.

His eyes barely tracked the card's progress as it sailed across the room, spinning like a miniature buzz saw. It hit the apple dead center, one corner easily piercing the skin and progressing until it almost reached the core.

Rusty stood there for a moment, looking at the half card protruding from the slit piece of fruit. Feeling both relief and a certain wistfulness for the days when he used to be able to slice an apple or potato clean through.

He was also wondering what it would feel like to hurl a card at just the right angle to blind Kenny Dixon in one eye.

24.

Tampa Nate sat at the corner stool of the Inlet Bar thinking dark thoughts about the Maryland Department of Health and Mental Hygiene. Said department was responsible for issuing a 2007 decree that banned smoking in any public venue selling food.

The Inlet Bar technically had a kitchen, but Tampa Nate didn't know of anyone desperately hungry enough to ever order anything from it. Even the peanuts lined up in little plastic trays along the faux wood bar looked inedible. If ever a drinking establishment had been built to accommodate the needs of patrons who enjoy tobacco products in consort with their beverage of choice, this was it. And yet Tampa Nate was legally prohibited from lighting a Kent 100 from the pack that lay on the bar in front of him, seeming to jeer at his dilemma.

He could step outside, but he'd have to leave his Captain & Coke in here. Which utterly defeated the point of enjoying both simultaneously. Plus, it was too damn cold out there.

Tampa Nate never wore a hat of any kind to keep his head warm, regardless of weather. To do so would be to obscure the dreadlocks he'd spent upwards of six years growing to their current state of ragged glory. There weren't too many dudes in coastal Maryland sporting dreads, and of that small number even fewer were white.

Tampa Nate knew once they blew this pissant town and started hitting the bigger resort spots along the Atlantic Coast, his look would become less unique. He'd most likely encounter any number of white boys with similar hairstyles down in South Florida, and upon seeing him they would all realize with a stab of inner despair what a real head full of dreads was supposed to look like. But that was their problem, not his.

The Inlet Bar was slow this late Saturday afternoon, slower than Tampa Nate had seen it at any point in the last six weeks. None of the few haggard patrons sharing the bar with him were born after disco, and none looked to be likely customers for what Nate had to offer. They barely had enough scratch to afford dollar drafts nursed at the rate of two per hour.

This whole town got sleepier every day, with the last traces of youth and disposable income vanishing back to wherever the hell they went in the colder months.

The temperature had dropped into the thirties with almost an hour of sunlight left, announcing November's imminent arrival in less than ten days. By that point, Tampa Nate would feel quite happy to be out of here. Hell, he'd rather be gone already. He couldn't wait to put this godforsaken burg in his rearview and leave it there for good. They'd overstayed their welcome already, something Nate knew with certainty but was unable to talk Fade into accepting.

He'd made his case no less than three times, or tried to, but didn't get so much as a nod. Why not? They had milked a healthy profit from Ocean City. The boardwalk and the dozen or so dives within walking distance had proved a more than fertile marketplace. Tampa Nate didn't have access to a full accounting, but he figured their profit margin had to be in the low six figures.

The sensible move now was to close up shop and vanish. There was too much pressure around here, thanks to a few pathetic losers who couldn't handle the product.

With all the shit that had happened lately, Tampa Nate didn't see any point in lingering. His idea was to start moving down south a little bit sooner than planned. Back to his home turf. Florida was still plenty warm in November, and the coastline was dotted with so many resorts they wouldn't have to stay in any one place more than a few days at a time. A hit-and-run approach seemed prudent from now on, considering the kind of wake they were leaving behind.

But Fade wouldn't budge. He refused to pull out of Ocean

City until the end of October. Overriding any argument, he insisted tonight's Halloween festival should produce a spike in sales big enough to merit any attendant risk.

As for the heat coming down from the killings, Fade didn't seem to sweat that. With the drugs stored well away from their bungalow on Ninth Street, where was the danger? The cops could kick in the door at any time and all they'd find would be a collection of equipment that might belong to anyone with a graduate degree in toxicology from the University of Maryland.

Fade had one of those, or so he claimed. Nothing illegal in owning test tubes and Bunsen burners, as he liked to remind Tampa Nate in that know-it-all voice of his. Fade kept the setup in such pristine condition between cooks that not even the smallest trace elements remained, a precautionary measure Tampa Nate wholeheartedly endorsed.

If only more such measures were being enacted.

For such an obviously smart dude, Fade showed a streak of recklessness that sometimes bordered on stupidity. Nate didn't like it. He got nervous working with someone who enjoyed flirting with disaster. But it wasn't the only thing he didn't like about how the operation had been going.

Tampa Nate was not a man of great self-reflection. He devoted considerably greater effort to building his physique (6 foot 5, 195 pounds with 7% body fat) than to inward analysis. Still, he could hardly stop from thinking about all the bad mojo of late.

Three people dead. In ways that weren't pretty. One of them an old lady, too. That's what disturbed his mental equilibrium more than anything else. Fucking Dixon. Tampa Nate didn't like to think of that asshole at all, because it invariably made him think of the old woman. She was the one loose end he couldn't tuck away in his mind.

He didn't give a rat's ass about the little tweaker Ronnie. That kid was born to die young. And as for the dude he shivved, Tampa Nate had never met the man so he wasn't going to waste any time feeling sorry for him.

The system he and Fade had worked out was based on one

simple rule: no product in the bungalow, ever. Which meant no sales conducted from the bungalow. That's why they had the stash house and a crew of runners to rotate from the stash house to various points of sale on the outside.

The crew was a pretty sorry lot from the start, always the weak link in the chain, but their job didn't require massive brainpower. From a peak of six they were now down to one runner. Whose skinny ass should be here by now, Nate thought irritably as he ordered another drink.

No product in the bungalow. Those words were like a mantra that allowed him to sleep at night. It was the first thing Fade and Nate agreed upon when they rented the place at the end of August, the cornerstone of their whole operation.

They'd both stuck to that rule, until last week. Tampa Nate still burned with chagrin for the poor judgment he'd exercised when the late Ronnie Wilson stopped by.

It was only a fluke that he had a few spare grams on hand that night—just some leftovers that hadn't been moved. He knew selling it to Ronnie was a mistake, and he should have just booted the weak little punk off the front stoop. Fade had been plenty pissed off when he found out, but in the end it didn't matter. Ronnie was dead less than forty-eight hours later, conveniently slitting his throat before he could come back to the bungalow again or, worse, give the address to anyone else.

Tampa Nate took a pull off his fresh drink and glanced up at the ancient fifteen-inch TV set bolted above the bar. It was halftime of the Delaware/Villanova game, a long-standing rivalry, and the Blue Hens were cleaning up. The game wasn't even interesting enough to watch in a morgue like this with absolutely nothing else competing for his attention.

A good system was only worth its design if you stuck to it. Tampa Nate wouldn't have devised such a good system if left to his own devices. That's why he continued to work with Fade, despite what he thought of him. The dude was smart; there was no argument about that. Not just smart enough to cook up the salts, but to make all the other decisions that helped them secure a foothold in the local drug economy.

Like boosting each batch with an extra meth kicker. That was inspired. Who even thought of doing shit like that? Sure, it made for slightly higher production expenses up front, but that was more than recouped by repeat business once people got a taste.

The kicker wasn't even necessary at first. For a good month they were moving plenty of product without the extra bump. But it was a crowded market out there; they weren't the only ones in the game. So Fade had the brainstorm of reformulating a sample batch with some meth in mid-September. The response from the street to a few free testers was sky-high, and demand kicked up overnight. Fade decided all future batches would come with the kicker, and had made it so.

Fade was pretty sharp when it came to branding, too. All dealers identify their product with some kind of name. Fade had a different idea. No name, just that little green image stamped on each bag. The snake eating itself with the crazy name Tampa Nate could never pronounce correctly (much to Fade's amusement, until Nate stopped trying altogether.)

The message it sent was subtle, Fade had explained, but people would pick up on it subconsciously. Like, this shit's so heavy you can't even *give* it a name. Like, words don't even come close to describing it.

Nate thought that was genius. He told Fade it reminded him of when Prince changed his name to that weird symbol, then immediately felt embarrassed by the withering look of contempt he got in response.

He was starting to suspect Fade had no sensible reason for staying in Ocean City at all. Except maybe some perverse satisfaction he got out of peddling the salts to the citizens of this place in particular, like he had some grudge to settle with the whole town. That kind of irrational motivation, which had absolutely nothing to do with good business sense, made Tampa Nate very nervous.

* * *

The Inlet's front door swung open, a blast of frigid air turning every head at the bar. Wallace ducked inside, bundled up in three layers of flannel. Tampa Nate looked irritably at his watch, which read 4:17.

Wallace took a stool next to him.

"Still can't tell time, motherfucker," Nate muttered.

Wallace didn't seem to notice, signaling for the barmaid to get off her stool and bring him a beer.

"Tell me you're here because you need to reload, Wallace."

"Hell no. I'm here to get some feeling back in my goddamn toes. Colder than an Eskimo's toilet out there."

Tampa Nate wanted to be angrier than he was, but it was hard to muster that reaction. Wallace was the only runner still on the payroll ever since that scumbag Kenny Dixon got cut loose earlier this month. Back in September, when it was still warm and the market was jumping, they had a legit crew working shifts, slinging hard in twice as many local bars and a handful of well-chosen spots along the boardwalk.

It had been a good run, for a while.

"I said it's fucking cold out there," Wallace repeated, reclaiming Nate's attention.

"So keep moving, make the rounds. Circulation's good for keeping up your body temperature."

"Ain't nobody out there," Wallace said, pulling deeply on his bottle of Bud. "Gonna be dark soon, and no one's dumb enough to hit the boards tonight. I don't care how bad they're jonesing."

Tampa Nate almost reprimanded him but knew he couldn't put up too much of a stern argument. Wallace was right: pedestrian sales were dead. Forget about the fucking Halloween festival—that hardly seemed likely to attract their clientele, regardless of what Fade might think. This was a seasonal town, and the season was over.

"Keep at it for a few more hours before you take a break. It'll pick up."

"I'm telling you, man. It's a morgue." Wallace seemed to consider his next statement with care. "Fact is, that's why I stopped by. You can have what I got left. No way I can move it now, and I'm sick of trying."

Any wisp of sympathy Nate may have felt for the runner's plight dissipated instantly. He turned his head a few degrees in Wallace's direction, not looking him in the eye.

"Fuck did you just say?"

Wallace again measured his words. Tampa Nate carried more muscle mass in one arm than he did on his whole frame.

"Just take it back. Only a half-dozen grams or so."

"Meaning you haven't moved any product all day."

"There's no fuckin' way to move it. That's what I've been ..."

"Shut up," Tampa Nate said.

Wallace complied, thinking he had pushed his luck a bit far. He'd be better off just dumping his supply and making the payoff to Fade out of his own pocket. At least that way he'd be done with it. Only problem was he couldn't cover the $120.

But Nate had tuned him out completely. He was staring up at the TV above the bar. A local newscast was on, filling the game's halftime interim. A square-shouldered cop with sandy-colored hair was speaking to some reporter chick.

Tampa Nate reached across the bar and grabbed the remote. He ignored a look of irritation from the barmaid and upped the volume.

"Everyone needs to know how dangerous this stuff is," the cop was saying as a graphic at the bottom of the screen read: Lt. James Biddison, OCPD. "A single dose can be lethal, not only to the user but to anyone who might encounter a person under the influence. These drugs have an unusually high capacity for inducing violent behavior."

The picture cut from the cop's face to a larger graphic that made Tampa Nate grip his cocktail almost hard enough to crack the glass. Filling the screen was a blowup of the serpentine shape he had seen thousands of times. The same green symbol on the corner of every gram they'd sold over the past two months.

"Jesus," Wallace uttered. "That can't be good."

"Shut the fuck up," Tampa Nate hissed, eyes glued to the TV. The female reporter's voice was audible over the graphic:

"The narcotics in question come in bags marked with this

stamp in the lower right corner and are referred to in street slang as the green serpent. Believed to be a particularly potent variant of the designer drugs known as bath salts, OCPD reports they are being sold in various locations around town, with the boardwalk cited in particular."

The TV cut back to a shot of the newsroom. The reporter wrapped up the story with a spiel encouraging citizens to contact the police department with an advance promise of anonymity for any useful information regarding the salts. Tampa Nate turned off the TV, generating a few angry slurs from down the bar he didn't even hear. He was too busy trying to think, fingers still clenching the cocktail glass.

Wallace felt like saying something, but he held his tongue. The news report seemed to validate his very purpose for coming here today. Namely, to tell Tampa Nate he was done with dealing. Part of him wanted to emphasize that point right now. Just hand over what he had in his pocket and walk out the door. But a more self-protective instinct told him this was a very poor time to make that move.

"Guess I'll get back to it," he said, finishing his beer.

"Stay where you are."

Tampa Nate was starting to form an idea of how to proceed, and he didn't want Wallace rabbiting on him now. Not until he could determine some kind of intelligent response to what he'd just seen on the goddamn TV.

He pulled out his cell phone and dialed Fade's number.

25.

At the exact moment Tampa Nate made that call, Rusty was intently pacing the unswept floor of his basement. Arms folded tightly over his chest. Head bent at a forward angle to produce clear thinking. A sense of mission propelled him, one he'd given up questioning.

He was getting inside that bungalow on Ninth Street. Tonight. Either by invitation or force, he would see the face of whoever went by the name Fade.

And then what are you gonna do?

A solid answer to that question still eluded him, but he knew one thing for sure: he'd be taking some weapons on tonight's foray. Choosing the right arsenal struck him as a paramount task.

He stopped pacing and planted both hands on the wooden worktable. Across its unvarnished surface lay a motley assortment of items—all designed for the purpose of entertainment, but they could be employed just as well for attack or self-defense.

Knives. Blindfolds. Smoke pellets. Flash paper, cotton and rope. A handheld brass propulsion gun loaded with four-inch darts, their tips containing a combustible mix of polymeric dust and multicolored nonflammable lubricants.

Not likely I'll be needing you, he thought with mild regret, moving the gun to the side of the table where a dozen other discarded selections lay.

The collection of throwing knives kept drawing his eye, gleaming in unison under the basement's sole dangling lightbulb. He picked up one with a razor-sharp 7" blade folded into an ivory handle and snapped it open. Then he set it back down.

Tonight's about gathering information, he reminded himself impatiently. *Not punishment, at least not yet. Don't overdo it.*

Guided by that logic, he leaned in the direction of limiting himself to defensive items. Anything apt to prove effective in helping him out of a tight spot, just in case he found leaving the bungalow more difficult than getting inside.

Smoke pellets were a no-brainer, given that he carried those around most of the time anyway by force of habit. He grabbed a trio from the table.

Figuring the sterling silver handcuffs were a good choice if restricting someone else's movement became a priority, he pocketed those as well.

Then his hand returned to the folding knife. This time it felt better to the touch, almost reassuring. He picked it up and slid it into the breast pocket of his long black coat.

Feeling sufficiently armed, Rusty emerged from the basement and grabbed his car keys. The sun was sinking behind the pines as he walked out of the house. Gunning the Lexus, he turned from Echo Run onto Ocean Parkway.

Just after making that first turn, he spotted it.

In his rearview. The same silver Dodge that had been an intermittently malignant shadow since all this shit started.

Good, he thought with a nod. *Perfect way to elevate the adrenaline.*

Instead of heading east toward Route 90 as planned, he made a quick right onto a quiet residential street he'd never been down before. So narrow and untrafficked it didn't even have a sign. A few houses lay far back from the road, their facades protected by trees and hedges.

Keeping his speed low, he continued for half a block. Then he cut the wheel hard left and stomped on the brakes. He slammed it into reverse and swerved back so that his car was effectively blocking the road in both directions.

The Dodge had halted two car lengths behind, neither attempting to pass nor moving away in reverse. Rusty kicked open the door and hit the street, running toward the tail car at full speed. His right hand reached for the knife in his pocket and flipped it open with a sharp snap of the wrist.

The Dodge's driver frantically tried to execute a three-point turn and retreat in the opposite direction. Rusty ran right up to the window, peering inside with wild curiosity to see his unknown pursuer.

He stopped as if struck by a falling cinder block.

Jesus Christ. I knew it!

Marceline Lavalle huddled on the other side of the window, looking angry and scared in roughly equal measure. Her black hair was untied so that it fell in long, graceful curls. Her dark coffee complexion shone even smoother than Rusty remembered from the countless times he'd gazed at it in dopey love-struck awe.

He pocketed the knife quickly. Then spoke her name twice, the three lyrical syllables ringing strangely in his ears.

Still in a state of agitation, she tried to back up. He quickly sidestepped to block the car.

"Marceline!" he repeated more forcefully. "Come on, slow down. Talk to me."

Seeing no exit, she put the car in park but made no move to get out.

"Forget you saw me, Rusty," she said through the glass, only flashing a brief glance at him. "Just let me go."

No way he was going to let that happen. Not just yet.

Almost three years had passed since he stood this close to the woman who had once rarely been too far away to touch. She'd stayed by his side day and night throughout their migration from Louisiana to Nevada until, seeking things he didn't think she could offer, he started creating distance. The gulf widened with startling rapidity, and one day he woke alone in his suite at Caesars and realized she was gone for good.

"For Christ's sake, Marcie," he now pleaded, gesturing for her to roll down the window. "What's going on?"

She lowered the window an inch.

"I'm sorry," she uttered, her voice as much of a familiar shock as her face. "Just let me get out of here. You won't see me again."

Her hand still clutched the gearshift, a look of impending flight in her eyes. Rusty couldn't believe he was seeing those eyes trained on him again, regardless of the emotion they conveyed.

"Just try to calm down. I only charged the car because I had no idea who you were."

"It's not your fault. I never should've …"

"Look, it's all right. Let's just catch our breath for a second."

"No. This was a mistake."

"Marcie, you came all this way for a reason. Why don't you kill the engine so we can sit down somewhere and talk."

"Where?" she asked after an uncertain pause.

"My place."

She seemed to relax just slightly, thinking it over.

"We don't have to go inside if you don't want," Rusty said calmly. "Let's just get off the damn street, OK?"

Five minutes later, they were standing in postures of mutual discomfort in the pebble driveway in front of his house. Neither said anything at first, both sensing any attempt at real conversation might prove cancerous, radioactive.

Finally Rusty asked the simplest question he could conjure:

"What brought you here, Marcie?"

She shook her head as if she hadn't given the matter much thought.

"Wanted to see you. To talk, maybe. Maybe not. Just getting a good look might have been enough."

"To make sure I'm still alive?"

"I've known that for a while. When I first heard you'd gone missing, I thought maybe you were dead. That wasn't hard to imagine, given how things were going out there."

"Hell of a way to get back in touch."

"I wasn't sure I *wanted* to get in touch. I wanted to get close enough to really see you, then decide."

"So you tail me like a goddamn stalker?" he asked, a trace of anger in his voice.

"Maybe it wasn't the best way. But you obviously don't want to be found by anyone."

Rusty had to concede as much with a nod.

"How'd you pull it off?"

"It's pretty hard to stay hidden these days, Rusty. Ten minutes on Intelius was all. I had a pretty good idea where to look. You've been listed at this address for months."

"Then why not call or just knock on the door?"

He really hated the facial response she gave in answer to that question.

"Jesus. Are you afraid of me, Marcie?"

"No. Just afraid of what it would be like to see you again."

"I guess I can understand that." A protracted pause, then: "Where have you been staying?"

"Some crummy motel near the boardwalk. I'm flying home tomorrow out of D.C. Would've left sooner, but it costs too much to change the ticket."

Another silence passed.

"So what exactly did you hear about Vegas?"

"Not much," she answered with a shrug. "Just what the press reported. Rising star magician vanishes, whereabouts unknown. Big mystery, for like a week. I got in touch with some old contacts at Caesars, asked around."

"Yeah? Like who?"

"Steve the valet. Rocco, naturally. Lynette at Nobu."

"I bet they had all kinds of theories."

"Just two that I heard. One was you OD'd."

Rusty almost found himself replying, *I know a few people out there who'd be happy if I did*, but a sense of better judgment stopped him.

"I never let myself believe that," Marceline continued. "Rocco said it was more likely you were holed up in rehab somewhere. He seemed to think you didn't have much choice about leaving town, like maybe someone wanted you gone. I couldn't get anything more specific out of him, and I doubt you're going to volunteer much."

Instead of responding to that, Rusty asked, "What did Prosper have to say about it?"

Marceline noticed the way he braced himself for her reply, and it amused her.

"Very little. He doesn't ever speak your name, to be honest."

"Your dad could turn holding a grudge into an Olympic event." Seeing her change of expression, he added, "I'm sorry, Marcie. You both had every reason to leave."

"You left *us*, Rusty. Vegas turned you into someone we didn't recognize. After a while I couldn't even remember that quiet kid I met in the Quarter."

"So you bailed without saying goodbye. I can't lie, that was some bitter medicine."

"You never came begging to get me back, did you?"

"No."

"I knew you wouldn't."

Rusty let those words, and the ones unspoken, land with full impact.

"Prosper still running the shop on Bourbon?" he asked.

Marceline allowed another small smile, this one warmed by affection.

"Of course," she said, adopting a sultry Creole patois. "Blowin' dem tourists outta dey fool minds six days a week. Most of 'em already blown on hurricanes, but you know he could dazzle anyone drunk or stone-cold sober."

Rusty nodded with a grin that matched hers.

"Still the best damn magician I ever saw, hands down."

"He says the same thing about you."

"Hey, I thought he never mentions my name."

"Almost never."

Another awkward pause ensued, just as the conversation was starting to feel marginally relaxed and natural.

"How are things with you?" Rusty asked.

"Good. I'm living in the Marigny now. Small place, but I like it, and close to Dad. I'm working in the maternity ward at Bon Coeur."

"Sounds nice. You always had a way with small things."

"Well," she replied, a hand reflexively rising to touch her stomach. "I figure the practice will come in handy."

This stopped Rusty cold for a beat, but he recovered quickly.

"Congratulations," he said, confirming with a glance she

wore no ring.

"Just found out last month. I think it's part of why I came here. I wanted some kind of, I don't know …"

"Closure? As far as us?"

She didn't nod or say anything, but Rusty sensed a kind of acknowledgment.

"I'm happy for you, Marcie. Really. I can see the glow on your face already."

He reached out and gave her hand a squeeze. She must have felt his sincerity, because she returned it.

"It's not just closure. There's something else I wanted to do."

Rusty didn't say anything, just waited.

"I can't do it right now," she continued, glancing briefly at her rental car. "Maybe it's not a good idea anyway."

"You're not giving me much to go on here. Whatever it is, must be pretty important."

Marceline seemed to shrug away a thought, her focus turning inquisitive.

"What happened out in Vegas, Rusty?"

He started to answer, could feel a rush words ready to tumble out. He knew once he started telling the tale he'd kept to himself like some kind of deformity unfit for the gaze of others, he wouldn't be able to stop. Not until he'd revealed every last detail of the unhinged free fall that had ultimately deposited him back here in Ocean Pines.

But the words didn't come. Rusty stood silently, feeling the knife pressing through the coat pocket against his chest.

"Look, there's something I need to do right now. Why don't we talk in the morning."

"That's all right. If you don't want to tell me …"

"No, I do," he said, meaning it. "This just isn't the right moment. You can stay here tonight, make yourself comfortable."

The look on her face prompted him to add, "You'd have your own room. No strings."

"I already paid for the motel. Might as well use it."

"OK, fair enough. How about coming back tomorrow, say around nine. We can talk as long as you'd like."

His proposal wasn't making much of an impression on Marceline, who seemed eager to get back in the Dodge.

"Come on, I've got chicory coffee direct from Cafe du Monde. You'll feel right at home."

"No beignets?" she asked teasingly.

"No, but I know a place that makes pretty good croissants."

She pretended to look offended by the suggestion, then nodded.

"I'll come, but only for a little while. I have to be at the airport by one o'clock."

"No sweat. And if you catch a later flight I'll pay for it."

Feeling unexpectedly relieved, he held the door for her as she got in the Dodge that had caused such anxiety before he knew whom it carried. Now he felt like he could kiss the damn car.

"Tomorrow morning," he said.

She nodded and put it in gear and pulled away, giving him a little wave. He watched until her taillights dissolved into a tiny crimson blur, still feeling like he was in a kind of waking dream.

Dusk was falling fast, with no one but him to witness it. The curtains of trees stood so thick along Echo Run that rays of sunlight broke through tiny spaces to create a star field of glowing amber dots on the darkening ground.

A sound broke the stillness, making him jump.

It was the deep, resonant cry of a bird echoing down from above. Rusty felt a chill run over him. The cry repeated, an ominous two-note rumble, and he smiled. He knew the sound well, having heard it innumerable times as a child, though he couldn't recall it finding him since he'd moved back to Ocean Pines.

He craned his neck back, eyes lifting and ears alert for the source of the cry. It came again, from the upper branches of an ash tree not ten feet away. His vision focused on a barren limb shorn of leaves.

Perched on the end, calling out to the twilight only the two of them shared, was a raven.

26.

The bungalow crouched before him across 9th Street. From his vantage point on the sidewalk, Rusty couldn't tell if it was occupied or not. Both front windows were concealed by blinds, a weak reddish glow emanating through the cracks. No sounds came from within, at least none audible from his spot some twenty feet away. The cargo van was the only vehicle in the driveway, no other cars parked at the curb.

The street lay emptier than the night he followed Ronnie here. Rusty chalked that up to the difference in temperature. Tonight didn't feel like it belonged to autumn in even the most distant sense. An encroachment of winter was palpable.

Rusty had elected at the last moment to leave the Lexus at home. His encounter with Marceline had him oddly spooked. The possibility that someone could track his car from the night he'd followed Kenny Dixon to the boardwalk still lingered. Dixon was out on parole and could be on the hunt himself.

Unlikely, perhaps, but not impossible.

Besides, the cab ride was only a little more than twenty bucks. Rusty had the driver let him out three streets north of here and took the guy's business card. He gave a fat tip for the fare and promised an even fatter one if he could count on a quick pickup sometime later tonight. The cabbie, an amiable Russian named Egor, made no promises but said he'd try to stay in the area.

Now, standing on the darkened sidewalk while seemingly everyone else in the neighborhood had the good sense to stay indoors, Rusty commanded himself to shit or get off the pot.

Still not too late to turn back.

Dismissing that inner voice of caution in his usual way, he crossed the street. He took a moment to memorize the number of the cargo van's Florida license plate: FL-RSTA.

Florida Rasta. Fits with the dreadlocks, so odds are it's the big dude's ride.

But was the big dude Fade himself, or just muscle?

Time to find out. Pushing open the gate, five paces got Rusty to the front door.

He paused, listening for any indication of life inside. A low, thumping hip-hop bassline dimly met his ear, but whether it came from a back room of the bungalow or an adjacent building he couldn't say.

He raised a hand and knocked on the door. Four brisk raps, the way he'd seen Ronnie do it. This prompted no response.

Just as he was ready to knock again, the door opened a crack. A security chain three sizes thicker than Rusty had ever seen connected it to the frame.

The behemoth who'd let Ronnie in the other night filled the narrow gap. His dreadlocks were hard to miss, even in the low light.

Tampa Nate stood there for half a beat, looking hard at the stranger on his doorstep.

"Who the hell are you?"

"An interested buyer."

"Of what?"

"The green snake."

"Fuck off."

The door slammed shut. Rusty immediately resumed knocking, using a closed fist to pound the wood at full strength.

The door yanked open again, rattling the chain.

"Looking to get curb-stomped, bro?"

"Looking to get high. Thought I made that clear already."

"Keep looking."

"Why? This is the right place."

A brief silence passed. Rusty felt himself being sized up.

"I don't know you, man," Nate finally said. "And I got a real good memory for faces."

"We haven't met before. Does it matter?"

"Tell me exactly what it is you want."

"I want some of the salts that come with the green stamp. A gram, two, whatever you got on hand. I'm prepared to pay."

He flashed a wad of twenties in one hand just briefly enough for the image to register.

The door closed, a bit more softly this time.

Rusty waited, thinking it probably wasn't going to open up again. He started to ponder the possibility of slipping into the place through a window. It should be easy enough. And probably just as easy to get shot the minute he stuck his head inside. Yet he felt like he'd passed some point of no return. The idea of heading back home without entering the bungalow by whatever means were required simply did not make sense.

He heard a chain sliding off a latch. A bolt turned. Then the door opened again.

"Step in."

The dreadlocked giant moved aside to let Rusty enter. Two steps got him inside. The door was quickly closed, bolted and chained.

Rusty found himself in a broad front room taking up half the bungalow's interior. It was so dark his eyes needed a moment to adjust, nothing but a pair of red-tinted lamps providing illumination. The air was heavy with some kind of incense, vaguely smelling like jasmine.

Tampa Nate stood with a pair of tree-trunk arms folded across his chest. He seemed to be waiting for Rusty to clarify his purpose, as if he hadn't already.

Rusty figured flashing the money again was better than anything he could say. He held out four twenties, not bothering with any optical flourish.

"Good for two grams, right?"

"Put it away. Have a seat."

"I'll stand."

"I said *sit*," Tampa Nate uttered, looking like only a great expenditure of will was keeping his hands off Rusty's throat.

He waited to make sure the instruction was followed. Rusty didn't want to sit, but had to calculate the upside of risking an altercation so early in the game. There wasn't any.

He lowered himself into an overstuffed leather chair facing the front door. A bamboo coffee table sat next to it, smoke undulating in patterns from the ebony incense holder at its center. The room boasted little in the way of decoration, all the walls bare. Almost certainly a rental property, one its current occupants didn't see any point in sprucing up.

Satisfied, Nate walked toward the rear of the bungalow. A door opened and then shut.

A few long minutes passed. Rusty's hand made idle forays into the pocket of his long coat every thirty seconds or so, regaining a sense of security each time he felt the slim heft of the folding knife inside.

He could hear a murmur of low conversation from one of the rooms behind. The tone was neutral, no hint of tension or a coming confrontation.

Will they sell to me? If so, do I walk out of here and give Jim Biddison one more chance to bust these guys?

No clear answer came to that question. He concluded all he really wanted to do was see Fade in person, to look the man in the eye. He'd done that now—presumably, the deadlocked man had to be him—but it provided no indication of what the next move should be.

A phone on the coffee table rang once, then stopped in the middle of the second ring. Rusty couldn't tell if someone had picked up the call in another room or if the caller had simply hung up. He spent a moment musing that he couldn't remember the last time he'd been in a residential space with a landline. The phone had to be at least twenty years old, its cord frayed and tangled.

Could just bolt right now, before I have to figure it out.

That was a hard impulse to deny, based on a simple desire for self-preservation. At least he knew with certainty where Fade could be found. Probably best to retreat and consider what offensive move would yield the biggest impact without inviting undue danger upon himself.

The decision made, Rusty was halfway out of the chair when he heard footsteps coming from the hallway behind. He turned, expecting to see the big man reenter the room.

Instead another man stepped in and took a seat on the couch across from him. Slight of build with close-cropped hair, a pair of round eyeglasses gave him an owlish look. There was something slightly professorial about him, offset by the unfinished roundness of his features, which seemed to suggest adolescence. He sat quietly, regarding Rusty with a kind of amused curiosity.

Sure as hell doesn't look like a drug dealer, Rusty thought. *Dude with the dreads fits the image to a tee. But this guy? A librarian, maybe.*

"What do you want?" the owl finally asked. His voice was as soft as his overall appearance.

"I told your boy already. Two grams, if you can accommodate me."

"Two grams of what?"

"The salts."

This provoked no reply.

Rusty added, "The kind with a stamp on the bag. I don't know if it has a specific name."

"You're referring to illicit drugs commonly called bath salts. I've interpreted that much correctly?"

Rusty just nodded. Whatever he'd been anticipating, this kind of effete reticence wasn't it.

"What an extraordinary thing to do. Knock on the door of a stranger's house asking to purchase narcotics."

On impulse, Rusty threw a curve ball.

"What kind of name is Fade, anyway?"

It was a guess, but he'd hit the target. The first glimmer of a reaction manifested on the owl's placid features, a look conveying disturbance. Embarrassment, even. He'd been taken by surprise but shook it off quickly.

"Funny, I was just about to apologize for not making introductions. I'll admit your appearance here has caught me a bit off guard. But the longer I have to think about it, the clearer it becomes."

"It's not murky," Rusty said. "I was told … well, let's say I was given reason to think this is a place where certain items can be obtained. So I'm here, cash in hand."

Fade didn't offer any reply to that. There was no sign of an impending transaction, and if Rusty didn't know better he might've thought he truly *had* come to the wrong place.

"Sorry for showing up uninvited. It's just the itch got a little too strong not to scratch. I imagine that's something you run into from time to time. Doubt I'm the first person to come knocking."

"In fact you are. Which makes everything you've said suspect in the extreme. If you really were interested in procuring, you'd know we don't vend out of this house. You could turn the place upside down and wouldn't find so much as a single crystal."

"So what you're saying is I've come to the right source, but I've gone about it the wrong way."

"I'm saying everything about you is wrong."

Rusty heard a new note in the man's voice, and for the first time he started to think a quick departure was not just a smart move but the only one at his disposal.

"If that's how it is," he said, "we don't have much to talk about."

He was preparing to stand when Fade stopped him with a question.

"You've sampled the product before?"

"I have."

"What did you think?"

"Back for more, aren't I?"

Fade didn't answer, just seemed to ponder the response with a good deal of concentration.

"I don't mean to give the wrong impression. Obviously, there are certain activities of which this modest little residence acts as a kind of central hub. The rules of operation are stated most clearly to anyone who finds a place in the chain, whether on the side of supply or demand. The loop is kept very tight, so the fact that you should even consider coming to this address for the purpose you've stated is either irregular to the point of absurdity or a flat-out lie."

He paused to pick a thread off the collar of his button-down shirt. Examining it for a moment, he let it fall to the floor.

"Now I ask you, friend. If you were me, which of those two options would strike you as most plausible?"

"A buddy of mine brought me the other night," Rusty said, figuring there was no harm that could come to Ronnie at this point. "I hung back while he took care of business. He made clear it wasn't cool to walk in with him. So I knew it was a little out of bounds to show up uninvited, but like I said, the itch was there."

"A buddy," Fade echoed. He nodded, smiling with the satisfaction of having solved some kind of puzzle.

"He said you don't like dealing with strange faces. That's why I waited a few days before coming over."

Fade was looking over Rusty's shoulder now, eyes slightly unfocused in a way that made it clear he'd stopped listening.

"So I'll ask again, Fade. Do you have anything to sell me or not?"

No answer came, and Rusty realized a sudden move for the front door was doomed to fail. He saw the bolt had been turned by a key rather than a knob. No way he was getting through that door without the express cooperation of Fade and/or the ape with the dreads.

"I'm a curious man by nature," Fade said. "It's been the guiding force in my life, a sense of curiosity. My studies, at which I excelled, always sprang from a desire to make known what was unknown to me. I applied that same instinct to my work in the professional field, the particulars of which wouldn't interest you. I no longer inhabit that field, working as something of a freelancer these days. But I remain a curious man."

Tensing his knees, Rusty decided his best option for escape was through the window to the left of the front door. A slight gap in the drapes revealed it was not barred. All he'd have to hurl himself through was glass. He'd done that a thousand times before, albeit in vastly different circumstances.

"Right now, for instance," Fade continued. "I'm incredibly curious about your appearance. That you should come here expecting to purchase drugs tells me you know nothing of who I am or how I conduct business. I can think of only a single person who may have given you this address. Alas, he can't provide any answers, and I'm not inclined to believe anything you say at this point."

This oblique mention of Ronnie made Rusty flinch. He felt the weight of the folding knife and had to shake off an urge to pull it out.

"But do you know what has me most curious?" Fade said, leaning forward on the couch. "I'm wondering what the odds are that you darken this door only a few hours after the police issue a statement warning the citizens of this backwater town to avoid my product."

Rusty's long-practiced facial control skills kicked in of their own accord. As surprised as he was to learn of the police statement, he also felt a small tug of relieved gratitude for an old friend.

You listened to me, Jim. Thanks. I just wish I'd known about it before walking in here.

"The result of all this curiosity," Fade went on in a tone of conclusion, "is I'd be very surprised if you didn't have anything to do with the issuance of that statement from the police."

Rusty rooted both feet on the floor. He didn't expect this weak little owl to impede his progress, but he wasn't going to give him any advantage either.

The window was five paces away. He'd be through it in less than two seconds.

"Like I said, we don't have anything to talk about."

He planted both hands on the arms of the chair and started to rise. His upward progress was halted by the billy club in Tampa Nate's massive hand, which swung downward to clip Rusty behind the ear.

It was a brutal strike, perfectly executed.

An instant of pain both dull and sharp exploded his vision into a white haze. He seemed to float weightless for a moment, too brief. Then the hardwood floor smacked him in the face, providing a perfect counterpoint to the blow he'd just taken on the back of the head.

27.

Remaining seated with no change of expression, Fade motioned to Tampa Nate.

"See what he's got on him."

Just barely conscious, feeling as if he was encased in ten inches of gauze, Rusty was vaguely aware of being rolled over onto his back. Hands frisked through his coat's exterior pockets. He felt the folding knife being removed and heard an appreciative whistle.

"Check this out," Tampa Nate said, brandishing the blade for Fade to see. "Nice little pigsticker."

"Keep looking."

Nate tucked the knife into his own pants pocket and then proceeded to turn out all of Rusty's. He helped himself to a roll of cash without seeing any need to call attention to it. Otherwise there was nothing.

"No wallet. No ID."

"Look inside the coat."

With a glare that hinted he didn't care to be ordered around by a man whose body weight he could easily bench-press, even if he'd gotten used to it by now, Nate continued the inspection.

Through his dull, painful haze, Rusty felt those two large hands rudely poking through the jacket near his ribcage.

Not the cuffs, he thought. Losing the knife was bad enough— it was part of a set that would be rendered woefully incomplete by its absence. He could live with that. But his monogrammed handcuffs were genuinely irreplaceable, the work of a talented silversmith in Nevada no longer above ground.

He heard them clinking as they were pulled out.

"Jesus," Tampa Nate said, sounding alarmed by the discovery. "Is he a fucking cop?"

"He's no cop," Fade answered with bland certainty.

"What are these for? Was he gonna make a citizen's arrest or what?"

"Doubtful. More likely he'd chain me to the radiator and do a little carve job."

"Why the hell would he want to do that?"

Fade sat back in the chair, a familiar look of superiority stealing over his face, undermined by a sense of regret that Tampa Nate was so slow on the uptake.

"I know you were listening just now. He said a 'buddy' brought him here. Now who do you think that might have been?"

"Little fuck Wilson, my guess."

"Exactly. This character was probably a friend trying to settle some ill-conceived score."

"I didn't think the little bastard had friends. Shit, out of how many people, he's the only one who can't follow the rule about coming here?"

Nate immediately regretted bringing up the incident, which by default reminded both men of his own role in it. Fade gave him a hard look, undaunted by the physical difference.

"It wouldn't have been a problem if you'd turned him away, would it?"

"OK, OK. Not again."

"In fact, it's turned out to be more costly than either of us anticipated. We wouldn't be dealing with this particular headache if you'd exercised better judgment."

"You want to hear me say I fucked up one more time?"

"Save it. It doesn't improve the situation."

"Look at the bright side. Little Ronnie ain't a problem no more."

"No," Fade said, glancing down at Rusty's prone form with further contempt. "But he is."

Tampa Nate finished his frisk. He hadn't thought to look in Rusty's boots, and had no awareness of the hidden pocket sewn into his pants.

"Nothing else on him. Not even a phone."

"Get some rope," Fade ordered. "Tie up his wrists and ankles, and make it secure. Then back the van up to the house."

Nate grabbed the keys and unbolted the front door.

"Get as close as you can to the stoop, understand?"

"Yeah, I *got* it."

Rusty heard the door open and close again. He was still weaving in and out of consciousness; the blow hadn't fully knocked him out. But something told him there may be an advantage in acting like it had.

The act worked. Fade took a last look down and was convinced he wouldn't be moving in the next several minutes. Rusty heard diminishing footsteps as Fade walked out of the room.

Then he started crawling across the floor, trying to make it to that unbarred window.

At the end of a short hallway leading to the bungalow's two back rooms, Fade punched in a four-numeral code to a digital lock securing the door on the right. It opened and he stepped inside. The lock was a superfluous bit of security, and one that wouldn't make the slightest difference if anyone ever raided this place. But it didn't matter, because Fade hadn't been lying when he told Rusty there were no narcotics in the house.

Stationed on the other side of that locked door, in what was intended as one of two small bedrooms, was a makeshift lab complete with burners, tubes, scales, funnels, beakers, rubber gloves—and an entire crate of gram baggies sitting on an otherwise unused bed.

This was a drug cooker's setup. A fairly sophisticated one, though small in scale. The greenest cop out of the Academy could determine as much with a glance. And yet there was not a single item in this room that was illegal for a private citizen to own. Fade had studied the case law well, and he knew exactly what was considered sufficient evidence to mount a successful prosecution for drug manufacture and distribution. Not even the presence of all those baggies, incriminating as they looked, was enough to bring a charge down on him.

That was Fade's conclusion, at any rate. Obviously he knew it was a calculated gamble, but there was no way to enter this type of enterprise without taking on a certain amount of risk.

He mitigated that risk by adopting an utterly methodical approach to cleaning the lab, a process he initiated as soon as a batch large enough to merit transport to the stash house had been produced. Using sterilized wipes, Fade went over every tube, every metal coil, every spoon and surface with almost loving care. He performed three passes. Once with ammonia to dissolve any lingering salt particles no matter how minute. Once again with a basic industrial-strength cleaner. And then a final pass with lemon-scented Fantastik bought from the local supermarket.

It wasn't enough for the room to be totally devoid of drugs. That precautionary measure would be rendered useless if the whole place reeked like it had just been scrubbed with ammonia. It needed to both look and *smell* like a perfectly legal home laboratory that could arguably be used for any number of innocuous purposes by a man equipped with a knowledge of chemistry. Fade was just such a man.

For all its cleanliness, this little room hardly compared to his old cubicle in the R & D unit of Tilly Pharmaceuticals. In some ways, Fade preferred the self-constructed bungalow lab to his former workspace. It had a decidedly unclinical, almost homey atmosphere.

And he found it important to be comfortable while working. More than the money, much more, Fade truly loved to cook. Here in the solitude of the back bedroom he made his own hours, often staying up till dawn in the middle of a prolonged session, enthralled by the process.

The first major step was always to mix the base components for alpha-PVP with red phosphorus and hydriodic acid, then filter out the red phosphorus and neutralize the remaining acid with a lye solution. Numerous other steps followed, then came his favorite part: adding Sephinordome-H as a bonding agent that kept all the chemical components together.

A beautiful thing, finding an entirely new use for the very solvent Fade himself had a hand in formulating. With the benefit of retrospect, he felt an unfathomable gratitude for his abrupt dismissal from Tilly last summer.

The corporate brass had decided that Fade (along with half his department) was no longer a vital cog in the machinery. In turn, he'd decided not to punch out his final time card without collecting something worthy of the countless hours he'd spent in service of expanding Tilly's footprint in the cutthroat world of Big Pharma.

With that mindset, he had "stolen" the chemical formulation for Sephinordome-H with the intent of using it for stabilization in a proprietary mix of bath salts he would sell to Delmarva's drug-abusing population. Starting with Ocean City, then moving southward with the advance of winter.

He'd been doing just that since September, and raking in profits that staggered him.

Utilizing Sephinordome-H for illegal ends gave Fade a sense of perverse satisfaction. And the stuff worked like a dream, much better than any comparable bonding agent used by low-grade cookers with no appreciation for the artistic side of pure chemistry.

As a matter of principle, Fade never stepped on his own product. With so little overhead, there was no need. He wanted everyone who had an opportunity to sample the green serpent (he'd chosen the Ouroboros symbol for branding on a whim, because it looked cool) to experience its full power. He'd be damned if he was going to dilute the batch with baking soda or baby laxative.

He tried to keep the cooks small to avoid excess inventory, producing roughly a hundred grams' worth at a time. Then came the boring bits—weighing, separating, and bagging each gram.

Fade would have liked to trust Tampa Nate with these tasks, but he couldn't do it. Just having someone of Nate's diminished mental capacity as a partner bothered him, though there was no denying the big man's usefulness. Fade certainly wasn't going to manage their haggard band of runners himself, or have any contact with them at all. He never let them in the bungalow, much less near the stash.

Of course he *had* made the mistake of letting that useless Kenny Dixon get too close. And look what happened. Fade caught Dixon with his hand in the cookie jar—skimming the goddamned product with no respect for the work involved in its manufacture—and cut him loose immediately. He didn't devote a nanosecond's worth of thought to Kenny until almost two weeks later when the idiot called to say something had gone wrong with one of the half-assed home robberies he seemed to think of as his specialty. Only a few days later, he was arrested for a very high-profile murder.

The news didn't surprise Fade, or make much of an impression at all. With a formidable capacity to filter out unhelpful notions, he never pondered the possibility that the old woman's gruesome demise may have some connection to his product. Not once.

He now stepped around the homemade lab and opened a closet to retrieve his leather jacket. It was cold out tonight, and they had some disagreeable business to deal with. Fade reached for the jacket on autopilot, averting his eyes from the closet's interior. On a shelf above the rack used for shirt hangers, an 8 x 10 glass frame threatened recrimination.

It was his masters in chemistry diploma from UM. Fade didn't consider himself sentimental, yet he'd been unable to throw away the diploma even though he couldn't bear to look at it. The damned thing had followed him like a stubborn conscience through a series of residences all the way to this cruddy rented bungalow.

Putting on the jacket, Fade allowed a brief glance at the diploma before closing the closet door. He told himself he'd get rid of it tonight when they swept this whole place clean. He would not be bringing any souvenirs of lost ambition with him on the southbound route to fresh markets for the green serpent. Time to let all that go and embrace his current situation with clear eyes.

Satisfied the lab was in tip-top shape for the moment, he stepped out of the room and pulled the door closed. The digital lock clicked into place automatically.

He walked into the main room and felt the briefest moment of panic. Their unwanted guest wasn't facedown on the floor where he'd been just minutes ago.

Turning his head at a small sound, Fade allowed a short sigh of relief. He almost laughed at the sight of Rusty crawling crablike across the floor toward the window next to the front door.

The sight amused Fade in an abstract way, but it disturbed him too. It illustrated the danger of taking anything for granted, even something as simple as assuming this guy would remain unconscious for a short period of time.

The front door swung open, missing Rusty's head by an inch. Tampa Nate looked down, a coil of rope slung over his shoulder.

"Dude's got some fight, I'll give him that much."

He bent down to whisper in Rusty's ear.

"Almost there, man. Keep going. You're home free!"

Rusty tried to answer with a few choice obscenities that came out as a jumbled groan. Nate pushed the door closed, laughing.

"Come on, tie him up."

Nodding, Tampa Nate stepped over Rusty and lowered himself, digging a heavy knee into the small of his back. Rusty suppressed a flinch, biting his tongue not to cry out. Nate grabbed his hands and pulled back roughly so they met at his lower back. Then he got to work binding his wrists.

Rusty was aware of what was happening, and it felt sufficiently familiar to react on instinct. Rotating both wrists away from each other—the left in a clockwise motion, the right counter clockwise—he brought the knobs in contact with one another, creating the widest possible space around which the ropes could be tied. Just a tiny bit of wiggle room that might make all the difference. He did this as slowly as possible so as not to attract Tampa Nate's attention.

Fade watched closely as the ropes were secured in similar fashion around Rusty's ankles.

"We're pulling out tonight," he said.

Nate looked up with happy surprise.

"For real?"

"Yes. You've convinced me of the inadvisability of remaining here. The power of your persuasive talents finally yielded the result you were after."

"Naw, it wasn't me," Tampa Nate said, pretty sure his chain was being yanked. "It was that thing on the news."

"Correct," Fade continued, trying to ignore his partner's stupidity, "combined with the fact that we have no idea how many more people now know this address. First, we deal with our friend here. Then we load up the lab. Sweep this whole place clean, every room. One last stop at the stash house and we'll be a hundred miles gone before the sun comes up."

Tampa Nate frowned as some thought occurred to him.

"That ain't gonna work. Not tonight."

"Why not?" Fade asked irritably. He was accustomed to having orders questioned, but never contradicted outright.

"Too crowded on the pier, all that shit going on down there. People everywhere, no way we can park the van close enough to move the product."

Fade didn't pick up his meaning at first. Then it hit him and he nodded briskly.

"You're right. There's too much activity for transfer tonight."

"Well, it's what we stuck around for, right? The festival?"

Face silently flushed with anger, refusing to answer. He looked around the room for something to break. Deciding on a cheap coral lamp on an end table, he picked it up and hurled it against the wall without sufficient muscle strength to shatter it. The lamp bounced off the wall and landed on the floor intact.

"No need to trip," Tampa Nate said, working to keep a straight face. "We'll do it tomorrow night. Laying low one more day won't sink us."

Fad grumbled something that wasn't quite agreement but a kind of wrathful acquiescence to the delay.

From his position on the floor, Rusty had been listening intently to everything being said. With the two men standing right there, he saw no possibilities for forcing his way out of the house. And he was still too sapped by the blow to his head to make a game effort of it.

"Let's get him in the van," Tampa Nate said, bending down and grabbing Rusty by the armpits. He waited for Fade to take the ankles so they could lift him off the rug.

Fade wasn't quite ready to do that, still fuming at the inconvenience this intruder had caused. He picked up the unbroken lamp and held it high over his head. Nate saw what he was preparing to do and almost said there was no need for that, dude was incapacitated already.

He didn't have time to say it before Fade flung the lamp down with both hands as hard as he could. It smashed into the back of Rusty's head, striking the same spot where the billy club had landed minutes before.

The lamp shattered this time.

Rusty didn't have to pretend to be unconscious anymore.

28.

The first thing Rusty became aware of was a sense of motion. A steady vibration coming from underneath. He lay cloaked in darkness that only receded marginally after forcing his eyes open. It took him a few moments to realize he was in a moving vehicle. The rattling hum of the engine was deep enough to indicate a truck of some kind.

The cargo van.

He was too disoriented to feel anything like fear, but he could sense its presence beneath the bleary ache enveloping his head and neck. The idea of closing his eyes and returning to a state of unconsciousness was disturbingly seductive. He shook it away and willed his lids to stay open.

He was lying facedown on the floorboards. Above him, the occasional flare of a passing streetlamp provided a brief view of this space. He determined it was the rear loading area of the van. His body was crammed in, knees bent underneath and pressing into his chest.

Only then did Rusty remember his wrists being tied just before the lights went out. He tried to move his legs and found his ankles similarly bound. Judging from the feel of the tight bonds clamping his hands together, it was some kind of standard hemp rope, maybe a half inch in diameter. That struck him as a bit of good fortune. If he'd been tied with plastic zipcuffs any chance of freeing himself would be considerably more remote.

Gingerly, making every effort at maintaining silence, he rolled over on to his back. Pushing himself against one side of the van's interior, he was able to squirm up to a sitting position.

OK. Wrists tied. Ditto ankles. In a moving vehicle.
I can deal with this. Right?

He remained motionless for another minute, trying to hear something that would give him an idea. Any hopeful notion of sharing this van with only one other person seemed ludicrous. At the very least, he'd likely have both Fade and the dreadlocked thug to deal with.

He heard no conversation, not so much as a cough. Nor was there any music coming from the tall subwoofers wedged against the back of the rear passenger seat. Rusty could just discern the outline of a man's head rising above the seat's rim. From the close-cropped hair and spectacles he knew it had to be Fade.

Maybe there was time to force a play. If he could move himself to a kneeling position behind the seat quietly enough not to attract notice, he may be able to launch a debilitating head-butt against the base of Fade's skull. If he landed it properly, and didn't knock himself out in the process, he could squirm into the backseat and hold Fade down with his own body weight. Whatever happened from there would depend on the driver's reaction.

Just as Rusty was repositioning himself to attempt this long-shot bid at altering the odds, Fade's head turned a few degrees in his direction.

"He's awake."

"Bastard don't stay out long," Tampa Nate uttered unseen from the driver's seat. Rusty thought he picked up a faint note of respect in his voice.

"Just as well. We'd have to rouse him soon enough."

Now rotating in the seat, Fade addressed him directly:

"We were just remarking that you seem to recover quickly. That's admirable, but it doesn't do much to help you out."

"Where are we going?" Rusty asked. He was dismayed to hear how thickly the words left his mouth. That knock on the head must have done more damage than he'd thought.

"Not far," Fade answered. "At least not in geographical terms. It may take you quite a while to find your way back home, if you ever do."

Rusty pondered that cryptic threat. He was pretty sure he knew what it meant, and his mind started churning in search of ways to avoid it.

"How long was I out?"

"Just long enough for us to make a brief supply stop. You started to stir a bit at one point, but I discouraged that."

"Don't you even want to know why I came to your place tonight?"

"I have a pretty clear idea. You tipped your hand rather clumsily. It has something to do with Ronnie Wilson. He was a friend of yours, no?"

"I know who you're talking about, but you've got the wrong idea. There's nothing personal about this."

"He was an acquaintance, if not a friend," Fade continued. "You obviously decided I'm responsible for the young man's death. Which is really foolish, I have to say. Do you honestly believe he was destined for a better end, even if he'd never come across my product?"

Rusty saw no point in answering that.

"The question wasn't rhetorical, but it doesn't matter. Your appearance tonight was an attempt at retribution of some sort. That's the best guess I can hazard, and I'm not inclined to devote much more thought to it."

"Wrong," Rusty said, pushing himself up against the van's interior wall after a bump in the road caused him to slip down. "You were on the right track before, about the police."

Fade shook his head, dismissing the suggestion.

"You're not a cop, despite whatever role you may have played in their statement. Maybe you provided them with a sample bag, and they used that to display our branding symbol, but that's it. Concerned citizen/do-gooder is my bet. A nuisance, in other words."

"I'm working undercover," Rusty said. "My movements are being tracked. You're in a bigger shitheap of trouble than you could possibly imagine right now."

Fade laughed.

"Not bad. You actually said that with something like conviction. Want to try another?"

"Lieutenant Jim Biddison knows exactly what I'm doing tonight. I'd be surprised if they haven't raided your place already. You've just brought down a handful of felony charges, starting with kidnapping."

Rusty couldn't see Tampa Nate's alarmed glance into the rearview mirror but heard him ask, "You think he's blowing smoke?"

"Of course he is," Fade answered irritably.

"I dunno. What'd he say, Biddison? That was the cop on TV."

"Which is exactly how he learned his name, for God's sake."

"Yeah, but what …"

"Just watch the road. The turnoff's in two more blocks."

Tampa Nate didn't reply to that. Rusty had to hope the big dude didn't cotton to being lorded over by someone he could crush with one hand. Maybe that would offer some kind of opening at the right moment.

Fade unfastened a small leather kit from the L.L. Bean knapsack on the seat next to him. From it he pulled a cellophane packet and a two-ounce bottle made of brown glass.

"Whatever's driving you," he said, speaking to Rusty again, "it seems you have a great deal of interest in the product. Well, there's no knowledge like firsthand knowledge. The best way is to let you form your own conclusions. Perhaps the experience will offer the answers you seek."

"Told you I already tried it."

"I doubt you've had a chance to sample what I'd call a proper dose."

Fade opened the cellophane packet. Balling it up and tossing it aside, he held up a 5cc Luer-Lok tip syringe with a 22G x 1" thin wall needle.

"Don't suffer any undue alarm. As you can see, I've unwrapped a fresh one. There's no chance of infection. Besides, that would be the least of your worries. Thanks to some fortunate timing, we have a small amount of some un-granulated product available. That's far preferable for introducing it to the bloodstream."

Fade inserted the needle into the rubber stopper at the bottle's top and partially filled the syringe barrel with dark gray fluid. Returning the bottle to the kit and refastening it, he slid a plastic guard over the needle tip and pocketed the syringe.

"You have a vote in how we proceed. I can come back there and give you the shot, assuming you don't attempt any resistance that's bound to prove futile. That's Option A. Option B is for you to resist, which will necessitate my driver pulling over and keeping you subdued while I administer the dose. I don't think he likes you, and he may exert more force than absolutely needed. It stands to reason that Option A is preferable from your point of view. The needle is going in, one way or another."

Rusty just nodded. His mind was too occupied by thinking of some way to change this course of events to speak.

"Good choice."

Fade slid around the end of the seat and crawled into the cargo area. Rusty moved down the wall a foot to give him some room. Crouching next to him, Fade produced the syringe again and pulled off the safety tab.

"Turn around so I can get at an arm."

Rusty still hadn't devised any countermeasure. His capacity to put up a fight was all but eliminated. The best he could do was thrash wildly and hope to land a blow with his feet, knees or head. And where would that get him? The driver would just dole out another beating while Fade prepared the shot. There was no gain in it at all.

So Rusty rotated himself on the floor until his back was to Fade. It reminded him of when he'd turned around to offer his hands at Officer Neely's command, and he tried not to think about what he'd gladly trade to be back in that position right now.

Fuck it. I wouldn't have done anything differently anyway.

He felt the shirtsleeves of his right arm being pushed up, halfway to the elbow.

"That should be sufficient," Fade said. "In any case, we're not going to bother with removing your jacket."

Rusty felt the fingers of a hand he couldn't see slapping the inside of his forearm, coaxing up a vein. Then the hand went away, and he knew the needle would pierce his flesh any second. His arm flexed instinctively, muscles constricting to their tautest point.

"That's a foolish thing to do," Fade said with exasperation. "I might break it off, which would not be a pleasant outcome for you. These aren't the easiest conditions for administering a shot. I suggest you do everything you can to help me. Or would you rather we revert to Option B?"

Rusty gradually relaxed his arm, submitting to the reality that if this man intended to stick him there was nothing he could do to prevent it. Like Fade said, resistance would only lead to a worsening of the situation.

"That's better. You're getting a bargain here. This dose has a street value of fifteen or twenty dollars and it won't cost you a dime. I only wish I could see how it goes to work on you. Sadly, this is just about where our paths diverge."

Rusty held his breath, trying to reach some kind of focused mental plane grounded in reality.

Whatever happens next, it's just the drugs. Don't forget that.

He felt the needle piercing his arm, digging deep into the vein. It stayed there, wobbling slightly as Fade depressed the plunger, making sure every last milligram found its way into Rusty's blood.

Then the sting went away as the needle was extracted.

Even before he had time to repeat his inner admonition about not forgetting, the liquidated salts started to take hold. It felt like an iron spring coiling tightly in the pit of his stomach, preparing to burst loose in an explosion that rocketed through every nerve ending in his body.

Just the drugs don't forget just the drugs don't ...

He didn't even notice they had stopped moving. Tampa Nate jumped out of the driver's seat and circled around to slide open the rear door. Rusty was just barely aware of being pulled from the van. A brief moment came when the floorboards disappeared, and then he dropped hard onto asphalt, feeling tiny pebbles that tasted like tar coat his tongue.

The driver's door slammed shut and the van peeled away, enveloping him in a cloud of exhaust fumes.

29.

Rusty rolled over on the gravel, lying on his side for a moment and determining he'd suffered no injury from being dumped. He turned his head to look upward. The cobalt sky was exceptionally clear, stars blazing down on him. The sound of squealing tires ripped the night as the van pulled away. Rusty bunched his knees together and maneuvered himself up into a sitting position.

On some level, he understood he had maybe thirty seconds left before any trace of coherent thinking abandoned him. He could already feel a sickeningly familiar rush of energy pulsating through his system. It felt similar to the initial stage of his controlled experiment in the basement, except he knew this was going to be much more intense.

He had to get himself someplace safe and try to ride it out. *But how long will it last?*

A few hours, like the last time? Longer?

Could he allow himself to think, even in a fleeting moment of panic, the effects might be permanent?

No, thinking that way was suicide. The thing to do was take protective action while he still could, and the most important step was freeing himself of these binds.

Luckily, his appendages had already decided to act of their own will. All those hours he'd devoted to practicing various acts of escapism, years of study in total, came to his aid now. Both hands went to work, acting on pure muscle memory.

The ropes connecting his wrists were tied tight, but it was the work of an amateur. Rusty had freed himself from hundreds of more constrictive knots in his time.

Remember it's just the drugs ...

By rotating his wrists when the ropes were bound back at the bungalow, Rusty had forced Tampa Nate to use a few extra centimeters in tying the knots. He now reversed the earlier motion of his wrists, flattening their fleshy inner sides against one another. This dual adjustment yielded a small but critical measure of slack.

Twisting his fingers to feel the grooves bunched beneath them, he determined the shape of the truss. It was a standard tight hitch with a pair of square knots added for good measure.

Good. This is doable. Not so bad. Just the drugs. Doable ...

Those words kept repeating in his head like a mantra at increasing speed until they lost all meaning. Just a repetitive sound that signified nothing. He was losing the battle with coherence, fast.

But his hands kept at it, ignoring the chaos blooming in his head. Each twisting rotation bought him just a little more wriggling room. At this pace he'd probably need another sixty seconds, tops. If he could keep his mind from completely fraying to tatters for that long.

Whatever happened once the salts kicked in full bore, Rusty at least wanted to have full mobility. With any luck he could run to some isolated area away from any other people.

Seventeen more seconds of focused wriggling produced a small pocket between the rope and the back of his left hand. Twenty-one more seconds and that hand pulled free of its noose. He tore at the coil wrapped around his other hand and it fell away.

Then came the ankles, which had been tied in a sloppier manner. Removing this length of rope was a much simpler endeavor, but not as simple as it might have been under other circumstances. Rusty had to stop twice, fighting off a nauseating sense that his hands were some kind of vile spidery creatures that didn't belong to him.

Just the ...

He finally got the ropes free and staggered to his feet.

Only in the act of freeing himself did it occur to Rusty that he may be better off with his hands tied up. That might limit the amount of damage he'd be capable of inflicting on himself.

Too late now! Old habits die hard!

Those were the last cogent thoughts to form before hysteria claimed him.

Running several ragged paces, he stopped abruptly. His breathing was all wrong in ways he couldn't identify. Jarred by this sensation, Rusty soon found himself shrieking laughter at something that escaped his comprehension the moment he tried to identify it.

Why laugh if you don't even know what you're laughing at, *maniac?*

A terrible thought, but it too dissipated as Rusty's equilibrium sank like a stone to somewhere just below his kneecaps. He found it bizarrely pleasurable, like having lead weights attached to each calf, stretching him painlessly into a tangled coil of boneless protoplasm.

It's not so bad just the drugs not so bad not so …

Struggling to raise each foot, he started navigating toward a cluster of lights in the distance that seemed to recede away with each tortured step he took toward it. All sense of time evaporated. He strained hard enough to raise the veins in his forehead just to advance a few inches, shuffling across the dusty ground like he'd been gut-shot.

It was frustrating and hilariously fascinating. The more he struggled to move, the harder movement became. His laughter resumed, raw and grating and too close to a scream for the distinction to matter.

A full thirteen minutes passed before he dragged himself to the edge of the parking lot where he'd been dumped. Breathless but energized, he howled in mad triumph like a drowning man reaching an elusive shore.

Then the drugs started to turn on him much more rapidly than he'd experienced the first time. A darkness he could feel as much as see closed in with the suffocating hold of an atmospheric burial shroud.

No! It's not so bad just the drugs not so bad …

Rusty recoiled away from the shadow of a tree that seemed

to stretch across the ground in his direction like some hideous liquid spill. Panic rose in his chest. He started running, legs no longer sapped but coursing with raw energy, knowing only that to stand still was to invite death.

With no concept of direction, he charged up a short flight of steps and found himself on the boardwalk. He was immediately surrounded by a blur of faces and bodies, pushing into him, staring with wide eyes, mouths releasing surreal noises he couldn't recognize.

An orange banner rippled in the wind above his head. It was familiar somehow. A tiny sliver of understanding wormed through his confusion, only to dissolve before taking shape. Rusty turned away from the banner, which now appeared as a massive snake, one he knew would start eating its own tail with slashing fangs if he kept looking at it.

He'd stumbled directly into the busiest junction of the Halloween festival. The event mushroomed outward in full riotous swing, taking up three blocks and attracting over a thousand residents along with a handful of tourists. Everywhere he turned, a phantasmagoria of bizarre sounds and images engulfed him.

Just the drugs just the drugs just the drugs …

That thought spooled out into a meaningless, repetitive curl of mental static. He'd started screaming the words aloud without realizing it or knowing what they meant.

Twisting in search of an escape path from this undulating river of bodies, images fresh from hell jolted him at every turn: Skull faces dripping gore from their eye sockets, teeth dancing in gaping mouths. A monstrous black cat, towering the size of a skyscraper, its foul pink tongue stretching a mile to wrap around him. Headless demons with yawning holes in their chests.

Everything was whooshing past in a hyperspeed frenzy. He had no awareness of his own legs moving but felt catapulted into a chimeral landscape bubbling around on all sides.

Gasping, out of breath, mouth on fire and each ragged inhalation a knife in his chest, Rusty spun in frantic circles. He could hear the sound of nearby voices but couldn't connect them to the mishmash of faces constantly reshaping itself in his vision.

"You OK, buddy?"

"Holy shit, this dude's freaking out!"

"He's gonna hurt himself. Someone find a cop."

Tears pouring from his eyes felt like acid running down his cheeks, scorching away flesh all the way to his skull. His hair was a mass of greasy snakes biting into his shoulders.

Have to get away! Away!!!

A pair of strong hands landed on his shoulders with the impact of a grenade.

"Try to relax, pal. Let's sit you down, OK?"

Rusty wheeled around to see the fat mustachioed visage of a Good Samaritan who resembled a decaying corpse. He swung wildly at the man's face, barely missing a direct blow.

"Whoa!" the Samaritan cried, wrapping Rusty up in a kind of standing tackle. "Someone help me with this guy!"

Then there were more hands on him. Rusty couldn't identify the owners; it looked like a mass of disembodied limbs was clawing at him, dragging him down.

No!

Pushing through the scrum, twisting free of the fingers trying to pin him, Rusty broke free to a small open pocket of the boardwalk. In front of him lay a narrow channel free of obstructive bodies. He started running at full speed, away from the densest area of the Halloween festival.

Through befogged eyes he could barely make out people lunging aside to avoid being run over. A woman pulled her young daughter out of his path just in time. He kept running.

Need to get away from the lights and the people. Find someplace dark and quiet.

That thought took root. It was the only thing that made any sense.

Charging another ten paces at full speed, he halted abruptly.

About twenty yards dead ahead, two bike patrol officers dismounted and started moving his way. They motioned brusquely for people to step aside. Rusty could see one of them unclasping a long black baton from his belt.

The other cop raised a small silver object in his hand. Rusty was able, even in his state, to recognize it as a Taser.

"On the ground," the officer with the Taser commanded. "Hands behind your back, now!"

Rusty started to reverse course but stopped quickly. The crowd he'd just run through was massing itself behind him. Spectators had grown emboldened by the presence of law enforcement, and wanted to see this deranged freak get taken down hard.

With the two cops directly in front, closing in carefully, Rusty wheeled and saw a new cluster of civilians—large men, most of them—advancing toward his right flank.

He was trapped.

"Get on the ground!" the officer with the baton yelled. "This is your last warning!"

The cops were now less than ten feet away. The lead officer pointed the Taser directly at Rusty's chest. His partner followed close behind, hoisting the baton high.

At the exact moment the lead cop squeezed the Taser's trigger, Rusty launched himself sideways into the group of men on his right. Using the broad shoulders of the nearest man as a fulcrum, he pushed himself off at a 45-degree angle. The momentum propelled him into the midsection of a smaller man with enough force to send both of them to the ground.

The Taser fired, nailing an elderly onlooker squarely in the solar plexus. The white-haired oldster shrieked and fell to the boards as 50,000 volts flowed into him.

Rusty was up off the ground and scrambling away from the group. The cop with the baton broke left to cut off his escape, muscling people aside.

The only way to avoid him was to run forward, into the dazzlingly bright dining area of Grotto's Pizzeria. Over a dozen patrons looked up from their slices and calzones as Rusty charged into the restaurant. It took less than two seconds for a panic to erupt, people rushing to get away from the goateed maniac.

Rusty knocked into an empty chair, almost following it to

the dirty linoleum. The overhead fluorescent lights exploded in his brain, making him scream. Intermingled cries of startled patrons rang in his ears. Upending tables and trays, he charged toward the back of the dining room.

The cop with the baton was just steps behind, ordering people to get on the floor. His partner with the Taser had rejoined the chase, running in through the front entrance.

Rusty barreled down a narrow hallway, almost falling into the steamy kitchen. Angry oaths rose from the five men working behind massive silver stoves, tossing dough and pouring sweat.

Both cops came bolting into the kitchen. They'd resumed yelling at him to get down, but he wasn't even hearing them anymore.

Rusty rotated his head furiously, looking for a way out.

Off to the right side of the room stood a narrow exit, its screen door open to allow as much fresh air as possible to enter the stifling kitchen. He took a step toward the exit and halted, his path quickly blocked by the baton cop.

In the hidden pocket!

What?

And now, ladies and gentlemen, in this pocket ...

The voice echoed in his head out of nowhere, a sliver of lucid memory emerging from his panicked haze. It was his own voice, speaking from the past. Reminding him of something.

Moving with liquid speed, the fingers of his left hand dug into the secret pocket sewn into the side of his pants. They closed around the familiar gummy surface of a one-inch smoke pellet.

He always suspected, deep down, there was a good reason to carry these things around other than mindless force of habit.

Rusty hurled the smoke pellet to the scuffed kitchen floor. There was a blinding flash of white light, which quickly faded and was swallowed up by a rising funnel of gray smoke.

Everyone was yelling at once. The cops, the cooks, maybe even Rusty himself, he couldn't say for certain. All he knew was he'd bought himself a few short seconds to make that door.

As blinded by the smoke as the rest of the room, he stomped in the direction of the exit. Someone tried to stop him, or simply got in his way. Rusty pushed off to one side, sidestepping this faceless human impediment, and kept advancing. He felt a gust of clean night air as the doorway came in sight.

Then he was outside, darkness spilling around him. No idea which direction to run, so he chose the left. A small alleyway lined with trash cans opened up before him like a pulsating tunnel into nothingness. He ran full speed, the panic still rising even though no one was in immediate pursuit.

Large plumes of smoke billowed out of the pizzeria's kitchen. Both cops emerged through the screen door, coughing and rubbing their eyes with the backs of their arms. Neither saw which way Rusty went. They split up, one loping back to the boardwalk and the other following down the alleyway.

Rusty had too much of a head start. The darkness and his own inner dread aided his escape. After running nonstop for more than ten minutes, only marginally aware of his surroundings but keeping to the shadows as much as possible, he fell to a breathless crouch behind a cheap motel on Dayton Lane.

Ragged inhalations gradually slowing, he stayed down on one knee next to a parked station wagon, shielded from the lights of the motel's first floor. Silence all about except for a tinny radio coming from an open window and the buzzing of cicadas off in the distance. There wasn't a human being to be seen in any direction.

Sitting down with his back against the station wagon, Rusty decided to stay there for some time.

30.

The world came back into focus, in stages. Long before his vision cleared, Rusty became aware that his heart rate had ramped back down to something close to normal. He realized he was lying on his stomach. One side of his face was cold and damp, the other starting to itch with heat.

Still alive, at least. Gotta be, to feel this bad.

He had to work on opening his eyes a few times before managing to keep them that way. The blinding wash of hazy sunlight was so harsh he'd have gladly paid a thousand bucks for a cheap pair of throwaway shades. Alas, a quick check of his pockets revealed he was cashless. He'd taken only a roll of bills with him last night, wisely leaving his wallet at the house. He didn't even have a quarter to call his new friend Egor the cabbie from a pay phone.

Looks like I'm walking home. But how far?

Before attempting to raise himself to an upright position, Rusty performed an inventory of his body. There was no particularly sharp pain screaming from any limbs or appendages, so he formed the hopeful conclusion of being in one piece.

Internally, his head was aflame with pounding discomfort, each throb bringing a fresh wave of dizziness. His stomach heaved and pitched with sour unease. Partially dried mud caked the left side of his face, and a nascent sunburn blossomed on the right.

I was knocked out, tied up. Came to in a moving vehicle. Drugged. Dumped out somewhere, got the ropes off my hands and feet. And then …

A shimmery vision of the Halloween festival danced briefly

before his eyes, then faded. No more lucid details presented themselves, and Rusty wasn't sure he wanted them to resurface.

The process of simply pulling himself upright required almost six minutes. By the time it was complete, he stood on a patch of muddy ground near the water's edge, looking out across Isle of Wight Bay. He was facing west, with the snug green expanse of Ocean Pines visible on the horizon.

Rusty cursed weakly. Judging from the landscape, he had to be several miles from Echo Run. With no wheels and no money.

Scanning his immediate surroundings, he saw that he was at the far end of a public park. Despite the mild weather, there was no one about. Which was fortunate, because if anyone saw him he'd probably be under arrest for public intoxication or worse.

Working to shake off the cobwebs, another strain of coherent thought hit him.

Marceline! Fuck, what time is it?

The sun looked down from a midday peak, telling him it had to be around noon. Hours past the time he'd asked her to come by the house. It wasn't even worth hurrying back; she had to be long gone by now.

Rusty estimated he'd been drugged for well over twelve hours. It must have been a monster dose, without any diluting agent to tamp down the ride. Of course, Fade wanted to give him a proper reward for trying to crash the party.

But what result had Fade intended to produce? That Rusty would end up killing someone? Killing himself? Not likely, or he wouldn't have been tied up. Maybe the hope was that he'd be apprehended for raving like a maniac. Sent away to the psych ward for some intensive observation and detox.

That would explain dumping him so close to the crowded boardwalk. Rusty had to smile through cracked lips as he contemplated the totality of Fade's failure.

He really should've gone to greater lengths to make sure I was dead or locked up. Because now it's all-out war.

That thought cheered him in a deviant way, and got his feet moving. Any counteroffensive required a calculated plan, something he'd been woefully lacking last night.

Starting across the empty park, Rusty asked himself what had changed. What knowledge, if any, had he purchased at such a steep price? It came to him—one crucial nugget of insight might have made the whole thing worth it.

Fade was closing up shop. The game was over. Rusty clearly remembered hearing that at some point before regaining consciousness in the back of the van. He strained to recall exactly what was said. Something about being a hundred miles from Ocean City by tomorrow night, which meant tonight.

Rusty's pace quickened as he stalked across the grass. It dawned on him that any chance of turning what he'd learned into actionable intelligence for the police was nil. Even if Jim Biddison didn't throw him in a cell on sight, there was still no point in approaching him. By the time cops showed up at the bungalow, assuming they could be persuaded to seek a warrant, it would be too late.

Unless Fade had been lying, the window for leaving this in Biddison's hands had elapsed. Any raiding police unit would walk into an empty property on Ninth Street. Not a trace of a drug-making equipment to be found.

And the salts themselves, Rusty thought as another small chunk of memory turned over to reveal itself. Fade said they were never in the bungalow at all. Stored in a remote stash house, most likely being transported somewhere else at this very moment.

No. Not this moment. Rusty seemed to recall the big dude with the dreads saying the salts had to be moved at night, after dark. Last night was no good because of the Halloween festival. And then Fade had grown audibly angered at the delay, because he'd agreed they would have to wait until tonight to clear out.

Rusty's strides continued to accelerate. He reached the park's entrance and turned west on Hitchens Avenue. The idea that Fade and his partner might slip away was biting into him in ways he could almost feel physically, though he knew that might have been a lingering effect of the dose.

Once they were out of town, any chance of tracking them would be gone. So the task was basic: draw Fade out onto open ground before he could collect the stash and depart tonight.

Rusty figured he might also have to settle the score with that dreadlocked son of a bitch, if the opportunity arose. But he was small beer, hired muscle who probably didn't make a single decision guiding the entire operation.

Taking down the top man was the priority.

He got back to Echo Run faster than expected, little more than an hour's walk. Overcoming fatigue, his legs were operating at a high capacity, fueled by hunger for payback and a gnawing certainty he'd missed Marceline.

As soon as he reached the driveway, he saw it. Sitting on a flagstone by the front door, a cardboard box about ten inches square. Taped to the top was an envelope with his name scrawled in a delicate hand.

Dubiously hopeful it might contain an offer to meet again, he ran to where the box lay and tore open the envelope.

A single sheet of paper was folded within, handwriting on both sides. Reading it slowly, a nostalgic pang hit him at the sight of her crisp, elegant penmanship.

> Rusty,
>
> I stuck around for 30 minutes before giving up. Maybe you forgot? Or maybe you had second thoughts, and you're inside waiting for me to leave.
>
> Can't blame you for not wanting to see me. I had no right to intrude on your privacy. It was wrong to sneak up like that. I just hadn't found the nerve to approach you directly.
>
> Still, I don't regret it.
>
> You want to know why?
>
> Because now whatever we had finally feels over.
>
> Just talking for a few minutes yesterday made the trip worthwhile. I always felt bad that the last time you saw me I was planning to leave and lying about it.
>
> Now I can feel like our last meeting was an honest one.

I'm flying back to NOLA today. Dad's been going crazy with worry. I lied about where I've been these past few days and didn't mention your name. That's for the best, believe me.

I hope you've found some kind of peace here. It's a beautiful place, just like you used to describe it to me.

In spite of everything, you deserve to be happy. We both do.

~ M

Rusty swore out loud, standing there on the stoop. He unleashed a protracted string of obscenities, enraged and powerless to do anything about it. He hadn't even mustered the presence of mind yesterday to ask for her phone number.

Fingers trembling, he almost tore up the note but thought better of it. Instead he carefully folded it and returned it to the envelope. As if keeping her handwritten words intact might maintain some lifeline of contact, one he could use in the future when all this shit was behind him.

Rusty picked up the cardboard box, retrieved a spare key from its hiding place beneath a flagstone, and let himself into the house. Moving on instinct, he went directly to the basement and set the box down on his worktable.

Peeling away a strip of tape sealing the top flaps, a flash of telepathic insight hit him before he had a chance to look inside.

Of course.

Centered within the box, swaddled in layers of protective wrapping paper, lay the missing coffin. An identical match for the one contained in the blue velvet case. Rusty didn't hesitate before pinching his fingers together and slowly opening the coffin's teak lid.

The object looking up at him through sightless eyes was too jarringly lifelike to be called a doll and too robust to be termed a figurine, despite being constructed in pocket-size dimensions and weighing less than two pounds. It was more like a handcrafted representation of actual life and death, rendered in astonishing detail with simple materials: body carved of polished cherry wood, long white gown sewn from lace and gingham, facial features lined with untold time and etched in an expression of tranquility suggesting a state beyond repose. A tiny pendant below the neck hung from interlinking gold-plated hoops.

Here in his hands was the long-absent partner needed to make "The Dance of the Deathless Lovers" come to life. The one thing Marceline had taken when she fled Vegas, knowing full well what a psychological blow her purloining of this particular object would have on him.

Unnamed by ancient lore attached to the illusion, Rusty had always called her The Bride, as he'd been instructed by Prosper Lavalle. Over the intervening years, watching other magicians perform a variation of the same routine, he'd heard the female figure referred to as Sheba, Annabelle-Lee and sometimes just Her. But to Rusty she was always The Bride, emblematic not only of magic at its most refined but of his own intended bride. The bride he'd felt sure Marceline would one day become.

Looking down at the figure, he recalled exactly how the two of them would unfold the illusion before clusters of camera-wielding tourists on Bourbon. It was a clever twist on the basic "two cabinets" trick, demanding total precision to work. Timing each other's responses down to the second, he and Marceline would take turns explaining the haunted legend of The Deathless Lovers to spellbound, not infrequently inebriated audiences.

Moving in slow circles around a small table holding the blue velvet box, they would open and close each side in sequence to reveal glimpses of the male and female figures within each coffin, gradually increasing the speed of both their patter and movements as the trick progressed. By virtue of the box's hidden false back and a host of misdirectional cues, The Bride and Groom would inexplicably switch places from right to left, gaining speed until they seemed to be dancing to the same rhythm of their two living surrogates.

When executed properly, it was a hell of a trick. Guaranteed to close any street performance with maximum impact, drawing rowdy applause and a shower of bills into the tip jar.

Rusty now placed The Bride back in her coffin, noticing a folded sheet of paper beneath. Torn from the same pad she'd used for the letter, in perfectly condensed script Marceline had written:

> You probably guessed what's in here already. I don't know if you want it, or if you can stand to have it in your home. I know I can't, not with the baby coming.
>
> Prosper doesn't even know I still have it. He'd make me burn it, probably want to tan my hide for keeping it this long.
>
> For me, it's got nothing to do with superstition. The only feelings I attach to it are feelings I used to have for you. It doesn't belong with me anymore, but I couldn't bring myself to get rid of it.
>
> Maybe it belonged with you all along.

Rusty lifted up The Bride's coffin and carried it over to the bookcase. He pulled down the blue velvet box and opened it, for once not wincing at the rebuke of the empty slot inside. He returned The Bride to her appointed place without bothering to open the adjacent coffin and take a look at The Groom.

Seen enough of that asshole for one lifetime. All that matters is they're back together.

The same never would be true of Rusty and Marceline. Even with no ring on her finger, she obviously had someone who'd planted the seed for the life about to come.

But just because they were done as lovers didn't mean they had nothing left to say to each other.

When the right moment came, he would be proactive about it. He'd be the one to make the effort, get on a plane to New Orleans and go knock on her door. Tell her everything, if she still wanted to hear it. And then listen to everything she had to say in return.

I promise, Marcie. Yesterday wasn't our last meeting. We will see each other again.

31.

Three hours later Rusty wasn't fully restored, but he felt like a respectable shadow of his usual self. A piping hot shower that lasted twenty-five minutes, some clean clothes, a plate of fresh fruit and four cups of chicory coffee hadn't exactly worked miracles, but they did help him to think clearly. To plan.

A sense of urgency kept his movements brisk and mind focused. He'd put on a pair of black jeans and a black T-shirt from the Fantasma magic shop on Seventh Avenue in Manhattan that always felt like a lucky garment.

By the grace of some unknown miracle, he'd sustained no major physical damage during his hallucinatory rampage. Some inner fortitude had prevented his hands from creating any of the wounds they'd been only so eager to inflict during his first experiment with the salts.

The worst remnant came from that tap on the back of the dome Tampa Nate gave him, accentuated by Fade's blow with the hurled lamp. A sharp edge of the coral had dug into the skin at the base of his neck. It hurt, but the dried blood washed away in the shower, and there was no need for a bandage.

For the first time since this whole business had started, Rusty felt certain of exactly what measures to take.

All he needed to set the wheels in motion was a little information. He anticipated some hurdles in getting hold of it, but none appeared. A minimal amount of web surfing was required, first hitting the Worcester County Department of Public Records website and then Google Maps.

Marceline was right. Staying hidden from public view

these days was pretty damn hard. As someone who valued his personal privacy to a degree well beyond the average citizen, Rusty was almost dismayed at how easy it was to track down the two residential addresses he was looking for.

One of them held particular interest.

115 Gerar Street. Less than six miles from where I'm sitting.

After gathering a fresh batch of materials from the basement—including a few requiring special care he never thought he'd have an opportunity to use—Rusty chewed over the last remaining variable in his scheme. Janice.

He'd been wrestling with the wisdom of bringing her onboard for most of the day. It was a coin toss. He could opt to proceed without her knowledge, maybe fill her in on a few selected details after it was all over.

But that didn't sit well with him. Rusty knew she had good reason to be involved with his plans on at least a peripheral level. How could he justifiably deny her the satisfaction of knowing what he intended to do, when it was her plea that nudged him deeper into this tangle than he was before meeting her?

Figuring it all out threatened to hinder his momentum, and he was running out of time. He picked up his cell phone and dialed her number, consoling himself with the notion that either decision was bound to nag him.

It rang three times and he was almost starting to wish she wouldn't answer. He'd gladly take that as a sign for him to proceed alone.

She answered on the fourth ring.

So be it, he thought. Then he asked how quickly she could get over to Echo Run.

"Jesus, you look awful."

Those were her first words when he met her at the door. It had taken Janice less than twenty minutes to get here from the Avalon Inn, indicating a rather loose interpretation of traffic signals.

"Thanks. Sounds better than I feel, actually."

"What happened?"

He didn't answer right away, leading her into the kitchen where a fresh pot of coffee percolated. She declined a mug so he poured another for himself, bringing his current day's total to five, and added the cream at a deliberative pace.

"Am I supposed to ask twenty questions?" she said, not sounding all that patient.

"Sorry. The synapses should start firing with a few more sips."

"You found something, didn't you?"

He heard it again: that cold way she had of making a question sound like a statement.

"Yeah. But I'm not sure how much I should say about it."

Janice frowned, not liking that.

"There's more to be done," Rusty continued, setting down his mug. "At least that's what I've decided. I think you'd rather not know too many details. Not until it's over, anyway."

He expected some protest, but Janice seemed to intuit the unspoken warning. She nodded.

"So what do you want me to do?"

"I'd like you to stay on standby tonight. Keep your phone on."

She looked at him like he'd just told her to keep breathing.

"I'm gonna need a pickup," he explained. "It'll be somewhere near the boardwalk, so it would be good if you could keep yourself nearby. It'll definitely be late."

"Not a problem. I keep odd hours."

Rusty returned her grin as he silently toyed with the idea of laying out his plan in full. Janice was possessed of a sharp analytical mind, and part of him was curious to hear her take on it.

Another part felt like that would only be inviting additional worries for both of them. She might recoil in disgust or eagerly tell him to go for it; he just had no idea how to gauge a potential reaction from this woman. He wasn't sure if he was protecting her or himself by playing it close to the vest, and that was the most confounding part.

"Anything else you want to tell me?" she asked. "I didn't come over here just for that, did I?"

"Actually, I'm a little surprised you're still in town. Thought you had to be back in New York to deal with those nervous clients."

She stepped closer to him, smiling.

"Really thought I'd leave without saying goodbye? Does that sound like something I'd do?"

"Guess not. My head's been a little scrambled lately."

"So why don't you tell me what's in that scrambled head. Maybe there's something else you need from me, other than a pickup?"

"Here's the thing. I'm gonna be in one hell of a rush when the time comes. Might not be in any condition to drive, and I won't be able to wait around for a cab. Understand?"

She studied him for a moment, considering what he'd said.

"You found who's making the drugs. And now you've got something serious in mind."

"What's your idea of serious?"

"Something that might not involve the police. Something not necessarily legal."

Her arms were around his waist, almost seeming to pull an answer from him through friendly persuasion. He liked her touch a lot. But he wasn't sure what it meant.

"Is that what you think?" he asked. "Or what you want?"

"I told you what I want. Justice for my aunt."

"Nothing else?"

"Nothing else."

Rusty thought it would be nice to believe those words. It wouldn't make any difference in the long run. Wouldn't affect his actions one way or the other. He'd reached a decision to see this to the end, and that had nothing to do with satisfying anyone but himself.

"Don't say any more," she whispered. "Tell me about it later, if you want to."

"You must really trust my judgment. I'm not used to that."

"I think you understand how important this is to me. If

you've figured out a way to take care of it, that's all I need to know."

"So I guess you're not going to try to talk me out of anything crazy."

Instead of answering, Janice leaned in and kissed him. Just like that, the fire was back. Rusty had never known anyone to blow hot and cold with such sudden turns. It was like she was listening for something, a kind of coded confirmation telling her what she'd waited to hear.

Janice broke the kiss.

"You still haven't told me how you did that trick."

"Which one?" Rusty asked, playing dumb as his fingertips continued a languid southern foray toward the small of her back.

"You know which one, faker. With my card."

"Oh, that."

He quelled further inquiry with another kiss. Moving in tandem, they slowly repositioned each other across the linoleum, edging toward the staircase leading to the second floor.

"I hope you don't think you're getting any until I find out," Janice grinned.

"I thought we'd reached a tacit understanding that probably wasn't gonna happen."

"I agreed to no such thing."

Turning away from him with mock disappointment, she started ascending the carpeted stairs. Following her, Rusty watched as she unbuttoned her blouse and let it fall. He picked it up and inhaled her scent, finding it more pulse quickening than a dozen cups of Cafe du Monde's blend.

She turned right at the top of the stairs and walked to one of the guest bedrooms. Rusty had only come in here maybe once and didn't even remember what it looked like. A glance at the floral wallpaper and pink sheets covering a canopied double bed told him this used to be Janice's room. The room where she'd stay when living here while growing up, when things were bad at home. This is where she'd sleep and dream about places beyond Ocean City.

He was glad she'd chosen this room.

Sitting on the bed and unclasping her bra, Janice halted him with a look.

"That's close enough, magician. Let's hear it."

"Don't you know the trick doesn't mean anything once it's explained? As soon as you know how it works, it loses all value."

"You're stalling."

Rusty sat on the bed. He laid one hand on her bare shoulder and cupped a breast with the other, thumb and forefinger closing cozily around a pink nipple.

"No, I'm just looking out for your sense of wonder. That's a fragile thing, Janice. It's worth protecting."

"I'll risk it," she whispered, applying her hands to lifting his Fantasma T-shirt over his head, fingernails gently raking his chest.

"OK, I warned you. It's a basic trick any self-respecting magician should know, called 'Torn and Restored.' There must be a hundred variations to it, and they all operate on the same principle."

"And that would be?" she asked, unclasping his belt buckle.

"It's not *possible* to restore something to its original form after you've ripped it apart. So you leave it intact and switch out a dummy card, or dollar bill, or whatever it may be."

"I only gave you one of my business cards."

"You thought you did. I palmed another one while I was pouring you a drink."

Janice's hands stilled for a beat, the unbuckled belt dangling.

"Disappointingly simple, isn't it?" Rusty said, pulling back to look her in the eye.

"No," she answered, shaking her head with a new smile. "What matters is you trusted me enough to share the secret."

With that, she started kissing him again, and there was no thought of any further conversation.

Rusty forgot all about last night's hellish events and whatever tonight may hold as they finished undressing each other. In easy unison they rolled onto the bed, which squeaked as if annoyed to find itself being put to work after a long furlough.

They took their time with it, as before. Rusty felt utterly

rooted in the moment, tasting and slipping deep into Janice. Content to know her like this with no words or misinterpretations to get in the way. They'd done enough talking, and he'd done enough thinking.

As they found the rhythm, backs arching, he reflected that this was just how he used to relax in the hours before a big show at Caesars. It never failed.

Just as when launching any well-rendered illusion, the groundwork for tonight's main event had already been laid. Now all that remained was to raise the curtain and blow the audience out of their seats.

32.

Kenny Dixon lay sprawled on a stained and scratched La-Z-Boy in the living room of his tiny two-bedroom house on Gerar Street in West Ocean City. One of several dozen prefab units quickly erected on a remote plot of land fronting the bay (deemed undesirable by most prospective buyers thanks to a robustly fecal stench rising from massive formations of green algae), it had been Kenny's home for the past seven years.

Kenny knew he should feel at least somewhat grateful for being here right now. He was out on $400,000 bond after being formally charged with killing Thelma Garrett. Kenny had to put up the house, his truck, and his beloved Sea-Doo 200 Speedster motorboat in order to secure the bond from A-1 Bail Masters in upstate Linthicum. It was the only bond agency willing to consider his assets of significant worth as a hedge against the hefty sum.

Many voices in Ocean City had expressed outrage that Kenny made bail at all. None louder than the Worcester County prosecutor, who'd argued vehemently that the suspect was an obvious flight risk based on the fact that he'd been apprehended while trying to flee a tri-state manhunt.

The public defender had countered that Kenny wasn't trying to flee, he was simply seeking temporary shelter with his sister Laurene Cobb (née Dixon). Surely, the public defender argued, if Mr. Dixon truly wished to escape capture, the last place on earth he'd choose to hide out was the residence of his sole living blood relative. Where else would the police be apt to start looking for him?

To audible gasps in the courtroom, Judge Edgar Andrews had sided with this argument. He'd set the bail high enough to hopefully dissuade any renewed criticism of him being too soft on individuals suspected of violent crimes.

None of which made much difference to Kenny right now. He was out of the slam and sitting comfortably plastered in his own home.

An empty bottle of Jack Daniels lay on the faux wood floor. The impact of its drained contents, now swimming through Kenny's bloodstream, rendered him sufficiently supine to consider spending the night right here rather than stumble into his bedroom. Was there any advantage to moving, given how comfortable he already felt?

Before working out both sides of the argument in his bleary head, Kenny passed out.

It was 8:03 p.m.

An hour and ten minutes later, Kenny tried to reemerge from his boozy slumber. It was a difficult endeavor. He knew something was wrong, but he couldn't determine exactly what that might be. A disorienting lack of equilibrium made him feel like he was going to keel over.

But how could that be if he was lying down?

Opening his eyes, Kenny was deeply dismayed to see nothing but blackness. He blinked hard several times, and not a trace of light appeared. For an appalled moment he thought he'd literally drunk himself blind, then became aware that some kind of soft cloth was draped over his face.

He tried to lift his right arm to remove whatever was blocking his vision, but a new problem presented itself. Kenny's right arm was completely immobilized. He felt some kind of constraint at the wrist, both wrists. And then he realized his arms were pinioned in a position over his head.

His legs wouldn't move either. There was a similar kind of constriction keeping them bound together at the ankles. He tried kicking with all his might but couldn't budge an inch.

Kenny's breath started coming in ragged gasps. A wave of utter confusion washed over him. He had no idea what the hell was going on.

Then he heard the voice.

"Save your strength, Kenny. You're not going anywhere."

He almost had a coronary at the sound of the words. On instinct his arms attempted a protective lunge forward, only to remind him of his state of confinement.

"Who are you?" he managed to sputter, head thrashing from side to side trying to locate the source of the voice.

"Stop struggling," Rusty said calmly. "We're going to have a chat, you and me."

"Who the hell are you?!"

"I'm here on behalf of Thelma Garrett," Rusty continued. "She couldn't make it herself."

The name caught Dixon off guard. It rang familiar in an unpleasant way, but he could not immediately make an identification. Then it came to him.

"Look, I didn't kill that old lady. I'm going to trial and I'll beat it, just watch."

"Maybe you will. That's up to a jury. But you're going to get square with me first."

"Tell me who the fuck this is!"

"We've met before. I still got the bruise to remember you by."

Dixon started to speak but apparently thought better of it. Any memory he retained of jumping Rusty behind the Morbid Manor was sketchy at best. He'd essentially willed himself to blot out everything that happened after he broke back into the old woman's house to retrieve the prescription bottle he'd left during his botched robbery attempt.

"Listen to me, asshole. I don't know what you think you're doing, but you're messing with the wrong guy. I'll give you three seconds to get this shit off me or by Christ I'll …"

Thunk!

Kenny felt an almost imperceptible brush of wind against the side of his face, immediately followed by a heavy thud next to his left ear. He promptly stopped speaking.

"What the hell was that?"

"Are you really sure you want to know?" Rusty asked.

"Untie me, goddamnit!"

A moment of silence passed.

Thunk!

The same whoosh and thud, this one on the other side of his head. Kenny could feel something hard and flat pressed up against his left temple. He had a sudden intuition about what it might be, but rejected the thought as insane. Both arms and legs resumed pushing against their binds, to no effect other than to render him breathless after a minute of futile effort.

He felt the fabric against his face rising slowly as Rusty lifted the hood. A wash of bright light shone into his eyes, coming from a lamp a few feet away from which the shade had been removed. Blinking painfully, Dixon gradually gained focus.

The sight greeting his bloodshot orbs didn't make him feel any better.

He was trussed up against the kitchen wall, opposite the doorway leading into the living room. Looking down, he saw a black sash binding his ankles, the long end nailed into the floor with a thick spike. He couldn't see his hands in their conjoined position above his head but knew they had to be bound in a similar fashion.

Directly in front of him, on the far side of the kitchen, stood a tall man with long black hair and a demonically tapered goatee. Dressed all in black, he held in one hand the velvet hood he'd just removed from Kenny's head.

Something metallic flashed in his other hand. He raised it in a slow, deliberative motion, then launched it forward with a powerful overhand throw.

For a fraction of a moment Kenny saw the knife spinning toward him. It slammed into the wall with that same *thunk!*

Barely an inch wide of his right shoulder, the blade pierced deep into the lightweight balsa wood.

"Jesus Christ, what are you doing?!"

"I should warn you I'm a little out of practice. Haven't tried this routine in a long time, and it only stands to reason my aim isn't what it used to be. If I were you, I'd keep that in mind."

"Listen, you crazy fuck. I don't know what you want, but you better untie me right now!"

"Not until you tell me what I came to hear."

"And what's that?"

"A full confession for the murder of Thelma Garrett. I want to know about the drugs, and how they fit into your crime. You're going to tell me about Fade, how his operation works. I know a lot already but I want to hear your version. Then you're going to do exactly as I say. After that, I'll untie you."

"Why should I tell you anything?"

"Consider the situation you're in. And consider something else. This isn't a court and I'm not here to sentence you. I'll let the jury handle that, and you better believe I'll be keeping a very close eye on the trial. I'm here for answers, nothing more."

Kenny felt some slight comfort at those words. Whoever this guy was, he didn't come here to kill him, not if he planned to let the trial proceed. It was probably just some dumbass relative of the old lady looking to put a scare in him. The knives were pretty effective in that regard, but Kenny felt reasonably confident he wasn't facing any imminent peril.

"Go fuck yourself," he said. "I'll have your ass locked up for this. You're committing about five or six felonies right now, and don't think I won't call the cops. I'm an innocent man accused of a crime someone else committed, and I'll be damned if I let you push me around."

"Wrong answer, Kenny."

Taking the hood in his left hand, Rusty pulled it down over his own head. Then he raised his right arm again, gripping another throwing knife by the tip.

"Jesus, don't ..."

"You really need to learn the value of cooperating with me."

"Don't!"

Vision completely obscured by the hood, Rusty hurled the knife with all his strength.

This time Dixon felt like he had a lot more time to watch it flying across the room, end over end. It was going to hit him;

he knew it. He screamed even before the blade severed his right earlobe as it smashed into the wood.

The scream was brief, followed by a stunned silence. Kenny was in too much shock to register any pain, vision strobing in the glare of the lamp.

Rusty removed the hood and took an appraising look at his aim.

"Told you I wasn't as good as I used to be. Want to try again?"

"You cut my damn ear off!!"

"Nah, barely grazed you. Won't even need stitches, most likely. Are you ready to talk to me now?"

Finding his voice though a series of whimpers and moans, Kenny nodded with wholehearted consent. He started talking so fast and in such a marginally coherent jumble that Rusty had to slow him down and walk him through the whole narrative.

"Yeah, OK," Kenny said, returned to a partial state of calm now that it looked like no more sharp objects were going to be launched his way. "I broke into the house on Heron. Not to hurt anyone, just to lift a few things. She wasn't supposed to be there, man! I'd watched the place for days, always the same routine, and she wasn't supposed to be there!"

His voice cracked into a kind of plea, a mix of terror and maybe a little remorse.

"So she surprised you. And you killed her."

"No! I didn't touch her. I just … you know, maybe knocked her down so I could get the hell out of there. She was gonna call the cops. What else could I do?"

The note of falseness in that statement was so pure Rusty saw no need to challenge it. He redirected the course of his inquiry.

"You got high before you started tossing the place, right? In the bathroom."

"I always bump up before a job, sharpens the focus. So what?"

"I'm tossing you a lifeline, Kenny. I'm saying you were out of your mind on those salts when Thelma walked in on you. I'm saying you might not have even known what you were doing when you killed her. It's the best defense you've got. You might want to remember it."

"I didn't kill her!" Dixon screamed with such raw force Rusty thought he was genuinely trying to make himself believe it.

"Tell me about the drugs. You got them from Fade, right?"

This second mention of the dealer's name made Kenny tilt his head as if pondering what to say. Then he nodded.

"I was on the payroll, man. One of his runners, slinging bags around town."

"More details."

"I needed cash, that's all. I'd been dealing for a few weeks, hitting some of the bars. Nothing too close to downtown, too much heat. But some of the joints on the boardwalk were OK. Fade always got the word out, where to sell and where to avoid."

"Let me guess. You started sampling and got hooked."

Kenny shrugged.

"Everyone dips into the stash a little. It's part of the game. I didn't know what the shit was like until I'd tried it. Then I just wanted more."

"Fade says there aren't any drugs at the pad on Ninth Street. Is that right?"

"Wouldn't know. Never went in that place. I always made my re-ups at the stash house."

Rusty stepped closer, finally hearing what he came for.

"And where's that?"

Dixon started to speak but stopped short, thinking better of it.

"You got bigger worries right now than spilling on this, Kenny. I'll make it easy on you. The drugs are stashed in the Morbid Manor, aren't they?"

Kenny didn't respond right away. He seemed to be calculating the wisdom of divulging too much, as if he'd been a model of circumspection already. Then his head nodded slowly.

"You had to go back to Thelma's house because you left your prescription bottle there. Needed to have a mixer, and besides, your name was still partially there on the label. So you got the bottle but you forgot about the corner bag you dropped when she walked in on you. You went from there to the Manor because you needed to score and the burglary was a bust. No cash, so you figured you'd steal right from the source."

A long pause as some mental clouds parted in Kenny's head. He looked at Rusty with a new understanding.

"You're the asshole who followed me that night."

Rusty didn't reply.

"Shit, I'd almost forgotten about that. I was still pretty ripped at the time."

So ripped you forgot about killing an old woman, Rusty almost said. But since that seemed practically a moot point at the moment, he continued with, "What's Fade's real name?"

"How should I know? Calls himself Fade is all. Bastard probably doesn't have a real name."

"How much product is still around?"

"Dude's sitting on a damn mountain. That's why I figured he could afford to let his soldiers have a taste every now and then."

Rusty took a seat in a folding chair next to the kitchen table. He needed a moment to think, still undecided about what to do with this lowlife. He'd extracted enough information to progress with tonight's plan—but that didn't necessarily mean he'd inflicted sufficient payback on Kenny Dixon.

What to do? Just let him go and trust the system to get it right this time?

"Hey, I answered all your questions," Kenny whined. "Are you gonna untie me or what?"

"Shut up, I'm thinking."

After another prolonged pause, Rusty nodded. There were a thousand ways he could punish Dixon right now, but none of them would do anything for Ms. Garrett. He'd give the jury a shot. And, as he'd promised, he would be keeping a very close watch on their verdict.

Rusty stood from the chair and walked over to Kenny.

"Where's your phone?"

"What for?"

"Need you to make a call, then I'll let you go. Where is it?

"Hell, I don't know. Somewhere on the coffee table, probably."

Rusty walked into the living room and rummaged through a pile of debris on a battered wooden table next to the La-Z-Boy. Underneath a cheese-encrusted pizza box he found a chipped Motorola flip phone. He took it back into the kitchen.

"Now listen very carefully. In a few minutes you're going to dial Fade's cell phone."

"I don't know the number."

"You better hope that's a lie, Kenny. Because otherwise it's bad luck for you."

He left it at that. Kenny Dixon nodded.

"OK, I know it."

"That's what I thought. You're going to call and tell him exactly what I tell you to tell him. No fucking games or I swear to God that cut on your ear's getting a whole lot deeper."

"I believe you."

"Good."

"Give me the phone."

"Not just yet. First we're going to practice a few times to make sure you get it right."

33.

If anyone was milling about the Ocean City amusement pier at two o'clock that night, they might have seen a man striding across its weathered planks with purpose. They might have noted his slight frame and round eyeglasses. Someone might also note the small valise he carried close to his chest in a protective pose like that of a mother holding a newborn.

But aside from a few gulls circling the pier in search of some stay kernels of popcorn ripe for scavenging, there was not a soul out at this late hour. And so Fade felt confident no one witnessed him make his way to the pier's terminus, where the Morbid Manor held its grim sentinel.

Pausing by the wrought-iron gate, Fade set the valise down by his feet. He pulled out his phone and dialed.

Tampa Nate answered on the first ring.

"I'm out front," Fade said. "You're clear to approach. No sign of anyone."

"No one here either," Tampa Nate replied. He was sitting at the wheel of the cargo van with the engine running, six blocks away. Parked in the same lot where Rusty had followed Kenny Dixon. His was the only vehicle in sight.

"Think he'll show?" Nate asked.

"Undoubtedly. He thinks he's in an enviable position for setting terms."

"Dude's a fucking tweaker, and he's looking at life. Never should have taken the call."

Fade shook his head, awed by what a weak sister his musclebound associate could be in the face of unforeseen developments.

"I told you, there's no advantage to be gained by spurning the offer. I sincerely doubt Kenny intends to follow through on his threat, but the best way to find out is to meet in person. We had to stop by here regardless, you'll recall."

"I still say we go in together," Tampa Nate urged. "Dude might be in there ready to jump you. Don't forget what he did to that old lady."

"Why should he threaten me?" Fade said, glancing down at the valise. "I've agreed to his terms."

"Sure, as far as he knows. I still don't like it."

"You worry too much. I'm not without protection."

"Right."

"Back the van up to the entrance, as close as you can get. If I'm not out with the first load in ten minutes, you know what to do."

"Copy that."

They ended the phone call. Fade picked up the valise and proceeded toward the Morbid Manor.

Circling to the back of the building, down the narrow passage bordered by the metal railing, he paused next to a boarded-up window on the first floor. Securing the valise under his left arm, he used his left hand to press against one of the vertical planks of wood that was part of the building's exterior.

The lower half of the plank gave way, rotating on a hinge, and Fade squatted down to squeeze through the opening. It was a tight aperture, and he had to set down the valise again to get himself securely inside. Then he reached out and grabbed it, pulling the plank closed behind him.

If he hadn't been in so much of a hurry, he might have noticed one of the shadows behind the Manor shift in the darkness. Rising to a taper the height of a man, the shadow remained in place until Fade was inside the building and the plank returned to its original position.

Then the shadow moved.

• • •

Tampa Nate hung up, setting down the phone on the van's dashboard. He lit a Kent 100 and exhaled a long plume of smoke out the open window. Fade always complained about the smell of smoke in the van. It was Nate's goddamn vehicle, bought with his own money and registered in his name, but he acquiesced on this small point merely to avoid hearing Fade bitch. They had a lot of driving ahead of them.

Try as he might, Tampa Nate couldn't relax. He'd been fairly wound up ever since the phone call from Kenny Dixon chimed in on Fade's cell a little over four hours ago. Nate had cautioned him not to answer it. What could that scumbag Dixon have to say that was of any relevance to them at this point?

But Fade, with typical bullheadedness, had insisted on taking the call. The conversation turned out to be brief, and by the time it ended Fade wore an expression Tampa Nate had never quite seen before. Speaking in such a way as to suggest he was suppressing an outburst, he explained the terms of the "deal" Dixon had just laid out.

Ten thousand dollars, cash. Delivered in person to the Morbid Manor. Tonight, two o'clock sharp.

There was no room for negotiation, Dixon had explained. This was strictly take it or leave it. In exchange for the ten large, he would agree to turn down an offer extended to him from the county prosecutor's office this very afternoon. The offer was simple: all Kenny had to do was sell out Fade as the man behind the rash of tainted drugs that had blighted Ocean City for the past month.

Apparently the police warning broadcast on the news last night made a bigger impression than they realized. That image of the snake stamped on the torn corner of a baggie had crystallized the recent crime wave in a way the residents of Ocean City could understand and react to on an emotional level. Calls to the OCPD and the mayor's office had tripled over the past twenty-four hours, with outraged citizens demanding to know what measures were being taken to eradicate the drug scourge that had polluted their town.

Listening to Kenny Dixon explain this in his crude four-lettered fashion, it occurred to Fade that the very type of subliminal message he knew the Ouroboros symbol would send to prospective buyers was having a similar effect on the law-abiding populous. It gave them something simple and concrete, a visual prop on which to focus their need to see order restored.

Fade was the living, breathing surrogate for the symbol. The man behind the green serpent. He was the one whose head the county prosecutor wanted on a pike. That's what Kenny Dixon had conveyed over the phone. Oh sure, Kenny would still go down for snuffing the old lady. No plea deal in the world would buy him a ticket out of that rap. But the prosecutor's office had promised to bump the charge down to manslaughter if Kenny gave them access to whoever was producing the tainted narcotics.

So Fade had a choice: pay up or take the rap. With the Feds' recent classification of bath salts as a Schedule I substance, the minimum sentence for distribution of as little as a few grams was ten years. With the kind of weight Fade was moving, he'd be going away for a very long time.

Fade didn't argue or try to change Dixon's addled mind. He said he'd be there with the cash, and then he ended the call.

Immediately after getting off the phone and repeating the terms to Tampa Nate, who'd reacted with predictable outrage, Fade explained there was no alternative but to go along with it. They had to swing by the Manor tonight anyway, to pick up the stash before leaving town.

Fade hadn't waited around here one extra day just to leave all that good product behind because of some misbegotten power play from the likes of Kenny Dixon.

Tampa Nate argued vehemently against the plan. For Christ's sake, they should just go grab the shit and leave town as soon as it got quiet enough on the pier to slip inside the Manor without being detected. Screw waiting around until the wee hours, eleven or so should do fine. And why kiss off all that cash?

Fade was not to be persuaded. Which came as no surprise, since he'd never allowed Nate to change his mind on any subject for as long as they'd known each other. Fade's view was that ten grand was an acceptable cost for buying Dixon's silence. It was barely a day's take, especially when they started hitting those Florida resort towns where the junkies practically outnumbered the straight citizens.

When Tampa Nate asked why the hell he believed Kenny would honor the agreement, Fade said the answer was simple. Dixon was lying; he had no intention of cooperating with the prosecutor. Once he got the money he'd leave town immediately. The payoff was some much needed getaway cash. The cops would pick him up just as surely as they had before, but the two cookers would be several states southward by that point. Kenny could blab all he wanted and it wouldn't make a whit of difference.

Besides, Fade assured Tampa Nate he wouldn't be showing up with nothing but a sack of cash and his dick in his hands. To emphasize the point, he'd produced a handgun from a cabinet in his desk. A Charter Arms .44 Special Bulldog Pug, it fit neatly in the pocket of his leather jacket.

Seeing the gun had the opposite of a calming effect on Tampa Nate. He didn't trust Fade to handle a firearm with any more proficiency than he'd be apt to display in the weight room. But there was no point in arguing, so he just tried to feel grateful for the fact that they were finally clearing out of here.

They'd locked the front door of the bungalow, having already loaded all the cooking equipment into the van and giving the lab room a thorough spraying of ammonia just for safety. Then they wiped the whole place for prints, turned out the lights, and pulled away.

All that went down a few hours ago. Now Tampa Nate fired the van's engine and turned right out of the lot, onto the abandoned boardwalk. He kept his speed low, headlamps off, taking the uneven surface with caution. Driving on the boards or the pier at any time of day or night was prohibited except for vehicles carrying police, firefighters, lifeguards or municipal contractors.

Nate wasn't too worried about it. The buildings within immediate visibility were all businesses shuttered for the season. The closest residential units likely to be inhabited were at least two blocks west, and the odds of someone spotting him at this hour seemed dim enough. Anyway, it had to be done.

Making a left turn onto the amusement pier, Nate continued slowly until the Morbid Manor stood no more than twenty feet ahead. He executed a three-point turn and backed up as close as he could get without touching the wrought-iron gate, then hopped out and opened the van's rear double doors.

With any luck Fade would emerge momentarily, carrying the first load and announcing all had gone according to plan with Dixon. From there, shouldn't take the two of them more than a half-dozen trips to transport the entire stash into the van. Then it was bye-bye Ocean City and hello to whatever came next, which by definition had to be an improvement in Nate's eyes.

The idea of driving hundreds of miles across multiple state lines with enough product and cooking implements to send both of them away for decades didn't give him much comfort. In fact, it scared the hell out of him. But right now he'd be satisfied just to get moving and put this worthless town in his rearview for good.

Jim Biddison awoke to the sound of his baby daughter crying. Her high-pitched wails burrowed into his dreaming mind, which interpreted them as sirens. He saw himself chasing after something he could not identify, with a dying victim and a murderous perp shrouded maddeningly beyond his power to intervene.

Then he felt his wife's small fist pounding his shoulder, and his eyes fluttered open. Kim held Danielle close to her breast, trying to calm the hysterical infant.

"For God's sake, Jim! What's going on out there?"

He had no immediate answer, sputtering out an incoherent growl. The flashing red and blue lights on their bedroom ceiling confused him. It made no sense to see them here, and for a disorienting moment he felt himself pulled back into the queasy unreality of his dream pursuit.

Swinging heavy legs off the bed, Biddison crossed the

bedroom in three quick paces. He lifted the mini blinds covering the room's sole window with a clumsy hand, still only half awake, and looked out into the night.

An OCPD prowl car sat in the driveway below, cherry tops ablaze. Another vehicle, unmarked, was just pulling in behind it. Jim barely discerned the shape of a uniformed patrolman disappearing from view. A heartbeat later, he heard the doorbell.

"What's happening?" Kim asked with alarm as she held the squalling baby closer to her chest.

"I don't know, honey." Jim lumbered into a robe and a pair of slippers. "I'm sure everything's fine, just stay here."

He closed the bedroom door softly and turned on a hall light to make his way downstairs. Kim got out of bed and carried Danielle to the window.

By the time Jim reached the front door, the patrolman outside had started using a nightstick to rap on it. Biddison undid the double bolts and yanked it open hard to see patrolman Brad Neely take a step back with a startled look on his face.

"Neely," Jim uttered, raising a hand to shield his eyes from the blinding colored lights. "What the fuck are you doing here?"

"Sorry, Lieutenant. Dispatch sent me over, said to double-time it."

"Why?"

"Um, seems there's a situation going on …"

Officer Neely tripped over his tongue trying to get the words out. Jim was very close to choking an explanation out of him when he saw Detective Theo Taylor approaching from the unmarked.

"Theo! What the hell?"

Taylor rolled back his shoulders in a deflective motion.

"Tried calling you five times, Jim. Couldn't get through."

"Phones are off. The baby's sick, needs her sleep. What's up?"

"We got a call at central."

Neely took a few more steps back as the detective positioned himself to face Biddison.

"It was …" Taylor paused for a fraction of a second. "It was a threat, Jim."

"A threat."

"Made against you personally."

Any traces of fog instantly evaporated from Jim's head.

"From the top, all of it."

"Came in less than fifteen minutes ago. Claudia in dispatch took it. Male caller, didn't identify himself. Demanded to speak to you directly."

"Why?"

"Said he saw you on TV last night. Guy was furious, raving about the green serpent. Said he was gonna come right to the station and waste the pig who put out the warning."

Jim's heart rate slowed just a bit from its elevated pitch.

"Well, I guess something like this might've been expected. Some tweaker sees me on the tube, thinks I'm ruining the party."

"It's more serious than that. When he heard you weren't on duty he said it didn't matter. Said he knows where you live and he'd do it here. Then he hung up. Might be a crank, but still …"

"What?"

"He did know the address. Claudia kept him chatting long enough to cough it up."

Biddison gazed out at the quiet darkened street, feeling a chill. All his neighbors had turned in for the night hours before, no illumination other than a street lamp or two.

"How long ago?"

"Like I said, can't be more than ten or twelve minutes. Claudia had someone grab me at my desk while she was still on the call. Soon as it ended I told her to send over the closest unit and I hit the road. A backup prowler's on the way."

"Thanks, Theo."

"Kim and the baby can stay at our place tonight, just to be safe. Linda's more than happy to have them."

"Yeah, thanks," Biddison repeated, his initial alarm turning into a kind of rage he knew would require tremendous focus not to unleash on the wrong person. Like that incompetent dimwit Brad Neely, who was making a big show of trampling the freshly sodded front lawn with his nightstick in hand as if expecting an army of gangbangers to storm the place any minute.

"Was Claudia able to trace the number?"

Taylor nodded.

"Residential line, address on Ninth and Marlin. That's my next stop."

"I'm coming with you. Give me two minutes to get the girls together."

34.

It was pitch dark inside the Manor. Fade stood in the last room visitors would walk through, when the attraction was still open, before being chased out the exit by a ghoul wielding a chainsaw. Despite the gloom, he was able to get his bearings rather easily. Using a flashlight app that turned his cell phone screen into a small lamp, he had enough visibility to see at least five feet in front of him.

Measuring his steps carefully, he navigated a narrow walkway in reverse, passing through a number of showrooms featuring macabre set pieces of one sort or another: A sawmill with a massive circular blade above a table on which a distressingly lifelike wooden maiden usually lay. A torture chamber filled with scattered bones and an emaciated figure stretched out on the rack. A graveyard covered with fake moss and cardboard tombstones painted to glow underneath tracks of black lights drilled into the ceiling.

All these props lay dark and dormant, more frightening now than they appeared when lit and animated for the entertainment of paying guests.

Fade moved quickly through each room, having made the trek in similarly low-lit conditions many times before.

It had been his idea to use the Manor as a stash house, and he still had to congratulate himself on the brainstorm. In a few days' time, nothing would be left. The very boards underneath his feet and the entire structure they supported would be razed by a wrecking ball. Just like that, any possible trace of evidence would be turned into rubble and carted off to some landfill like it never even existed. Fade could only hope he and Nate would be able to find similarly convenient places to store the product as they moved southward and set up shop in any number of small towns along the way.

It took him a solid five minutes to traverse the entire two-story walkway that led to the house's largest room, a foyer of sorts on the ground floor just inside the front entrance. This was where guests would congregate after buying their tickets until some Manor employee in a death's head mask nudged them on their journey into the house of horrors.

The foyer was musty, smelling of mold and aged wood. Advancing to the corner opposite the chained front door, Fade set down the valise and stood still for a moment, listening. He felt certain someone else was in the room with him, but a sweep with the cell phone's LED glow revealed no one.

"Kenny?" he said in a hushed tone. "Are you in here?"

He thought he heard a quiet chuckle, but it might have been the wind pressing against the creaky boards of the Manor's front wall. He called out for Dixon again and got no reply.

Fade was positive he could hear breathing. It sounded to be less than a few feet away, but the direction of its source was hard to identify.

"If you're here, speak up!"

"I'm here."

Fade almost dropped his phone. The voice seemed to materialize from an empty spot where he'd shone the light just seconds before. It definitely didn't belong to Kenny Dixon.

Fade turned around jerkily and pointed his phone in the direction from which the voice had spoken.

A tall hooded figure sat in a high-backed chair in the far corner of the room. Dressed in black, from steel-toed leather boots all the way to the hood drawn over his head.

"Kenny couldn't make it," Rusty said, face hidden beneath the hood. "Sent me in his place."

He gave Fade a moment to gather himself. The chair he occupied was a phony antique, made of cheap plywood in a fairly convincing Victorian style, one of the Manor's many breakaway props. Twin posts on either side of the chair's high back were topped with grinning skulls.

"I came to meet someone for a simple exchange," Fade said. "If that person chose not to show, I'll be on my way."

"You're not going anywhere. Not just yet."

Now Fade recognized the voice, confirming his suspicion. He turned off his phone, figuring he could use the darkness to his advantage as well.

"How'd you like that taste?"

"It was a hoot. Biggest buzz I've had in a while. I owe you one."

"I'm glad you see it that way. After all, you can't fault me. I had a stranger in my house, armed with who knows what kind of hostile intent. Every man has a right to protect himself."

Rusty stood. Quickly turning his phone back on, Fade retreated a step, tensing. Waiting for an aggressive move that would spur him to pull the .44 from his coat pocket. He didn't want to do that before getting a better handle on the situation.

"I'm impressed you're back on your feet so soon."

The hooded figure took a few steps across the room. Fade tracked his progress with the LED light, keeping him visible.

Rusty stopped next to a low table holding more than two dozen 12-ounce ziplock bags.

"Nice stash. I'm surprised you've got so much inventory on hand, the way you've been moving the salts."

"I get carried away with the cook sometimes," Fade shrugged. "Once the process takes hold of me, it can be hard to stop."

"I know exactly what you mean."

"So what do you want? Did you come to steal my drugs, or collect whatever you think I brought for Kenny Dixon?"

He shone the phone's light over toward the corner where he'd first entered the foyer. The leather valise sat on the floor.

"There it is. Take it."

"Ten grand, right?" Rusty asked.

"That's the figure I agreed to on the phone. You must know that, if this ludicrous plan was your idea."

"Can't be too ludicrous. It convinced you to show up."

"Let's admit it strains credulity to think the county prosecutor would reduce a high-profile murder charge just for some intel about my practices. But stranger things have happened. I've concluded the Ouroboros has left quite a dent on the collective imagination of this town, such as it is."

"So you figured it was worth a sack full of bills, just for some peace of mind."

"Spare change. A minor business expense to mollify a disgruntled former employee."

"Fair enough," Rusty conceded. "You're getting away cheap, if you take Dixon at his word. Must really trust the guy to think he'll clam for ten large."

"There was no sense in trying to haggle. It'll teach me to be more rigorous in screening potential runners from now on."

He stepped closer to Rusty, feeling ever more confident about the situation.

"But something tells me Kenny's never going to see that payday. I don't know how you convinced him to make the call, but your methods must have been persuasive."

Rusty decided there was no need to maintain the front of being in collusion with Dixon anymore. It had worked in getting Fade to appear, and that was all he wanted.

"You can relax. That fucking worm Dixon has no intention of talking to the prosecutor, even if an offer had been made in the first place. He actually thinks he's going to walk on the charge. That's how much your shit's fried his brain."

Fade nodded, glad this subterfuge had come to an end.

"So pick up the money and leave. I'll do the same with my product."

He was disturbed to see the hooded man make no move for the valise, or even look at it.

"Why'd you add those extra elements to the mix?" Rusty asked. "The bonding agent in particular."

Fade nodded with surprise at the question's accuracy, still not pulling the gun.

"No great mystery. Sephinordome-H is an extremely reliable

bonding agent. I should know, it's the result of my own sweat, more than two years' worth. Not that chemists get rewarded for that kind of innovation at a company like Tilly. It's back to the hive with the rest of the worker bees, with a pat on the head for keeping the pipeline humming."

"That's what this is about? You're cooking up lethal drugs with one of their chemicals because you couldn't get a fucking promotion?"

"Woefully scarce job openings exist for people with my skill set right now. Tilly let me go, and I took something with me that I have every right to claim. I've found a new outlet for employing my knowledge. It strikes me as eminently fair that I use Sephinordome-H as part of the process."

"What about the extra dose of meth? Just for a bigger high, and to make it more addictive?"

"It's a buyer's market, friend. People all over the place are making salts in their bathtubs, or trying. Every cooker needs to distinguish his product in some way or another. It occurred to me that upping the fuel base with some meth was a surefire way to stand out in the marketplace."

Rusty took a slow half step toward Fade.

"And if it turns people into fucking psychopaths, that's just too bad. Right?"

Both men froze at the sound of heavy footsteps from above. A shimmer of white light flashed from the second floor landing.

"The odds aren't getting any better for you," Fade shrugged. "Should've taken your little payday and walked. I'm not sure I can control what happens from here."

Each rickety stair cried a shrill warning as Tampa Nate's weighty frame descended from the second floor, using his own cell phone to light the way. Stepping into the foyer, he appraised the situation with his customary command of the obvious.

"That ain't Dixon."

"It's all right," Fade assured him. "This doesn't need to get ugly. The agreement with our friend here stands, just as if he were Kenny himself."

"What's with the hood?" Nate asked.

"Fashion statement," Rusty replied. "I was wondering when you'd show up. Now we can get started."

Taking two rapid steps to the front door, he pulled a chain he'd rigged near the jamb earlier tonight. The door flew open with a groan. A bolt of cold air blew into the room riding a wide patch of brilliant moonlight.

"Fuck you doing?" Nate demanded with as much unease as anger.

Fade's hand tightened on the pistol inside his jacket but he refrained from bringing it out, wanting to see where this was going.

"Relax, guys," Rusty said calmly. He pointed toward the open front door, through which the rear of the parked van was visible just beyond the Manor's gate.

"Thought I'd make it easier for you to move all that product. We don't want to spend any more time in this scary place than necessary, do we?"

Theo Taylor's champagne Crown Vic pulled up to the curb in front of the bungalow on Ninth Street. Biddison jumped out without waiting for it to come to a complete stop.

Before leaving his house, he'd gently ushered a bewildered Kim and a still-screaming Danielle into Officer Neely's patrol car and told him to drive them to Taylor's house on Seabass Lane. The tone in which he gave the instruction made it clear he was holding Neely personally responsible for the safety of his wife and child.

Another OCPD prowler had arrived by then. Detective Taylor told the two officers inside to park down the street and monitor Biddison's house. Anyone who set foot on or even came near the property was to be taken in for questioning.

"Looks empty," Taylor now said, walking up the driveway to join Jim by the bungalow's stoop. All the lights were out, no vehicles parked in front.

Jim reached for the doorknob, figuring it was sure to be locked and more than prepared to kick it in without the legal support of a warrant.

He was surprised to see the door inch open at his touch.

Biddison and Taylor traded a look, both reaching for their service arms. Jim pushed the door open further and quickly stepped inside, gun raised.

"Police. Anyone in here?"

He stepped carefully across the hardwood floor of the front room, aided by some moonglow coming through an east-facing window. Theo located a light switch near the door and flicked it on.

The sight that greeted Jim's eyes startled him so badly it was a minor miracle he didn't discharge his weapon by accident.

Sprawled along the couch was a woman's body, severed in two at the waist. The half second required for the policemen to realize she wasn't real seemed much longer to both of them. A stream of red confetti signifying blood dangled from the narrow gap separating the wooden mannequin's two halves, spilling over the couch and onto the floor.

"Well, shit," Taylor said under his breath.

Jim took a step closer, noticing the small red object under his left foot too late to avoid stepping on it. A piercing squeak broke the stillness as a two-inch rubber ball compacted beneath his weight.

The wooden body on the couch jerked upward in two directions, both halves pulled roughly apart as if by an invisible hand. A spray of red confetti erupted soundlessly from the gap, floating briefly in the air before slowly falling.

"What the *fuck*?" Taylor barked, gripping his sidearm tightly.

Biddison didn't answer, still tensed and waiting for the next shock. Half expecting some kind of explosive device to detonate.

Three seconds passed, nothing audible except the two men's constricted breathing. Five seconds, and only more stillness.

Jim relaxed just slightly and glanced over his shoulder at Taylor, whose face was starting to regain some color.

Kneeling down, Biddison picked up the flattened red ball beneath his foot. Running his fingers over the surface, he saw it was attached to a length of fishing wire that stretched tautly all the way to the couch.

"Some kind of trip wire. Rigged to pull that … thing apart."

"Sure," Theo nodded humorlessly. "Why not?"

Moving closer to the couch, Jim saw something in the gap separating the woman's legs and torso. It was a cardboard placard, obscured behind the body until he'd unwittingly stepped on the ball and set off the makeshift dissection.

Painted on the placard in crude lettering were the words:

HEY PIG—BET U DON'T KNOW WHERE I CAME FROM! HAHAHAHA!

"I'll be damned," Taylor said, stepping forward for a better look. Jim was already moving toward the other end of the bungalow, firearm at the ready.

It took him less than two minutes to canvass the rest of the place—kitchen, bathroom, and one of two back bedrooms. All were empty, filled with what looked like impeccably well-ordered rental property furniture.

He noticed a high-tech alarm system drilled into the wall by the door to the second bedroom, and tried the knob with heightened interest. It was locked, but two heavy kicks opened it easily enough. Jim stepped inside cautiously and turned on a light.

The room was as immaculate as the rest of the bungalow, but a powerful scent of ammonia hung heavily enough in the cloying air to make his eyes water. Some great effort had been recently made to wipe away the traces of whatever happened in here.

Back in the large front room, he found Theo still looking at the inanimate body on the couch with bemusement.

"Christ, Jim. What kind of nutbar are we dealing with?"

Biddison stepped around for another inspection. He lowered himself to a crouch. Though obviously fake when viewed from up close, the severed woman unnerved him, her painted eyes and mouth stretched wide with soundless terror.

"I know where you came from, honey," Jim muttered,

reading the placard again and feeling a sliver of recognition light up inside his head.

Sheathing his gun in its holster, he strode to the door.

"Where we going?" Detective Taylor asked.

Jim didn't answer, already outside and moving for the car.

35.

Tampa Nate carried four more ziplock bags through the Manor's front gate toward the parked van, the bags stacked vertically on top of each other. He wasn't happy, and grumbled his discontent even though no one was around to hear him.

Nate added the bags onto a pile already filling one side of the rear cargo space. For the last six minutes, he'd followed Fade's precise instructions on how to load up the stash in such a way as to secure the cooking equipment so that nothing would break during the drive.

It was a tight fit, but workable.

Growing more frustrated by the minute, Nate decided he'd held his tongue long enough. Encountering last night's visitor here at the Manor came as a nasty jolt. He never expected to see that guy again, and couldn't imagine how anything good might come of them crossing paths. If the situation were reversed, and Nate was the one who'd suffered the effects of a monster dose forced into his vein, he'd sure as hell be looking to dish out some hurt.

Inexplicably, Fade assured him tonight's deal remained intact: hand off the cash, collect the drugs, and make southbound tracks out of Ocean City. None of it made sense to Tampa Nate.

Fade now approached with two more bags, handing them over for stowage in the van.

"This has gone quicker than I thought. We should really thank our friend for getting that door open."

"What's he doing in there?"

"Says he wants to stay until we're loaded so we can all leave knowing the deal is done. No loose ends, so to speak. I have to salute his sense of decorum."

"Still haven't told me why he's here," Nate fumed between clenched teeth.

"Calm down. He's a surrogate for Dixon, that's all. Nothing's changed."

"The hell you say. We're supposed to trust this guy after last night?"

"Why not? For all he knows, this is easy money. He's thinks he's walking away with ten grand."

"Is he?"

"What do you think?"

The question sounded rhetorical to Nate's ear, and Fade confirmed that by withdrawing the .44 Bulldog from the inside lining of his jacket.

"Jesus," Nate sighed, plagued by a renewed sense of certainty that going into business with this warped little bastard ranked among the worst decisions he'd ever made. Hell, leaving Florida was a mistake from the get-go.

"I'm going back for the last two bags," Fade said, "and the money. Start the engine. This won't take long."

Nate shook his head in weary disgust. Things had gotten all out of whack. He wasn't exactly thrilled about injecting the guy with what could have been a lethal shot last night, but at least that didn't qualify as straight-up murder.

"Forget it," he said. "Let's just bail."

Fade's placid expression turned to one resembling amazement.

"And allow that cretin to fleece us of what we've earned with our own sweat? I don't think so."

"You said it's chump change, right? Just a minor business expense?"

"That was before I knew whose pocket it was going into."

"What fuckin' difference does that make?"

Dismissing the question as unfit for a reply, Fade slid the gun into an outside pocket for easier access.

"Just start the van."

He turned away and started walking back to the Morbid Manor. Watching him disappear through the open doorway, Nate nodded with a feeling of tired resignation. Maybe just showing the gun would prove sufficient for liberating the cash. What did it really matter to him anyway, as long as they were leaving?

Rusty stood in the Manor's foyer as Fade reentered. He'd positioned himself in the same spot as the process of moving the stash unfolded, off to one side and saying little.

He now watched Fade move to the table holding the last two ziplock bags. Both bags had been sliced open by Rusty a moment ago, powder spilling all over the table and making tiny foothills on the floor.

Fade noticed it but said nothing. Instead he turned to face Rusty, the gun held at waist level.

"I told you before, you should have left while the offer was still in your favor."

The .44 didn't surprise Rusty. He figured Fade was too much of a coward to come here unarmed, regardless of who he thought was waiting to collect the money. The man's discomfort at brandishing a weapon was palpable.

But even a nervous shooter could pull off a kill shot at this range.

"Just curious," Rusty asked. "Were you planning to use that if it was Dixon who'd showed up?"

"Doubtful," Fade replied. "Risky putting a bullet in someone with such a prominent profile in this community. Even if the authorities welcomed being spared the expense of a trial, eliminating Kenny would attract too much attention."

He took a step closer, the muzzle pointed at Rusty's midsection.

"You, on the other hand. I'm guessing you're eminently disposable."

Sure I am. I've been as good as dead for a year.

Having anticipated the need for a distraction, Rusty now employed one. The fingers of his right hand flipped a switch strapped to his palm. In a split second, the whole room transformed itself with an explosion of searingly intense light.

A flaming torch arose instantly, turning Rusty's hand into a spitting ball of fire fifteen inches in diameter. Known in the trade as the "Mephistopheles Electronic Special," it was strapped to his wrists and concealed beneath his jacket sleeve. Two AA batteries, some flash cotton and lighter fluid were required to create the effect.

Spraying tiny embers as it assumed full ignition, Rusty held the torch in front of him far enough to avoid being scorched.

Fade reacted with blinded confusion. Using one arm to shield his eyes, he squeezed the .44's trigger and pulled off a shot.

It sailed a good yard to the right of where Rusty stood.

He didn't have time to get off a second shot. Rusty rolled across the creaky wooden floor in a somersault, careening into Fade with all his body weight. The impact was like being hit by a battering ram, driving the smaller man off his feet.

Fade held onto the gun as he went down, firing another shot.

Then Rusty was on top of him, knees pinning his shoulders to the floor. Easily twisting the .44 away with his left hand, his right keeping the torch aloft, he tossed the gun into a darkened corner.

He reached down to grip Fade by the collar and dragged him across the floor. Fade's glasses had been knocked off and he kicked and squirmed but failed to free himself from the strong hand clutching him.

With an upward yank, the cooker's chin was brought level with the pile of crystals overflowing from the sliced bags on the table. Rusty lowered the torch close, watching with grim satisfaction as he fumbled like a mole tossed rudely into the sunlight.

In panic, Fade reacted as if Rusty was going to push his face directly into the flames.

"No! No!"

But Rusty didn't intend to burn him. Twisting Fade's head and squeezing pressure points at the base of his neck, he buried him nose-deep in the salts.

"Breath in nice and deep," he commanded. "We want to make sure you get a proper dose."

Fade's whole body shuddered with a series of hacking coughs. Rusty lifted his head briefly to prevent total suffocation. Handfuls of yellowish grains were smeared all across the cooker's nose and chin.

"Please," Fade gagged, his voice reduced to a strangled whine. "I'll pay you …"

The sound of his high-pitched wheedling only stoked Rusty's anger. He shoved Fade down into the salts again, pushing harder on his neck.

"Oh, no. You haven't had nearly enough yet. It takes a greater amount to enter the bloodstream though insufflation than injection with a needle. But you know that."

Trying to thrash away from the pile, Fade seemed to realize he was lost. With a shudder his body went slack. His lungs and sinuses filled deeply. No way to avoid inhaling great gulps of powder.

Figuring he'd had enough, Rusty jerked him upright and shoved him against a wall, holding the torch close.

"Now … what?" Fade managed to articulate, his mouth twisting into a crooked grin that told Rusty the first wave was already hitting him.

"We wait. Won't be long."

Fade had stopped resisting, bodily movements limited to a few desultory twitches.

"That's right, go with it. You're gonna love the way this shit turns on you."

Two minutes passed, Rusty pinning Fade to the wall with one hand and monitoring his reactions. Calculating how much time remained until the guy with the dreads returned to see what was happening.

"See, I didn't come here to kill you. Or even shake you down. I just thought you should get a taste of your own product before you leave."

A tightening of the skin around Fade's mouth indicated the rush was growing more intense. His pupils were widening rapidly, black pits filling each cornea. Rusty let more time pass, counting the seconds.

Fade's head suddenly jerked backward in a fresh wave of panic.

"Let me … go …" the words trailed off. A mewling sob escaped his lips in shower of spittle, both eyes staring at the ball of fire with abject terror.

Rusty released his hold. Fade slid to the floor, then used the wall to buttress himself as he rose to a shaky stance.

"Go ahead. Get out of my sight."

He grabbed the leather valise with his free hand and shoved it firmly into Fade's gut.

"Don't forget this."

Fade tucked the valise under one arm instinctively, though his befuddled gaze indicated he didn't know exactly what it was.

Rusty gave him a rough shove toward the Manor's open entrance.

The cooker took a few steps then stopped by the doorway. He looked around in confusion.

Figuring he might have to physically move the son of a bitch through the door to get him outside, Rusty stepped over to do that.

He didn't see it until a half a second too late: the fire extinguisher he'd left by the entrance to douse the torch with as soon as both cookers were out of the Manor.

It was in Fade's hand. Swinging toward him in a wild arc. Rusty ducked, but not fast enough. The thick metal canister struck him just above his right ear, yielding stars before the pain registered.

He fell dizzily to one knee, barely aware of the sound of Fade's retreating footsteps across the front porch and onto the pier.

Then the stars faded to blackness and he was on the floor. Rusty's torch-bearing hand fell directly onto a pile of spilled salts. The pile sizzled for a moment before igniting with a burst of smoke.

• • •

Theo Taylor piloted his Crown Vic at high speed down Baltimore Street, making a hard left onto Sixth.

"Walk me through it again, Jim."

"I think someone might be sending us on a hunt. Why? I don't fucking know."

Taylor frowned, one arm draped over the steering wheel.

"Of course we're gonna follow up on this," he said, measuring his words against the obvious fury Biddison was making an effort to maintain. "But I'm not seeing the angle."

"The guy said he wants to off me, right? Maybe he figured coming to my house is too dangerous. Luring me out onto the pier might seem like a better plan."

"I guess," Theo muttered, not sounding like the idea held much merit. He was a long way from convinced that grotesque prop had been left at the bungalow specifically to be found by Biddison, or any member of the OCPD for that matter. A dozen other explanations impressed him as more likely.

He turned right from Sixth Street onto the boardwalk, heading south.

"There's another possible slant," Jim said, picking up on the detective's doubt.

"Yeah?"

"Different kind of setup. Someone wants to hurt whoever's pushing the salts."

"How so?"

"I don't fucking *know*, Theo. Maybe we'll find out when we get there."

"Rival dealer, you're thinking?"

Biddison shrugged.

"Maybe."

"Sounds like a stretch, Jim."

Taylor got no reply to that except a fuming silence that told him to keep any other skeptical comments to himself. What the hell, he could hardly blame the lieutenant for being on edge.

They turned left from the boards onto the pier. Driving

slowly, both policemen scanned the immediate area. No movement was to be seen among the abandoned attractions, their colorful paint jobs visible in the clear night.

"Looks pretty dead," Theo offered, but Jim had already spotted the van parked in front of the Morbid Manor.

"That's not a municipal vehicle. Want to tell me what it's doing here at two in the morning?"

Noticing the black cargo van, Theo started to reply it could have been left here by the demolition crew planning to tear down the building in a few days.

Then he noticed the van was running, a small gray cloud rising from the tailpipe.

Without another word to Biddison, Theo Taylor grabbed the radio and called dispatch to request immediate backup.

36.

When Tampa Nate heard the first shot, he reached for the door handle on instinct. He was halfway out of the van when the second shot fired, and he stopped.

It had to be over. He'd doubted Fade possessed enough sack to pull the trigger, expecting him to come back without the valise and spin some bullshit about how it was smarter to part ways with the ten grand after all.

Nate had judged his partner wrong, and it seemed they'd be leaving Ocean City with another body in their wake. More to the point, he was now an accessory to a homicide. That fact didn't sit well, but there it was. Nothing to do about it but start creating distance.

He lit a smoke and didn't bother to exhale out the window. Hell with it. Let Fade bitch, and see what kind of reaction he got.

Two minutes passed. Three. Nate flicked away the butt, anxiously clocking the rearview so he'd see his partner approaching the van. What was taking so long?

An uneasy intuition crept into Nate's gut. What if Fade hadn't fired those shots? All too possible the other man might've liberated the gun from his weakling grasp. A grade-schooler could get the job done if sufficiently motivated.

At the end of the fourth minute, Nate decided he didn't really care. Fade might be dead already, and another three rounds remained in the Bulldog if his assailant planned to finish the job out here. On top of which, almost the entire stash was sitting snugly in the cargo van.

Tampa Nate put the transmission in drive and cast a final

reflexive glance in the mirror—just in time to see Fade staggering out of the Manor.

So be it. Nate kept a foot on the brake, expecting him to clamber in and crow about his entry to the ranks of stone-cold killers. It didn't happen. Nothing happened. Fade just stood a few feet away from the passenger's door, peering inside with a glazed expression.

"Get in," Nate said, rolling down the window. "Want to stay out here all night or what?"

Fade lifted the valise from beneath his arm and held it up for close inspection. He threw it to the ground with a cry of panic like it was a rabid animal dripping froth from its fangs.

"The hell's with you, man?"

Nate almost repeated the question, then noticed the yellowish smear all across the cooker's face.

"For Christ's sake," he rumbled, not able to compute what he was seeing but starting to get an idea. "Just get in the van."

Fade stood frozen on the boards, either not hearing or failing to understand. Now well beyond pissed, Nate hopped out, circled around and forced him into the passenger seat with both hands. He banged the door shut without taking care to ensure all limbs and digits were safely inside, then retrieved the valise.

Back behind the wheel, Nate slammed it in gear. Didn't even bother trying to pry any more info from the passenger, who was babbling like a rhesus monkey and clawing at the air.

It wasn't hard to figure. Nate knew Dixon's stand-in had more in mind than a simple trade-off. He was torn between amused admiration for Rusty's move and puzzlement about those two shots he'd heard. Was the guy still alive in there or what?

Leaning on the accelerator, unconcerned with the fragile cooking equipment, Nate sped down the pier. The van's tires bumped roughly over uneven boards. He heard a plink of breaking glass and didn't slow down.

The mouth of the pier opened up fifty yards away. If he could make it that far, then traverse six blocks north along the boards until reaching an actual street, he'd have it made. Just keep it at a safe, careful speed all the way out of town.

At the first possible moment, when he spotted a place south of Ocean City that looked secluded, he'd dump Fade's tweaking ass on the curb, along with the lab gear.

And the stash? Nate would be keeping that for himself. All of it. Nice little profit center to help him get reestablished down in FLA. He figured it highly unlikely that Fade would muster the gumption to track him down and show up looking to settle things. But if that happened, Nate could deal. Hell, he'd be waiting for it.

As this plan formulated in his head, he found himself smiling for the first time all day. That goateed motherfucker had done him a solid by turning the tables on Fade. Put everything in perspective just like that.

This happy train of thought derailed as the van progressed to within twenty yards from the boardwalk. Swearing, Nate hit the brakes. A more complex shattering of glass erupted from behind, but he didn't even notice.

All his attention was on the champagne Crown Victoria that had just pulled out from behind an obstruction at the pier's mouth. Blocking all access to the boardwalk. Eradicating any hope for getting away clean.

"Goddamn son of a bitch …"

Fade twitched upright in his seat, gaping at a faded billboard advertising suntan lotion. Nate also noticed the reflection of flashing lights on the billboard, then saw an OCPD patrol car roll up next to the Crown Vic.

"Get out of the van with your hands up," a stark voice reverberated through a megaphone. Impossible to tell if it came from the black-and-white or the unmarked. Not that it mattered.

Nate bit down his anger, forcing himself to think. He knew this was coming, all along. That was the worst part. He could only blame himself for not breaking away from this insanity days if not weeks ago.

Actually that wasn't true. He could easily blame it all on Fade.

"I repeat," the megaphone boomed. "Get out of the van. Hands above your head."

Nate felt his foot pressing down on the gas. Adrenaline surged. He was going to ram right through both those goddamn cars. Twist metal, send bodies flying in pieces, never decelerate until Ocean City was nothing but a bad memory.

He glanced over at Fade, seeking some kind of affirmation for his unspoken escape plan. All he got from the passenger seat was a wide-eyed look of terrified bewilderment.

A gunshot ripped into the night air, jolting Nate from his fantasy of vehicular carnage. Fade screamed. The van sunk a few inches on the passenger side as the blown-out front tire collapsed.

"That was a warning shot," said the megaphone. "Out of the van, now."

Nate killed the engine, taking a protracted look out the window to his left. Ten feet away stood a tall chain-link fence blocking off a maze of darkened amusement rides on the pier's southern flank.

These pissant cops wouldn't shoot an unarmed man, especially one who was fleeing with his back to them.

Without a word to his unhinged ex-partner, Nate jerked open the door and made a run for it.

Smoke forced Rusty from the depths of unconsciousness. His nose and lungs drew in stinging microscopic particles that pulled him awake with a groaning cough.

He'd been out less than three minutes, but the foyer was already choked with billowing black and gray clouds. He raised his head painfully, still seeing the extinguisher rising in Fade's grip and feeling its leaden impact. Before he could curse his own stupidity for allowing it to happen, another ashy plume smothered the words in his mouth.

The mound of salts on the floor had turned into an incandescent pyre. The table from which they spilled was entirely ablaze, all four legs and rectangular top covered in flames. The torch in his right hand had burned out, all the flash cotton expended.

The visual information around him stunned Rusty as he swayed upright. One of the many facts he'd gleaned from his online research was that bath salts ignite at roughly the same rate as powdered coffee creamer. Meaning not particularly fast.

Clearly, Fade's product was more inductive to fire than garden-variety salts. Rusty spent a blink wondering if the solvent from Tilly was responsible for the increased flammability.

What fucking difference does it make?

A shower of sparks leapt up from the burning table. It traced across the darkened air, landing on the nearest wall. Almost immediately, a column of flame stretched upward toward the ceiling.

With speed that seemed to defy physics, smoke started curling around an overhead beam on the other side of the room. The beam dripped burning embers below, landing on the foyer's cheap breakaway furniture. They too were enflamed with surreal dispatch.

Rusty knew the building had been deemed unsafe and due for demolition. But he had no clue it was a literal tinderbox. Built forty years ago of cheap pre-code materials, this entire room had turned into a giant cube of flames in minutes.

Going into a crouch, he madly scanned the floor for his extinguisher. It had rolled over by the staircase and lay there on its side, the rubber nozzle detached.

Almost reaching for it, he rejected the idea. No chance of putting down this blaze now. He had to get out before nothing was left but cinders.

Striding hard for the front door, a piercing creak directly above stopped him. It sounded like two rafters giving way.

Rusty had barely half a second to lurch back before a massive overhead beam crashed to the floor in front of him. Landing at a forty-five-degree angle, its burning flank filled the front door's opening. Blocking his exit path as effectively as a steel gate.

That's when he realized he was trapped inside the burning building.

37.

Tampa Nate's brawny fingers clawed at the crisscrossed wires of the chain-link fence. The sheared top, fifteen feet in height and unprotected by barbwire, looked down at him from the distance of only a few more lunges.

He heard multiple voices yelling for him to drop but kept climbing. It seemed stupidly easy. One more long reach would get him there. Toss his legs over and just fall. Let them yell all they want.

Another sound was tearing through the air. The hysterical screeching of Fade, and he ignored that too. If he ever found himself alone in a room with the little bastard, things would go from zero to ugly in no time at all.

Taking Nate's cue, Fade had hurled himself from the van but was too befogged by the drugs to progress much farther than that. Each direction appeared equally hostile, alien, impenetrable. He was only partially aware of Jim Biddison moving in on him, gun drawn, shouting orders to lie flat.

Nate reached his right hand up as far as it would go, fingers just inches from the top of the fence. No idea what he'd do once he made it over, all that mattered was getting there.

A bright spotlight fell all around him, illuminating the rides and kiosks on the fence's opposite side. Nate could clearly see the gaudily painted horses of the carousel, motionlessly prancing in what looked like delight at his dilemma.

He heard a voice commanding him to get down from the fence or be tased. Without turning his head, Nate knew the cop had to be close enough to rule out any chance of missing with the Taser. And what exactly did he plan to do once he'd gotten over this fence anyway?

Releasing his grip with a defeated snarl, Nate dropped to the windswept boards below. Responding to more barked directions, he placed his hands behind his head and got down on his knees. The cuffs were on him in less time than it took to fully sink in that he was going to jail.

Over near the van, Lieutenant Biddison kept closing in on an increasingly deranged Fade. From a distance of ten paces, Jim could see the unfocused glassiness of his eyes. Obviously high, or maybe just off his meds and unresponsive to orders to surrender.

One cautious step at a time, sidearm raised protectively, Biddison tried alternating to a less confrontational tone.

"No one's gonna hurt you. I promise that, OK? We just need to talk."

These words broke through to some dissipating core of Fade's lucid mind. He gaped at the broad-shouldered man moving closer.

Jim could not possibly imagine how he appeared within the raving suspect's fragmented vision.

Emitting a shriek, Fade recoiled in preparation of launching a well-telegraphed attack.

Jim didn't give him the chance. Lowering a shoulder like he'd always been coached, he took the diminutive cooker down with the finest tackle he'd executed since playing middle linebacker for the Blue Hens in the late '90s.

Both men landed hard on the boards, but Fade took by far the worst of it. All the wind left him and he thrashed around noiselessly, mouth stretching into a repeated oval like a fish tossed onto dry land.

A uniformed patrolman ran over to offer assistance as Jim stood. His lower back cried out in angry distress, but he wasn't worried about it. He waved off the patrolman's helping hand and instructed him to cuff the suspect. That took some doing, given all the pained gyrations happening on the ground.

Once securely manacled, Fade was shoved into the backseat

of the prowl car. Right next to Tampa Nate.

The dreadlocked brute's reaction to his presence was so violent, head-butts and knees flying, that after thirty seconds a freshly bleeding Fade had to be pulled from the prowler and deposited in the back of Detective Taylor's Crown Vic for his own safety.

Theo walked over to join Biddison at the cargo van. Found him rifling through the cab for anything that might link this vehicle to the trip wire prop they'd encountered in the Ninth Street bungalow.

"So," Taylor said, sticking his head in the van. "Guess we can dial down the panic alert on that threat. The leprechaun's got to be our caller, don't you think?"

"Maybe," Biddison said dubiously, not looking up from his search. "Why would he do it?"

"You saw the guy, didn't you? He's renting lakefront property on Mars right about now."

Taylor got no reply to that, so he pulled the keys from the ignition and went to open the rear doors. Jim heard him whistle like a naked woman had just strolled by.

"Oh, James. Come take a gander at this when you find an idle moment, won't you?"

Biddison stepped around and beheld the largest cache of drugs he'd ever laid eyes on, packed tight against all the equipment needed to produce them.

"The Lord knows I'm no betting man," Taylor intoned sagely, "but if I had a silver dollar to spare, I'd wager what we have here is the green serpent. In bulk."

Awaiting some reply, or at least a grunt of satisfaction at their monster haul, Theo faced Jim. But the lieutenant had already turned his back on the van to look down at the far end of the pier.

"The damned Manor's burning," he said.

No time to hesitate. Taking a step forward, Rusty kicked hard at the beam that blocked the entrance. Bashes from the steel-toed boot on his right foot didn't move it an inch. The flames on the fallen beam had spread to the doorframe itself, turning the only way out of here into an impenetrable slab of fire.

He spun around, closing the hood over his face with one hand. The smoke was growing thicker, limiting visibility even more than just moments before. He could see maybe three feet ahead of him.

Only one other option for escape: the hidden back entrance through which he'd followed Fade into the building. Having only a general sense of which direction to move in the ascending clouds of ash, Rusty started across the foyer. He had to reach the stairway at the opposite corner. Once there, it should be relatively doable to retrace his steps through the mazelike path that would deposit him at the far side of the house.

Getting there would entail climbing to the second floor, which was bound to be filled with even thicker rising smoke than the ground level. A more direct route used by Manor employees to traverse the building may have existed, one that didn't require going upstairs. But Rusty had no clue where that might be and didn't have time to look for it.

Nine staggered steps brought him to the stairway. Flailing in front of him, his left hand brushed against the bannister. He used it for guidance to navigate the upward climb. He counted each step, saying the number aloud.

The steps were unusually tall. Rusty calculated there couldn't be more than fifteen or so.

By the time he got to seventeen and was still climbing, a throe of panic shook him. But he kept advancing, counting aloud.

Three more steps brought him to the second-floor landing. From here it was a blind guess which way to turn. He started to the right, then a long-buried memory flashed in his brain.

I've done this before, countless times. Been decades, but I knew this place like a second home.

Spinning around, he started left and soon found himself within a cramped passageway. He knew he was on the correct path and his steps quickened. He could feel the heat rising through the floorboards, scattered trails of smoke sneaking up through the gaps to attack his lungs.

The hallway twisted further left, its floor slanting at an angle to create a disorienting off-kilter sensation for guests walking through the Manor. The hallway opened into the torture chamber, and from there followed the sawmill. The floor leveled out and Rusty crossed both rooms at a full run, barely noticing the empty table beneath the circular blade where he'd stolen the two-piece maiden earlier tonight.

By his recollection, he'd reach the gaping haunted forest in another ten or twenty paces. He got there in twelve, recognizing the cavernous space of tilted mirrors and fake cement trees. Not too much smoke had entered this section of the building, so he moved even faster, twice smashing into a full-size mirror and having to change course.

Out of the forest, only two more rooms to navigate: the graveyard and the crypt. He passed through both in a sprint, unable to see anything in the blackness.

The bannister of the back staircase appeared faintly up ahead. Rusty ran for it, going too fast and failing to secure his balance with a hand on the bannister. He stumbled at the top of the stairs and started falling. Impossible to stop his momentum. The best he could do was curl into a ball and let gravity carry him, hoping he was lucky enough not to split his head open on the way down.

Slamming against each step, he landed hard on the lower wooden floor with a thud that knocked the oxygen out of him. Several seconds of dismay passed as he couldn't inhale. His lungs had seized up completely. He couldn't even cough out the vile black dust that seemed to permeate through his pores.

With a strained gasp he finally drew in some air. He looked down to see one sleeve of his thick leather jacket afire from the elbow upward. He batted the flames with his other hand, partially extinguishing them.

Not even trying to see where he was going at this point, he charged toward the rear exit. After ten paces he collided with a row of wooden planks. The jolt of pain in his forehead came as a blessing; he knew he'd reached the back wall. Now all he had to do was find that one loose plank and he would be outside.

He moved down the wall blindly, using two fists to pound on each board. Hitting three or four times to make sure he found the right spot where the hinge allowed the plank to tilt open.

After the seventh plank he had to drop to a knee, the constriction in his lungs too intense. His left arm had started burning again, heat smoldering through the jacket.

He struggled back to his feet. Swinging an arm wildly, he felt the next plank give a few inches. Moving his hands lower, he pushed with what was left of his strength. The plank swung open, letting in a whiff of clean air he could taste.

Made it. I'm out.

Too exhausted to feel any emotional response to that realization, not even basic relief, he crouched down to squeeze through the opening.

Then the floor buckled beneath him. The fire had eaten through the bottom planks of the Manor to reach the ancient wooden pilings supporting them, their ends buried deep in the sand. With a splintering groan the entire structure started tilting to one side, its foundations giving way.

Two massive beams fell from the ceiling, one striking Rusty at the base of the neck almost hard enough to knock him out. Seeing stars, he heard the room-rattling creak of another beam preparing to fall as the house shifted off its axis.

Taking one step back and bending his knees for momentum, Rusty propelled himself into the loosened plank. His body weight pushed it open on its hinge, and he felt himself emerging into the narrow passage behind the Manor. Stumbling two steps forward, he reached out to stop himself on the same metal railing he'd clung to after being attacked by Kenny Dixon.

Two of the pilings beneath him shuddered. The end section of the pier started to cave in under the weight of the Morbid Manor. Rusty felt the rear wall of the house pushing toward him, then he was in free fall.

Time didn't slow for him as he dropped twenty-odd feet into the churning waves below. It seemed to speed up, robbing him of a chance to breathe before hitting the cold, briny stew.

He entered headfirst, clenching his jaws tight to prevent inhaling gulps of salt water.

Rusty thrashed his legs, trying to keep his head above the surface. Large hunks of debris fell all around, sending up smoky fountains like cannonballs striking the froth.

Looking upward, he saw a monolithic mass tumbling down at him. The Manor's worm-eaten back wall was collapsing in a tower of ash and flame. Taking one last breath through the frayed netting, he submerged himself as deeply as possible as an avalanche of burning wood followed him into the sea.

38.

The waves tossed him about like a piece of driftwood. Rusty didn't resist. He made no motions except those required to keep his head above water. High tide was in, nudging up the coast at about 10 knots. The surf was choppy and rapid. Rusty went limp in the water and let the tide do the work, dragging him northward along the beach line.

The frigid ocean water had extinguished his flaming jacket upon impact. His arm had been spared any burns by the density of the jacket's fabric. A thin column of smoke rose from his shoulders, dissipating into the night air.

His kept drifting, figuring this would put ample distance between himself and the pier. Floating out past the break point offered an excellent view of the fire and the activity at the pier's mouth. He kept a close eye on the Manor as he continued north, remaining well out of sight of anyone who might happen to be strolling the beach.

The flashing lights of at least two police cars animated a tall billboard where the pier met the boardwalk. A blur of bodies moved underneath. Rusty couldn't tell how many. He didn't see the cargo van, but the police presence gave him a surge of hope they'd arrive in time to intercept the cookers.

His plan, such as it was, tilted substantially toward the side of fortuitous timing as opposed to calculated precision. Not exactly the way he used to operate onstage at Caesars, but eerily familiar to those unscripted early days on Fremont Street.

That thought yielded a sardonic smile as Rusty tread water, letting the tide carry him. In the increasing distance, the Morbid

Manor was rapidly transforming from a brilliant orange glow to a huge mushroom cloud of smoke and soot. The damned thing went up so fast, it really was a hazard. Rusty figured it had to be a major blessing the place hadn't burned down years ago, God forbid, with people inside.

Hearing the first bleat of engines, he spotted two long red trucks pulling up to a stop at the mouth of the pier.

Nice to see you, boys. Not a moment too soon.

Rusty felt himself relax just slightly. With the firemen on hand, the blaze should quickly be contained. Nothing would be left of the Manor, but the same would have been true soon enough even without the events of tonight. What the hell, he'd probably saved the owners a bucket of dough in demolition fees.

He emerged onto the wet sand about a quarter mile north of the pier, where Twenty-seventh Street intersected the boardwalk. Covered in greasy black soot, he was pleased to have chosen an utterly empty section of the boards, with only a few seasonal restaurants in the immediate area.

Stepping into a dark space between two small condos, he stripped off the hood and outer jacket, both of which still smoldered. He dumped them into a trash can and started walking north in search of the nearest payphone.

It's over, he thought. *Just about all of it, anyway.*

Rusty felt safe in taking an optimistic view that any physical danger of the night was behind him. Only one last detail remained to be ironed out. Weirdly, he dreaded it more than the rest.

When he found a payphone five blocks north, he used it to call Janice.

Fifteen minutes later, he leaned against a wall in a secluded parking lot on Thirty-fourth Street. The lot was small, less than ten spaces. It backed a copy shop that was utterly dark, not even a service light on in the rear. It was as good a place for a surreptitious pickup as any.

Rusty's legs were so tired they didn't even hurt anymore. He didn't want to think about all the kinetic use he'd put them to over the last twenty-four hours—running, kicking, propelling through walls, treading water in heavy surf. He planned on spending the vast portion of tomorrow lying on a couch with his feet up on a pillow.

A car nosed into the lot, headlights off. Rusty started walking toward it even before he had time to confirm it was Janice's rental sedan. He could see her slender outline behind the wheel as she carefully pulled to a stop in the nearest space. The sight caused a brief pang in his chest that he chose to ignore.

He opened the passenger door and slid into the seat.

"My God," Janice said, rolling down her window. "You smell like an incinerator."

"Sorry about that. Hope I'm not ruining the upholstery."

Janice gave a wry grin.

"Don't worry, it's a rental. I'll send you the bill."

Rusty just nodded.

"Thanks for meeting me."

"I was going nuts waiting for the phone to ring. I know you said late, but still." She reached over to take his hand. "I was worried about you."

The stench of burnt wood and ocean brine kept filling the car, and rolling down the windows wasn't going to make it any better. Rusty wondered if she was going to ask about the fire, then realized she probably couldn't see it from where they were parked. This lot was well over a quarter mile from the pier, and several blocks inland.

"You wanted me to get at whoever was making the drugs. To do what the police wouldn't. Right?"

"Yes," she said, a note of caution in her voice.

"And I promised I would." He turned to her. "I'm finished with making promises I don't intend to keep, Janice."

"Rusty, I won't press you for details. I'll leave it to you to say as much as you want."

"I can tell you this much. The man indirectly responsible for your aunt's death is in a very bad way right now."

Janice paused, holding her breath.

"Alive?"

The way she said it didn't sound like she really hoped to get an affirmative answer.

"Yeah, alive. He may wish otherwise at the moment. But no permanent damage, I don't think."

"I'm sort of at a loss. I suppose I should thank you."

"Something needed to be done. We agreed on that much. I'm not sure if this was it, but something."

"Justice for my aunt," Janice whispered, and the hollowness of those words almost made Rusty wince.

"It's not exactly an eye for an eye. Then again, he didn't kill her, and the man who did is looking at a life sentence. I'm glad if it feels like justice, since that's what you were after."

"I guess so," she said after a long pause, releasing his hand. "I'm just relieved it's all over."

Rusty sat in silence for a moment, feeling his head throb with dulling pain and pondering whether or not to say the words on the tip of his tongue. Did he need to see the reaction they would yield, or could he live without knowing that?

He decided he couldn't, and so he said them:

"As for your other concern, I'm afraid that won't work out the way you were hoping."

"What other concern?"

"Your client."

"My *client*?" Janice repeated, placing a confused emphasis on the word that didn't quite ring true.

"Uh-huh. They may be looking at a fairly heavy shitstorm when all this goes public. Probably need to lawyer up, and I'd imagine running their campaign's going to get a little tricky for you."

"Rusty, what the hell are you talking about?"

"Tilly Pharmaceuticals. Valued top-shelf client of Rawling + White. It's almost certain to come out that they're connected to the violent deaths of at least three people. Can't be good for the corporate profile, or stock price, when the press reports one of their former employees was cooking up hyper-toxic drugs using Tilly's own solvent."

Janice gave no reply, as if what she'd just heard didn't

compute. It probably seemed like a genuine enough reaction, to someone who didn't know better. But Rusty did know better, or was at least 99 percent sure of it.

Having spent literally years studying the diverse range of tells that a person is most apt to employ in the act of lying, he trusted himself when it came to identifying one. Especially in a woman with whom he'd been intimate, who was sitting just inches away from him. He wished he was wrong, but couldn't trick himself into believing he was.

"Is that really what you think I was worried about?"

"Does the name Fade mean anything to you?"

She shook her head. Rusty judged this response, at least, to be genuine. It didn't change his view of the matter. For Janice to know the man by name would've struck him as highly unlikely. Fade's connection to the company—just the possibility of that connection—was the salient point.

"I didn't use you, Rusty. No matter what you think."

"Never said you did. But you sure got interested when I told you about what I'd learned at the university. All of a sudden, you weren't so content to let the cops handle it."

"If that's what you thought, why didn't you say anything?"

"Didn't occur to me right away. I got sort of distracted that night, as you may recall." Rusty smiled. "That was some pretty good misdirection on your part. I gotta tip my hat."

Janice looked at him in quarter profile. Her whole upper body was rigid as a stick, hands holding the wheel tightly.

"What exactly do you think I wanted you to do?"

"I think you wanted me to make the problem go away. To make sure no one ever knew Tilly came within a mile of this nasty business. Find the cooker before the cops did and take him out, by any means necessary. And I think you pegged me as just crazy enough to do it."

"You son of a bitch," she said quietly. Her voice was tonally flat, no emotion indicated at all.

"Look at the bright side. Even if your client takes a big hit and you end up losing the account, there's no way you can be tied to any of this shit. Just a terrible coincidence you happened to be in Ocean City when it all went down."

Rusty could see her piecing it together in her mind, figuring out how much she needed to know.

"Tell me what happened tonight," she eventually said.

"Nah, you don't want those details. Less for you to deny, should the need arise. The important thing is, we spent the whole evening together at my place. Didn't we?"

He waited a moment to see if she would answer in agreement, or perhaps fire something else back at him. More denials, or an admission of some sort.

Deciding he didn't really need to hear it anyway, he opened the passenger door.

"I'm sorry if I read you wrong, Janice. But I don't think I did."

Rusty got out of the car and started walking. It was too dark to see if she was watching him go, and he wasn't inclined to turn around and look.

39.

At 1:37 the following afternoon the Wilhelm Diner was almost empty, as usual. Jim Biddison was wolfing down a stack of pancakes and glancing at a copy of this morning's late edition of the *Ocean Gazette*.

By the time he and Theo Taylor had finished booking the two suspects and turning over their van's possessions for logging with the Evidence Unit, it was almost four in the morning. Jim had then accompanied Theo in the Crown Vic to the Taylor home on Twenty-seventh Street, where he'd joined Kim and the baby in the guest bedroom to grab a few hours' sleep.

This morning, he'd patiently explained to her that last night's evacuation had been a false alarm, and it was safe to return to their house. Kim demanded emphatic assurances there was nothing to worry about. He gave them, without mentioning that an unmarked until would be monitoring the house whenever he wasn't home for the foreseeable future. Danielle slept peacefully as they thanked the Taylors and was still napping in her crib when Jim kissed her goodbye to head back to the station.

Lieutenant Biddison figured he deserved a hearty breakfast today, but Kim had stubbornly insisted on feeding him granola and yogurt. She was growing concerned about the state of his waistline and had recently started to enforce some alarming dietary measures. Breakfast was Jim's favorite meal, and if he had to enjoy it at some greasy spoon in the middle of the day rather than at home in the morning, so be it.

He pretended not to notice when Rusty walked in the Wilhelm's door. Jim kept attacking the flapjacks as his old friend sat down across from him. It was the same window booth they'd occupied during their last meeting here.

"Since you didn't ask to meet me at the station," Rusty said, "I'm guessing this isn't police business."

"Don't be so sure about that. Maybe I just wanted to question you informally before dragging you in."

A waitress came over and asked what Rusty wanted. He mulled giving their mediocre coffee a second chance. Deciding he was living proof everyone deserves a second chance, he ordered a mug.

"I know I've been a stone in your shoe these last few weeks, Jim. But you did the right thing by putting out that public warning."

Not even looking him in the eye, Biddison gave no hint of needing Rusty's affirmation that he'd done the right thing.

"And I really did get the message when you booted me from the station," Rusty continued. "You cut me more slack than just about anyone else would, and I appreciate it."

Now Biddison looked up, wiping his mouth with a napkin.

"Contrition doesn't wear well on you, Rusty. Makes me think maybe you've got something to hide."

"Have I bothered you lately? No. I've been keeping my nose clean. Minding my own business."

"That so?"

Jim turned the *Gazette* to the front page and slid it across the table. The banner headline read:

MORBID MANOR BURNS; BELOVED PIER ATTRACTION DESTROYED BY FIRE DAYS BEFORE PLANNED DEMOLITION.

A sub-headline read:

Two men arrested on scene with sizable drug cache; suspected to be behind crime wave tied to tainted narcotics.

Rusty glanced up, brows raised.

"You caught them?"

"Try not to sound so surprised," Biddison answered, unable to suppress a small grin. "We sometimes manage to close a case or two."

"I don't doubt it, but you're sure these are the right guys?"

"They're cookers, anyway. With a shitheap of product to answer for. If their stuff matches what's in the toxicology report you gave me, it's them."

Rusty didn't say anything in reply to Jim's passing acknowledgment of his contribution to the case. He quickly skimmed through the *Gazette*'s article, zeroing in on the final paragraphs.

> OCPD officers were on hand even before fire trucks arrived and took two men into custody, along with a considerable quantity of narcotics and narcotic-producing equipment. The men are considered suspects behind the wave of "green serpent" bath salts linked to a series of violent crimes. Their names have not yet been released as questioning continues.
>
> Bayview Entertainment intends to rebuild a new, improved version of the popular attraction in time for the 2015 summer season. In addition to the Morbid Manor, a small section of the pier was damaged and must be rebuilt.

He set down the paper, nodding.

"Lot of action around here for an off-season town."

Biddison was holding his fork a few inches from the plate, a slice of pancake impaled on its tines. His eyes studied Rusty closely with no attempt at hiding it.

"Is that all you want to say to me?"

"No, I should also say congratulations. Great work, really. I knew you'd catch the fuckers."

Jim grunted through a mouthful of pancakes, making clear it wasn't praise he was looking for right now.

"Are they talking?" Rusty asked.

"One of 'em is. Big muscle head, obviously not the decision maker of the pair. He's only too ready to spill on his partner.

Says he's got some tale to spin about how the drugs were made, something he thinks will buy him a lighter sentence."

The waitress brought Rusty's coffee. He took a sip and raised a brow.

"This stuff isn't quite as bad as I remembered it."

"The other guy's a little runt. Name's Leslie Fadowski, Salisbury address."

Rusty took another sip to conceal any trace of a grin.

Leslie. No wonder he called himself Fade.

"Does that name mean anything to you?" Biddison asked with an intent look.

"Never heard it before," Rusty replied truthfully. "Did you find anyone in your records with that name?"

"No. I looked, but we have nothing on file. Fadowski's not all that far from Fade, is it?"

Rusty shrugged. He hadn't felt so relaxed in weeks, maybe months. This morning he'd sat cross-legged on the bedroom floor for a solid forty minutes of meditation, and it came to him as effortlessly as it ever had. Focus, clarity, calmness—all still within reach, to his immense gratification.

"Where'd you hear that name again?" Jim asked. "Fade, I mean."

"You know where. The kid who killed himself. Ronnie."

Biddison nodded absently, as if he'd just been checking to see if Rusty gave a different answer this time.

"Anyway," he said, "we haven't gotten shit out of Fadowski yet."

"Won't give without a lawyer, huh?"

"No, that's not the problem. The guy was completely out of his mind last night. Raving like a loon, said he was attacked by a man who set himself on fire. That's how the place got torched."

"Original defense. Think it'll hold up in court?"

"We'll see what he has to say when the drugs wear off. Can't figure why he'd get so wrecked on his own shit if he knows how dangerous it is."

"People are hard to fathom."

Jim's face grew an even sharper edge of skepticism.

"Want to hear something weird? I wouldn't have even been there if someone hadn't called the station an hour earlier."

"Tip-off?" Rusty asked, draining his coffee.

"No, not a tip-off. It was a death threat made against me."

He let that sink in for a minute, stubbornly waiting for Rusty to say something.

"That's terrible, Jim."

"Scared the hell out of my wife. We had to evacuate the house. Baby was up half the night, total fucking nightmare."

"I can imagine," Rusty muttered, breaking eye contact for the briefest of moments.

Biddison didn't seem to notice. He was shaking his head as if pondering some inscrutable puzzle.

"Thing is, it made all the difference. Far as the bust goes, I mean. These guys were getting ready to split town. No chance we would've grabbed them if someone hadn't called in to threaten me."

"I don't follow."

"The call came from a landline, real easy to trace. When we got to the residence, no one was there. But they'd left the front door open, making sure we'd get inside. Never guess what we found in there."

Rusty just offered another shrug.

"A prop stolen from the Morbid Manor, rigged with some kind of message."

"A message?"

"Yeah. Like, taunting me."

"That's definitely weird."

"Totally fucking illogical is what it is. We don't know who made the call. Maybe Fadowksi, maybe not."

"Could've been him, I guess. If he was out of his gourd on the shit, like you said."

"I'm guessing no dice," Jim replied, shaking his head. "It's looking to me like a tip-off in disguise. Like someone left a trail of breadcrumbs leading me to the Manor, just in time to catch the perps before they split."

Rusty furrowed his brow dismissively.

"Obviously I don't know jack shit about law enforcement, but that sounds pretty far-fetched."

Biddison offered no comment on that observation, just polished off a last few bites of hash browns.

"Out of curiosity, what were you doing last night?"

"Are you asking as a cop or a friend?"

"Would it change your answer?"

"Nope, just wondering. I was entertaining a lady. All night."

"At your place?"

"Yep. Made her some of my famous Cajun gumbo, secret recipe I learned in New Orleans. I should whip up some for you sometime, if you've got a stomach for spice."

"I'm sure the lady in question would be willing to corroborate that, if anyone felt like asking her."

"She went back to Manhattan this morning, but I can give you her number. Not sure why you'd feel the need to check, to be honest."

"Well, I've been chewing it over all day, Rusty. This fucking prop we found, whatever you want to call it. Seemed familiar somehow. Couldn't figure it out at first. Then I remembered. It was just like the shit you used to pull at school, when you were in a mood to prank someone."

"I gave up pranks a long time ago, Jim. Like to think of that as a sign of maturity."

"We're having a tape of the call analyzed for voice recognition. If it's a match for Fadowski, fine. But I'd be surprised."

Biddison paused, leaning in just slightly closer.

"Promise you this much, one old friend to another. I won't quit till I find out who made that fucking call. Whatever it takes."

A long moment passed, each man holding the other's gaze. Over the course of the last two bizarre weeks, Rusty felt like he'd never had to employ his poker face under such scrutiny.

Biddison finally returned his attention to the remaining pancakes. Rusty accepted a refill of his coffee from the waitress and waited to see if this line of discussion would be resumed.

It wasn't. Maybe the lieutenant had decided to believe him.

Or maybe he was just sandbagging for now, waiting for another opening to pursue his inquiry.

"Ravens are playing Pittsburgh on Sunday," Biddison muttered. "Home game. I got some pretty good seats near the 40. The baby has a cold so Kim doesn't want to get a sitter. You free?"

The invitation genuinely surprised Rusty. It was pretty much the last thing he expected to hear, and he didn't have an immediate answer.

"I'll check with my secretary. Don't think I have anything too urgent that day."

"Forget it," Jim said, wiping his mouth with a fresh napkin. "You never much liked sports, did you?"

"I always liked cheerleaders."

"So you want to go or not?"

Rusty drank some coffee, then nodded.

"Sure. I could use some new scenery. Can't remember the last time I was in Charm City."

His answer seemed to please Biddison.

"Game's at one thirty. I'll pick you up at nine. Maybe on the drive you'll spill some stories about what the hell you've been doing the last twenty years."

Rusty pondered the suggestion.

"Anything's possible."